SONG
ON A
BLUE
GUITAR

A Novel
Dorothy Cave

SUNSTONE
PRESS

SANTA FE

Other books by Dorothy Cave:

Mountains of the Blue Stone
Four Trails to Valor
Beyond Courage

Sunstone books may be purchased for educational, business, or sales promotional use. For information please write: Special Markets Department, Sunstone Press, P.O. Box 2321, Santa Fe, New Mexico 87504-2321.

Library of Congress Cataloging-in-Publication Data:

Cave, Dorothy.
    Song on a blue guitar: a novel / Dorothy Cave.
        p. cm.
ISBN: 0-86534-349-7
        1. Ranchers—Fiction. 2. New Mexico—Fiction. 3. Male friendship—Fiction. 4. Real estate developers—Fiction. I. Title.

PS3553.A9656 S66 2002
813'.54—dc   2002021205

Published in SUNSTONE PRESS
Post Office Box 2321
Santa Fe, NM 87504-2321 / USA
(505) 988-4418 / *orders only* (800) 243-5644
FAX (505) 988-1025
www.sunstonepress.com

For my mother for her 100th birthday,
for Ralph and Kathy, Kate and Tom,
and as ever, for Jack.

They said, "You have a blue guitar,
You do not play things as they are."

The man replied, "Things as they are
Are changed upon the blue guitar."

— Wallace Stevens

PROLOGUE

IN THE CANTINA THEY STILL TALK of the night Toro Duran cut the fences and blazed his trail into the misty land of legend and of song. As with most legends, the bits and pieces vary with the narrator and the hour; but the core of legend is truth, and that burns undimmed in the memories of those who were there.

Sometimes, as the evening ripens and the talk slows into a buzz of easy fraternity, someone, great with wine or nostalgia, senses an errant ghost that sometimes sweeps through thumbing his nose at the world in general. Like Toro.

Then once more they tell the story, with grins and chortles and blinked-back tears, and always with a lilt of pride. For Toro was one with them and they with him, in virtue and in villainy, which is to say, in humankind.

It is a short and simple story, for Toro's defiant charge streaked brief as a meteor over the mesa. But truth is not measured by permanence. Meteors are as real as mesas, and Toro's coup burned its bright tail through the heavens before it cooled to legend.

To hear it firsthand now, you must wind north from Santa Fé along the Rio Grande to a high plateau that spills from mountain range to river bluff. Cupped in its lap you will find a certain village that nestles against an ancient pueblo and draws from it some of its own strange mysticism.

From the village plaza a lane winds westward through scattered mud-brick houses where geraniums in coffee cans bloom in wood-framed windows and hollyhocks rear in summertime against the walls, and the tattered seats of abandoned pickups rest beneath cottonwoods or junipers. Past the houses and the junkyard and the little *grocería* the lane meanders to a small cluster they call Tuceros, and ends at a bleached blue door, unmarked by sign or number. Here is where it all began.

The cantina may once have had a name, but no one can remember, not even Arabela, who reigns, muscular and magnificent, behind the bar. Should anyone ask (though no one ever did), Arabela would cock her black-maned head, chomp heavily on her wad of spearmint, and shrug with a buck-toothed grin.

Laughter rises, and jokes—sometimes a lively fight—and over it pulses the guitar's sweet throb, soulful or heroic or in gay fiesta mood. But these fountains of sound will dry like summer drought when you, a stranger, walk in. Tecolote's guitar will muffle to tuneless chords. Eyes will sidle. Arabela, grinding her cud, will serve you silently.

But a friendly "¿Como se va?" to one, a "¿Qué tal, señor?" to another will ease the silence and soften the stares. And should you ask about Toro Duran, the eyes will mist, the mouths will curve, and talk will flow again like an *acequia* in spring. And sometimes, if the air feels right, Tecolote will raise his hooded eyelids, thwack his strings a thumping chord, grin like a wicked angel, and sing for you his *corrido*. His song of Toro.

Joe Steele could tell the story most completely, for he was party to the whole affair. But you won't find Joe at the cantina. He's long since headed back south to his ranch at High Lonesome. And if you found him he probably wouldn't tell you anyhow.

Or maybe, if you caught him right, he would. Joe talks in a slow loose way, the way he walks, and his nose aims the smallest fraction to the left, a tribute to one of the best fights he ever had, and to Toro Duran who so realigned it and became—until the other thing happened—his best friend. It was Joe who told them in the cantina how Toro, finding himself in Uncle Sam's army shortly before Pearl Harbor, had taken on the drill sergeant, bravely and creatively, and thus set his foot on the first rung toward heroism.

But that was a story far in time and geography from Toro's *compañeros* in the cantina; and besides, as Toro himself maintained, handling the sergeant was only in the line of his natural duty. Tiger he may have been in the war, a real hot tamale—they expected no less—but heroism, like charity, begins in one's own cantina; and it is Toro's glorious deed there, among his own amigos, by which they remember him. For they were a part of it all.

And so they talk. The night deepens and jokes grow funnier and memories mellow. Then someone recalls the night Toro cut the fence, and what came after, and Arabela, wiping the counters with her bar rag, will slow her muscular stroke a little, push back a damp tendril, and grin toothily— maybe even stand a round on the house. If it isn't too crowded. And they talk too of Joe, of how he came to Tuceros bringing a curious little box, and then took it home again, and they scratch their heads and shrug their shoulders and agree that Joe knew more than he ever told.

Ysidro will follow his paunch through the bead-curtained door behind the bar. Then, spying Chico and Rico at their usual table beneath the red neon Coors sign, he'll flip his toothpick to the floor and, pregnant with fellowship, he'll amble over to join them and begin some idle yarn.

Sooner or later their talk will turn to Toro, and it seems they can still see him, with his dark eyes that sparked in fun or fury, his black Stetson perched on the back of his head. And his fine red boots. He could dance like a flame in those boots—could kick ass with them too. Like on that August night.

Then with a chuckle and a tear the old *compañeros* will lift their beers to Toro; and down at High Lonesome they fancy Joe will be lifting his own. And they know too that Toro will be joining in the mystical communion on whatever far and fenceless mesa he may be.

Here is how it all began.

1

ON A TUESDAY MORNING IN LATE August Joe Steel tossed a small wooden box onto the seat of the blue Olds, hitched his jeans to a comfortable spot, and climbed behind the wheel. He removed his Hopi bola, hung it over the mirror, and tossed a two-fingered salute to Beth waving from the ranch house door. Cocking a sardonic eyebrow at the tightly taped box beside him, he shifted into drive and headed for the northbound highway. A couple of his dogs ran beside him, then fell back in his dusty wake, and soon he was cutting through the drought-scorched New Mexico desert.

Joe was on a mission, which was in itself odd, because Joe was not a mission-trotting type.

It was the tail end of a rainless summer, one of those August days when desert floors crackle with white heat and clack-winged grasshoppers leap carousing against the coming death; when meteors streak the sky above night-black mesas, and old ghosts may become insufferably high-handed.

About noon he reached the river. Tired and half-hearted it moved, low even for August, and along its banks the dusty-leafed cottonwoods awaited their yellowing fate. A small breath of September whispered pine-scented from beyond the peaks ahead.

Then began a series of ridges. He wound along the river, began to climb between black lava and red sandstone, redder in the afternoon sun, crenelated with dry washes; and then the river veered west and left the highway. Joe topped the last rise, swept his gaze across the expanse of late-summer yellow to the sharp black gorge through which the river cuts deeply, and he thought again as he always had in this spot that if God had a face it was in this vast sweep of carved immensity. To his right reared the Sangre de Cristos, ancient and arrogant, carmine in the sun; and beyond the river rose the blue-veiled Jemez.

Then below lay the village, captured between mountain and gorge, and west beyond the river rose the mesa, dark and solid and still against the bright tumbling clouds on the horizon—a threat, a challenge, or a freedom—*¿quién sabe?*

He wondered again why he had come on this damn-fool mission, then glanced at the box, decided he'd gone loco, shrugged, and drove on. He'd deliver it, put it behind him, and go home where he belonged. To High Lonesome. To Beth, who put up with his quirks—until she'd had enough. Then she could be a spitfire. Joe grinned remembering.

Nearing the town he began to see the signs, a belligerent array of money-green billboards heralding the JD Emmenthaler Realty and Development Company. Like acne on the face of God, Joe thought, and wondered who in hell's outhouse JD Emmenthaler might be. Another sonofabitching developer? In this little adobe village that hadn't enough water for the people who already lived here?

Those signs were the only green thing he'd seen all day in this drought-plagued land. He thought again of his own ranch, dry and brown, and his wells falling lower and lower trying to keep the stock tanks filled.

At the edge of the tourist-glutted town another green sign loomed. Crude red letters marched across it: "WHERES MY DAMN PAY?"

He first saw Toro Duran in the middle of a traffic jam. Several cars ahead of Joe, dead center in an intersection bounding the town plaza, a red Ford pickup clotted the single village artery, and from it spewed a sinewy little man, smoke-brown, white-haired, red-booted, and yelling mad. Charging like a Mexican bull he lit waving his arms like a windmill in March. A small pouch dangling from his belt bobbled with each wild gesture.

Traffic in the narrow street snarled, stopped, seemed almost to throw itself in reverse. Horns honked and tourists shouted, impatient of the congestion in the quaint narrow streets whose quaint narrowness they had come specifically to see. Some raced their motors. In the bed of the red pickup a dog barked with all the importance of his species, which seemed preponderantly shepherd. But his master roared louder in a shaggy voice.

"I got the by-god rightaway!"

"Who got the rightaway is who I say got the rightaway, and it ain't you!" yelled back a fat man with a bristly moustache who seemed to be directing traffic. Above him a disabled traffic light seemed permanently stuck on red. From a fast-convening crowd of local citizens someone cried "*¡Hijo!* Let 'im have it, Rico," and the crowd cheered.

"You ain't the by-god police," bellowed the little bull.

"Tell 'im, Toro!" The crowd cheered again. *Toro?* A gnat whined in Joe's brain but he swatted it away.

"—and you ain't the sheriff either!"

Sweat rolled down the fat man's face. "He's gone fishing and you damn well know it." Both men seemed to be enjoying the altercation immensely. The bystanders yelled democratically for both contestants.

"Get 'im, Rico!"

"*¡Andale*, Toro!"

Spurred by the crowd, Rico warmed up. "You don' like how I handle traffic, you stay the hell home."

"*¡Chale!* Some of us got bi-ness, *chingo!*" The man called Toro spat furiously and where the globule landed a small puff of dust spurted like a miniature volcano. The crowd cheered again.

"You want I should haul you into court for contempt?"

"This ain't your goddam court, *piojo!* This here's a public street—"

"Resisting the law!"

"—and I'm a by-god tax-payin' citizen on my way to the Uni' States post office to get my by-god mail, that you are obstructin' the delivery of, which is a by-god crime."

The argument was going nowhere, and neither, Joe could see, was the traffic. Wedged behind a white Toyota with a Mississippi license and a dented Ford pickup angled optimistically into the snarl from a side street, he cut the motor—and with it his air conditioner—glanced at the little box again, and shrugged. After forty years it could wait another hour.

The late August sun gilded the plaza and reflected off windshields and glazed the stir of dust raised by the day's traffic. The heat rose. Joe unstuck his damp shirt from the back of the seat and stepped from the Olds. The smells of dust and exhaust fumes rose from the asphalt. To his right a tall plywood-paneled fence masked a building being razed or reconstructed and greenly proclaimed it the property of the JD Emmenthaler Realty and Development

Company. The shrieking whine of a power saw split the air.

"Christ a'mighty," drawled Joe.

He pulled a briar pipe from his pocket, nodded to a passerby munching a candy bar, and gestured toward the fracas in the plaza. "What's their problem?"

"*No problema.*" The power saw screeched again. Swallowing the last of his Butterfinger, the man tossed the wrapper, hooked his thumbs in his belt loops, and leaned against Joe's fender. "They just like to fight."

"Yeah?" Joe fiddled with his pipe. Something about the jackhammer energy pumping from the irate little man ahead recalled a flash of old memory.

"Yeah. Him and Rico—he's the magistrate judge, Rico is. Also he's Chico's brother. Chico's the sheriff. And he's gone fishin'."

A thud and a grind of metal distracted their attention as a high-nosed yellow van with a Texas license, trying to pull around the line of cars, backed into the hood of a Minnesota Volkswagen, then shifted and lurched over the rear fender of a black New York Cadillac, plowing an imposing furrow in its trunk. Trying to disengage, the Texan shifted into reverse, then forward again, and the coupled vehicles began to hump like copulating turtles. The New Yorker poked his head from his shell and glared stupidly before he began to yell.

Joe grinned. "Looks like some entertainment's making." He sucked asthmatic noises through his pipe and fished for his can of Prince Albert.

Abruptly another exasperated driver wheeled over a curb, proceeded around the honking mass scattering the pedestrians with a blast of his horn, and shot forward unconcerned, his right wheels on the sidewalk, his left in the gutter. A few tourists jumped aside unbelieving as he careened down the walkway, but the villagers parted without surprise or comment.

"He's in the legislature," explained Joe's companion.

Rico had ignored the whole action.

The power saw screamed again.

The battle ahead continued. A line of epithets roared from the little bull's throat and spattered like bullets on a rock against the unimpressed Rico, who stood alternately blowing his nose and wiping sweat from his balding head. Traffic had meanwhile begun to inch around the red pickup and somehow to more or less sort itself out.

The New Yorker now stood looking morosely at the dent in his trunk, which, graced by a yellow blob from the Texas van, resembled nothing as much as a large tortoise shell. "Where are the goddam police?" he yelled above the power saw.

"Gone fishin'," someone said. It didn't matter anyhow, because by now the yellow van had disappeared.

Ahead, with a red-booted kick, the man called Toro sent a rock in his path flying, hurled himself into the pickup, yelled a parting obscenity, and yanked the door shut. The dog ran barking from side to side in the pickup's bed, joyously adding to the din. A glint of sunlight flashing from the rear window seemed to flare from the furious man within.

"And fasten your damn seatbelt," yelled Rico.

From the pickup window shot a hand, the middle finger thrust indelicately skyward. The engine roared, and through a hole in the now crawling traffic the red truck sped like a burning comet. Behind the departing little rebel the bystanders continued to brawl happily. The tortoise-marked Cadillac crawled slowly down the street.

Joe opened his door, then turned back. "That man in the pickup. Didn't they call him—Toro?"

"*Sí*, Toro. Toro Duran. Victorio on Sunday or in court. Toro for everyday. Lives out to Tuceros."

Toro Duran. My god, it was! The man Joe Steele had left the comfort of his well-heeled ranch at dawn and driven three hundred miles to this little mud-pie town to find. The man he'd come to deliver a small box to because he'd made a half-assed promise once, and all the way half hoping he wouldn't find him. It was the little bastard himself.

Joe had been trying for forty years to forget Toro Duran.

2

IT WAS TOMCAT LITTLE, OR Tomcat's ghost, that, when Joe heard of his old buddy's death, had goaded him into finally making the pilgrimage.

Tomcat's appearance capped a summer of vexations. They started in June when Joe was riding fence one day. Except at branding time he did little of the physical work on the ranch anymore. His son was pretty much in charge now— Mike loved the ranch like he did—and he had plenty of good hands. But Joe did like to ride fence, usually in the old Ford pickup, sometimes in the saddle, and always with a dog or two trailing along. He liked the desert. Liked the summer heat that rose in shimmery waves. Liked the frozen crackle of dry winter weeds. Liked even the bitter sweep of spring gales and the sharp sting of blowing sand against his face. He liked the loneliness, where a man can think, or not think if he didn't want to. Where there was space and time for the mind to fly. Where freedom rose each morning with the sun and renewed itself at each day's end. Joe had come home from the big war asking only for peace, a good well, and rain in July.

These wide high plains were his country. Joe's father, an eastern physician threatened with tuberculosis, had come west as a young man for his health. His lungs healed. But the spell of the desert didn't and he elected for the life of a country doctor. Jonathan Steele claimed he'd tended as many horses as humans.

From the time Joe was a kid he liked making ranch calls or tramping the hills with his father, and over the years he acquired the same love of the land, a decent respect for fences, and a passion for locating water.

He was thinking these thoughts on that hot June day, riding fence, when he found the barbed wire cut, neatly and deliberately. Some fired ranch hand, he guessed. Or a government snoop. Few things angered Joe like cut fence unless it was a misused horse.

He didn't care much for Texans, either—gobbling up the precious downstream river water, angling their damned wells under New Mexico's border. It was a sentiment he liked to needle his sister with whenever he saw her, which was as seldom as either of them could manage. Aileen had married a man with some oil money in Dallas and spent her days playing golf and bridge at one of the better country clubs. (Joe claimed she paid more attention to her fingernail polish than to the state of the Union.)

July came on the heels of a June hot enough to barbecue a man, and no rain fell. The grass dried and hardened in lumps like scabs on the burnt soil, and the level of his well kept sinking, and the windmill clanked and groaned and turned in the wind sucking desperately for water. Thunderheads built sometimes, promising like politicians, and rain streaked the far sky, but always it evaporated before it reached the ground. Then the winds rose and the hot sand blew and the clouds fled.

In July came the letter from Tomcat's son. "Just before he died," it read, "Dad told me, 'Ask Joe if he ever got that damned box to Toro Duran.'" That was when the long-dead promise resurrected itself and Tomcat began to dog him, along with other ghosts of memory, and set throbbing that small vein of brooding Joe had inherited from his mother's Scottish ancestors. It was a thing he'd always tried to suppress. He had consciously followed his father's habit of turning introspection inside out in the name of practicality and he nursed that habit with a dry humor.

But sometimes the Gaelic ghosts still sneaked peering over his shoulder, quiet and insistent and mocking. Like Tomcat.

Sometimes Joe felt him in the pickup, not talking, just looking at Joe with that grin, the way he'd done when the Japanese planes roared in from the China Sea and his crew got ready to fire the big guns, that let's-get-on-with-it grin and flashing a V-for-victory sign. Tomcat didn't talk now, but he might as well have, because Joe knew what he meant.

And Joe had no answer.

Still he rode the fence and the wire stretched long and taut and it was a rightness. Except sometimes he thought he came on Tomcat tangled in its barbs like a trapped tumbleweed.

There had been three of them—Tomcat and Toro and Joe—and then four with the tall Indian they called Chief who came from the pueblo near Toro's village and was assigned to their artillery unit. Best buddies they were almost from the first, when they'd trained together at Fort Bliss. Alive with the animal joy that had not yet faced its own mortality, they had gotten into Saturday night fights prowling across the border in Juarez —fights usually started by Toro and finished by Chief unless the MPs interrupted their fun first.

The Fearsome Foursome they were called in their newly federalized home-state Guard regiment. Toro, the bull. Tomcat, so-called for certain proclivities at which he was talented. Chief, always handy in a scrape. And Joe. GI Joe, who never started a fight, never walked away from one, and never took any of it very seriously. Joe, with a humor as dry as the land he'd grown up on, friend to everyone, close to few.

The Fearsome Foursome went with their regiment to the Philippines, traded forays in Juarez for forays in Manila when they could get passes and in nearby barrios when they couldn't, until the Mitsubishi bombers came dropping war from the skies like swift and sudden hail. Hot damn! The war was on and it promised to be their best brawl yet.

Until, outnumbered, out-weaponed, and out-provisioned, they retreated onto the peninsula of Bataan, where they dug in for what became one of the great delaying battles of the world. Then the foursome banded together more tightly to perform with guts and gusto some truly creative escapades.

When the food ran low they helped themselves to ammo and disappeared into the jungle to bag a crow, a monkey, an iguana, or—when they could find one—a Jap sniper. They scouted enemy positions. Toro, anticipating a booby trap, barbed wire, or a chance to rob a Japanese cache of rice, always hung a hatchet from his belt, a length of rope, and wire cutters. They volunteered (or more correctly Toro volunteered them) for whatever adventure might relieve them from the daily chores that plague a soldier's life.

It was on the last mission that the thing happened.

But Joe's memory stalled there, and he shoved the war under a pile of manure. Until forty years later when Tomcat came buzzing into his consciousness like a persistent horsefly.

That same July—that was in 'eighty-five—Joe's father had a heart attack. In the Catholic hospital in Roswell, still and lumpy between white sheets, he opened an eye suddenly and asked Joe what was bugging him.

"Nothing." Joe had thought the old man asleep.

"Horseshit," growled Jonathan Steele. "When you come on a rattler, kill the sonofabitch." Sister Hilda waddled in about then to take his vital signs. "Sister," he asked, "will I live through the day?"

"Oh my goodness, yes."

"Then bring me a newspaper." He and Sister Hilda had vied in friendly combat for years.

"Would you like anything else?"

"Yes. A bottle of good champagne."

"Now don't be naughty, doctor."

"Dom Perignon preferably."

"You know you can't have champagne."

"Then stop asking me what I want." He turned back to Joe. "You heard me, son. Get rid of your snakes."

Jonathan Steele died that night. But first he read his newspaper, and winked a fading eye at Joe.

A week later Mike confronted him at the stable. "What the hell's got into you, Dad?"

"What the hell makes you ask?" Joe continued moving his hands over the new cutting horse, feeling his shoulders and legs.

"Well, something's sure as shit put you on edge." Mike leaned against the stall gate, arms crossed.

"I told you. You paid too damned much for that stallion."

"I don't think so." Mike stared hard at his father for a few seconds and walked off.

In August Joe's wife delivered an ultimatum.

Like Doctor Steele, Beth had started out an easterner. Joe had courted her, back before the war, while he was working on a degree in hydrology at Penn. (His mother, an ex-Philadelphia socialite, had insisted Joe receive an Ivy

League education.) There, eclectically and democratically, he mixed English Lit and Greek grammar with the sciences of water and the serious pursuit of coeds.

He met Beth at a frat party. He had a petite red-headed music major in tow, with whom he was engaged in a solemn discussion of the relative merits of Glen Miller and the Dorseys, T. and J., when a frothy deluge came cascading over his head. Whirling, he grabbed the instigator by the elbow. Her spike heel had caught in the carpet.

"Lost my balance," she said giggling.

"And your beer."

Seeing his face decorated in foamy rivulets, she couldn't stop her giggles from becoming gales. "I really am sorry," she gasped and then went off into another round of whoops.

"Can't think of a better way to drown my sorrows," he drawled grinning, "than in a bucket of suds." Dabbing a handkerchief at his face and neck, he sized her up. Tall, rose-cheeked, hair the color of desert sand. Suddenly the music major, who had already drifted to another group anyhow, seemed frumpy.

By evening's end Joe had secured rose-cheek's address, phone number, a recital of her major peeves and priorities, and a date for the next weekend.

Beth was a freshman at Bryn Mawr, which Joe privately considered the dead center of crackpottery, but he courted her the rest of that year and by the next they were engaged. But war was in the offing, his regiment was being federalized, and he went home to rejoin it. The wedding, along with a lot of others, was postponed. Beth quit school after Pearl Harbor to do her patriotic duty in a munitions factory, which at least, Joe thought, rescued her from the lunatic excesses of academia. After the war Joe renewed his courtship and rescued her again from progressive education. But, he admitted, had she not been slightly loco she would never have come west with him to take up ranching, about which he knew little and she knew less.

He'd come home with some money, borrowed more on the G.I. Bill, and with some help from his dad bought the ranch at High Lonesome. It wasn't a large ranch, but it was good grazing land (when it rained in July) and it had ties to his boyhood, when he used to spend time there with Ben Chapman whose dad owned it. Ben stayed in town with his grandmother (who lived next door to the Steeles) while school was in session and spent the rest of his time on the ranch, bringing Joe with him when the boys could manage it.

The Chapmans had weathered the Depression. When the war came they lost their three sons and most of their hands to the army and finally sold the ranch to a draft dodger from Mount Gilead, Ohio, who was glad to unload it after the war when Joe came looking. So the world he had wanted became his world—the moods of the desert and the realities of its heartaches and its demands on his manhood, until he and the land seemed one.

Except for the weekly forty-mile trip to town for necessities, intermittent treks to the mountains for some good fly fishing, or an occasional trek abroad when Beth could pry him loose, Joe seldom left High Lonesome. The ranch was his center, where the land stretched forever in the deep sounds of peace— the everyday sounds of cattle and horses and dogs, the regular sounds of family and ranch hands going about their activities, the night sounds of wind and coyotes and the comforting creak of the windmill.

It was those sounds—the endless creaking of the windmill and the wind that drove it—that had at first driven Beth to desperation, that plagued her days and invaded her nights until sometimes sobbing she woke Joe to ask if they would ever stop.

"They better not," he always said. "That's our water. Our life." In time she learned to tolerate those sounds, eventually to rely on them, and even to miss them when away from the ranch.

She had learned to put up with his eccentricities too, Joe admitted. To most she paid no heed; for Beth, despite Bryn Mawr, had basic common sense and a large helping of humor. But on occasion her safety valve blew—most recently when the cook quit after Joe had thrown a bunch of dirty socks in the dishwasher. That was on Friday.

"So get a new cook," he said and leaned against the kitchen counter in grand unconcern, tamping Prince Albert into the bowl of his pipe.

"To lose Carlita—after thirteen years—"

"Long enough for any cook." He touched a match to his pipe and let a few smoke tendrils curl from the corners of his mouth. "Hell. Lots of wives don't stay that long."

"And leave for less reason."

"Well, it's only a cook."

That set her off. "You've been every bit as charming lately as an ailing tarantula," she began, and she ended by telling him to get rid of whatever burr was under his saddle. "And that, mister, is an ultimatum."

Joe didn't take much to ultimatums.

Tomcat wasn't through with him either.

It had been Tomcat who entrusted him with the packet for Toro, to be delivered in person. That was at war's end when, reunited after three years of pure hell, he found Joe among the thousands of newly freed POWs at the staging area on Luzon awaiting transportation home.

Only Tomcat wasn't going home.

"What do you mean, not going?" Joe punched him in the shoulder. "You loco?"

"I mean I got me a little gal."

"That supposed to be news?"

"Cutest little Filipina you ever see."

"So?"

"So this one I'm going to marry. Settle down right here on this bea-u-tiful island—what's left of it—and fish!"

"What about all those gals pining for you in El Paso? And their kids that probably look just like you?"

Tomcat grinned hugely. "Why the hell you think I'm staying this side of that big bea-u-tiful ocean?"

"Christ a'mighty," said Joe.

So they went for a few beers and a lot of catching up—Tomcat had escaped the Death March and joined a guerilla group—and after a night of swapping stories and carousing, Tomcat laid the box on him.

"Wha's so almighty important about it?" Joe was trying to focus his eyes.

"Long story. Toro'll tell you. If he's still alive."

So Joe put his arm on his old buddy's shoulder and in a rush of alcoholic brotherhood promised to deliver it. In person.

He hadn't, though. There was always his old friendship with Toro, severed now like a cut fence, and the nagging question, like a rattler under a rock, of how much blame might be his own. Then his Scottish ghosts and his

Presbyterian conscience rose again to plague him. By nature he might have cleared his soul in confession. But by rearing he disdained to do so, asserted his father's no-nonsense approach, and managed for the most part of forty years to ignore, and for long stretches even to forget, the box and the promise.

He'd pushed away the memory of Toro's craggy face that could change like a lightning's flash from twinkling devilment to shaggy long-eyed sainthood. He forgot Toro's exploding like thunder over the way the Japs worked wounded horses, beating them mercilessly until they sank dead to the ground. He forgot Toro's voice like shaggy juniper bark, and the tattoo Toro had gotten in Juarez—a burro it was, on his right arm.

And he forgot the box and his promise.

Until Tomcat waylaid him again. "For Chrissake," drawled the voice in Joe's mind, "plant your skinny ass on a fast horse and spur that critter north!"

His father, Beth, Mike, Tomcat. Even the windmill's creak seemed to be mocking him. Joe had had enough.

That was on Saturday. On Monday, declaring himself drought-driven, ghost-goaded, and wife-witched, Joe drove into Roswell, pulled the old package from his safe-deposit box, and with it the long-stashed Silver Star he'd never told anyone he had.

By first light Tuesday he was on his way.

There were no vacancies in the tourist-glutted town, but a blonde clerk in one motel told him to check back after six. There might be an unclaimed reservation. He found Toro Duran listed in the directory, dropped in his coin, started to dial, and then thought better of it. Better face a live Toro than wait for one more ghost to plague him. No matter what it might stir up. The safest place for the fly to land, his dad had always said, is smack on the swatter.

But he wanted to know something else before Toro Duran tried to lay a guilt trip on him. It was still high afternoon and there was one person he suddenly wanted to see first. If he could find him. Someone who might tell him what he wanted to know, and from a less partisan viewpoint. Chief had been around when the thing happened.

And Chief's reservation lay just beyond the town. Joe rubbed the heels of his hands down his flat hips, patted his wallet pocket, and headed for the pueblo.

3

SO HERE HE WAS WANDERING
about the pueblo looking for an Indian he had known once in a war Joe Steele
had long ago put behind him. How many times had he driven through the
village without stopping, without seeking out Toro or Chief or anyone else who
was part of what was over and done with, dead silage from the compost heap?

It was Joe's nature to leave the rest of the world and his own dark side
pretty much alone. Why poke up a nest of spiders? Even as a boy he hadn't liked
the dark areas of things. He remembered once visiting his grandmother in
Pennsylvania when she sent him to fetch a jar of pickles from her cellar. She
kept all sorts of stuff in that cellar. It was nothing but a small cave scooped out
under the house, and to enter it you had to lift a door outside the house and
crawl down under.

That day his sister had closed the door on him, and he sat for what
seemed like hours huddled in the dark among the spider webs. He thought he
might even die down there, and then she would be sorry, but it wouldn't do him
any good because he'd be too dead to enjoy it. But he wouldn't make her happy
by pounding and yelling either, so he sat in the dark huddled in fear of the
creepy-crawly things and told jokes to himself—even made himself laugh at
them—until she finally grew bored and let him out. He said later he hadn't
been scared. But he never went into that cellar again.

He'd put the war and his own darkness behind him the same way.

And now, because of a jug-headed promise made when he was stewed,
here he was ambling around like a tourist wondering where to look first. Then
suddenly the damn-foolishness of this mission began to amuse him and he
laughed aloud, and despite old quarrels he began to wonder about Toro. What
paths had he walked? What doors through the years had he opened and closed?
Would the little bull recognize Joe Steele, and if he did would he run happily
to greet his old buddy, or would he paw the ground and charge in red-eyed
rage?

Joe had really lit into him that last time he'd seen him, had said some pretty harsh things. Toro's eyes had blazed like dry kindling, but he hadn't said anything. He'd just turned and stomped off. He might stomp off again; or punch Joe in the nose as he had that time in Juarez. Well, Chief could fill him in. If he could find him in this wasp-nest of sightseers.

He pushed through the crowd and focused on the blocks of earthen homes that rose in stair steps in the yellow light and on the sun-fired mountain behind that lit the pueblo like a halo. From its slopes spilled a breeze, and cloud-made shadows chased over the ground and across the tiers of pueblo walls. Splashes of early-turning aspens shone yellow like scattered suns from the pine-green slopes.

Joe circled a hive of buzzing tourists. An overweight kid dragged by a sunburned woman beat monotonously on a toy tomtom and whined for a Pepsi. A tow-headed boy popped his sister with a bean shooter. She squalled, he ran, and their plush-bottomed mother yelled at both. The father, training his camcorder on a ladder rising from a kiva, ignored the commotion.

Joe walked toward the shallow stream over which a wooden foot bridge connected the halves of the pueblo. At the water's edge a knot of soft-chattering women dipped pots and buckets for the evening meal. Suddenly the tow-headed kid darted among them. Yelling shrilly he brandished his weapon, drew a bead, and launched a nut-sized rock. "'Nother Injun bites the dust!"

The stone flew straight into the posterior of a tall Indian crossing the bridge. He turned, looked down at the culprit as the eagle spots his prey, dropped to the ground where the boy stood transfixed, and without a word calmly lifted the miscreant in clawlike hands and gently deposited him waist deep in the cold stream. The dark women on the banks giggled.

The tow-head thrashed yelping in he water. "Dirty Injun! Mama—"

Mama ran up panting. "Brandon! What're you doing?"

Brandon pointed. "He done it! Dirty Injun threw me inna—"

She gasped and turned on the man. "You attacked a little child—"

The Indian nodded and turned away, Mama in pursuit. "—an innocent little child who—"

"Who shot that man in the butt," said Joe. His voice was dry.

She turned on him. "That hulking savage—"

"Should've pushed your kid under." He grinned. "I would have."

The Indian turned back amused. It was a good opening. Joe stepped toward him. "Pardon me, but I'm looking for—I knew a man from here."

The tall Indian nodded. His face was thin, his eyes dark, direct, far-seeing like the eagle's above his beaked nose, and housing some very private joke.

"We called him Chief in the army," said Joe. "Name was Placido—"

"Yes." The Indian crossed his arms over his chest. "Bataan." His right finger started tapping on his left arm.

"He was in my outfit. We also called him Eagle-eye, or the Eagle, because he could spot enemy planes so far away."

"Yes."

"You know him?"

"Yes." The finger kept tapping and Joe remembered how Chief tapped his arm whenever he was thinking, or listening.

"Are you related?"

"Related?"

"Yes. Kin—family."

The Indian smiled. "I understand you."

"You resemble him."

His smile grew broader. "All us Indians look alike."

"I didn't mean—"

"I know." His mouth was wide, thin, and twitching with humor. He wore jeans and a denim shirt; his feet and ankles were moccasin-shod, and two long braids hung below his shoulders. Like many of his race he seemed neither young nor old.

Joe pulled his pipe from his breast pocket, then put it back again. "I'm Joe Steele. I'm looking for my friend."

"I know." The man's dark eyes probed Joe's blue ones a moment. "Okay. Come with me."

They wound through the milling tourists, past the church and through the plaza, and Joe wondered again if he really wanted to hear what Chief might tell him. Well, he'd saddled this horse; he'd ride him, like it or not. And he probably wouldn't.

He'd relived that mission from his past so many times when the night winds moaned or a coyote howled and the windmill creaked, and old thoughts like dead tumbleweeds blew through his mind, thoughts of the four of them, buddies, from Fort Bliss to Bataan, until—

Until the thing happened. And Joe, remembering—trying to remember, or maybe trying not to—was again crawling through the jungle, he and Toro and the kid Cholly, crawling on their bellies, and him shaking with malarial chills all the way, behind the Jap lines. He remembered, too, some barbed wire—a flood of light—shots exploding and the confusion of ambush and fever, and more shots, and crawling—only Cholly wasn't with them anymore—and somehow, at the end, just before Joe collapsed, Chief. And then the memory blacked out, as if he'd stepped from a kaleidoscope of noise and light into darkness and echoes, and only the burning flame of the thing he couldn't forget and couldn't remember was left, like an old half-forgotten song that whined in the night with the windmill.

Joe had long ago quit trying to remember, had locked it away as he'd locked Tomcat's box in the safe-deposit vault along with the medal he'd won in that escapade he couldn't remember except for bits and pieces. Still it came sometimes, like a lost ghost scratching at the window, a faint persistent fear that he hadn't earned that medal, that it might be a false badge for a courage he hadn't had.

So he buried the insanity of burned-out war and turned to a world restored. He and Beth and Mike had the ranch—its miles of rangeland secured within miles of fence, its day consuming chores and challenges and the eternal prayer for rain in July. He had his books—a library full, and always a stray volume or so thrown in the pickup or tucked in a saddlebag. As a boy Joe had devoured the books of Eugene Manlove Rhodes, and took to reading on horseback as Rhodes had done. His early amusement had, with age, become a habit.

His fellow ranchers thought him an odd duck but they liked his wry humor, respected his intelligence, and enlisted him to lead the eternal crusade for water conservation. He was a good rancher, they knew, for all his bookishness.

Joe had grown up with books. His father had an extensive library of scientific tomes and whodunits, his mother had literary tastes, and Joe gorged on whatever he found. Shakespeare and Homer mixed genially with medical journals, and with the Thurber and White and Mencken he found in his mother's *New Yorker*s.

Beth claimed she could plot his boyhood development by leafing through his old books. Like an archaeologist sifting through artifacts, she said. Those most dog-eared yielded the best clues—a popsicle stick in *The Boy's King Arthur*, a mustard-smeared *Robin Hood* with a hot-dog wrapper for a place mark. *Huckleberry Finn* yielded a fourth-grade report card, with Deportment marked "poor." His absolute favorite (evidenced by its broken spine and loose pages, chocolate fingerprints, two Band-Aids, and a paper airplane) seemed to have been *Treasure Island*, she reported—the one with the N.C. Wyeth illustrations.

Puberty was marked by a well-worn *Iliad*, into which was tucked a note asking, "Why didn't you punch him out?" and signed, "Yours forever, Alice Ann." *Macbeth* had a phone number for "Sue" scribbled in red ink on a matchbook cover. Somewhere about that time he must have discovered Steinbeck. Inside *Tortilla Flat* Beth found a condom.

So many things there were in the world around him that sparked Joe's eclectic imagination—the Bermuda Triangle, paleolithic cave art, aerodynamics, and the Cavalier poets. El Greco's skeletal figures and Rubens's round ones, the Shroud of Turin, the Trojan War, and the behavioral patterns of dolphins. Southwestern archaeology and Greek drama. Things that didn't directly touch his life. Or maybe in their own strange way they did.

His credo was simple. You mended your own fences, kept your cattle inside them and yourself inside the law (or reasonably so), you paid your taxes and your grazing fees, and you never wasted water. You believed in God, but you didn't try to read His mind or analyze His intentions, and you damned sure didn't go pestering Him for favors. Except sometimes for rain in July.

You might not love your neighbor as yourself, but you didn't rustle his cattle or covet his Ford 350 Supercab or seduce his wife (which, considering most of his neighbors' wives, required no great strength of character or purity of soul).

Joe had small use for real-estate developers—the land rapers he called them—or Democrats, rattlesnakes, the Bureau of Land Management, or the Dallas Cowboys. But for the most part he was a temperate man. He studied many things, meddled in no one else's business, and fervently believed that if everyone would dig his own postholes, leave his neighbor's alone, and lynch any sonofabitch caught cutting fences or wasting water, the world would turn a lot smoother. And that went for governments too. Especially for governments.

So now it was time to examine his own fences. An old promise and a new ghost had triggered his mission, but he knew—had known for a long time—that sooner or later he'd have to challenge that closed gate of his memory to learn what it was that butted to get out of that corral in his mind.

Get rid of your snakes, his father had said.

The Indian stopped in the plaza to talk to another man in their own tongue. A few steps beyond a skinny long-haired woman pushed a squalling baby in a go-cart. She had that look-at-my-baby-and-tell-me-how-cute-he-is smile and people passing by were, like well-trained seals, intimidated into responding. A Cub Scout leader in shorts was lecturing on pueblo life to his small charges, none of whom were listening because their attention had focused onto a lively dog fight in the plaza. Joe and the Indian walked on saying little, and Joe thought again of Jonathan Steele.

He'd gone on a call with his father on that last weekend furlough. It was August of 'forty-one—just before he'd shipped overseas, orders sealed, destination unknown.

They bumped along a gravel ranch road. "Any idea where you're going?" Jonathan asked.

Joe shrugged. "Sailing from Frisco's all I know."

"Alaska, do you suppose? Hawaii?"

"Maybe. Or farther." Joe squinted into the distance. "You know, Dad, there may be a war."

"I can read." The doctor spat an arc of tobacco juice out the window. "Well, I guess you won't piss in your pants at the first shot."

"I guess not."

"Give 'em hell, son," said Jonathan.

He said the same thing, only with a question mark, four years later when

Joe came home. "You give 'em a good dose of hell?" They were drinking an after-dinner cognac on the veranda of the ranch house Joe had just bought. His mother and Beth were still inside.

Joe looked away and his voice was flat. "We were surrendered." His jaw muscles tensed as he remembered walking through that last hot night, with great balls of red fire gushing, rolling toward infinity as one by one the ammunition dumps blew, and they knew they too would be part of that same infinity when the Jap tanks rolled at dawn, because this would be their last stand against the crushing odds, and they all prepared to die, but they'd sure as hell die fighting.

But they hadn't. "We were surrendered. But we didn't surrender. Our generals did."

"Hell's catoot, what else could they do? You can't rope calves with fishing line." The doctor's pale eyes darkened for a minute and he looked hard at Joe the way he used to when Joe was a kid trying to explain some misdeed. It was that level blue don't-lie-to-me look.

Joe looked toward the low rise on the eastern horizon, at the rose-pink clouds fading to dusk and he breathed in deeply. "Dad—" He stopped, unable to talk further.

"Don't explain, son. Things happen in wars can't anybody understand." Jonathan had fought in France in 1918. "Maybe not even us that it happened to. Maybe especially not us."

Joe reached for the decanter on the table between them, poured another splash of cognac, looked again at the darkening horizon and thought how night fell and day rose everywhere—universal, but particular too, because every man saw it differently, so it was his alone. He looked a long time at the changing sky and when he looked back Jonathan was watching him.

"You only have one man to answer to, son," he said. "And that's the guy in the mirror."

Joe smiled a little. "Not the one up above?"

"Maybe it's the same thing."

Joe and the Indian came to a low adobe wall within which rested the pueblo's silent dead, and the silence seemed somehow to push the noise of the crowd into some far distance, reduce it to insignificance.

The clouds scudded from the mountain more thickly now, cool with coming autumn. A mist began to drape the peak and a faint scent of rain teased Joe's nose. Autumn came early in this high country. Summer would still bake High Lonesome for another month or so.

The man pointed to a mound. "Placido."

Placido. Chief, who more than once had steered the Fearsome Foursome clear of the MPs in Juarez or Manila. Chief, who on Bataan could hear the Mitsubishi bombers coming before the radar could. Chief, who glitter-eyed would steal into the jungle night searching for enemy snipers and sometimes return with a smile of success. Chief, who caught Joe when he collapsed on the Death March, held him, made him keep going because the Jap guards bayoneted those who fell, and when Joe could no longer walk, carried him. Chief, who had somehow appeared when they needed him during that mission when the thing happened.

Joe reached for his pipe, fiddled with it, gestured toward the mound. "How long?"

"Three years about." The Indian stood cross-armed.

"There were four of us. Two left now. Just me and—" His eyes followed the mists moving down the mountain. "And one other."

"Toro Duran?" The finger began to tap.

Joe darted a quick sharp look at the man and his jaw tensed. "Yeah." *Who is this man who seems to know who I am?* "Yeah. Toro Duran." He looked again at the grave, sucked at his empty pipe making noises like an asthmatic ghost. "Toro—only guy in our outfit that could outshoot Chief." He smiled a little. "We were together—Toro and Chief and I—when they surrendered us. Ordered us to dismantle our rifles. Most of us did. I wrapped mine around a tree. But Toro—"

"Toro didn't." The Indian laughed. "Hid it in the weeds."

"You've heard that story?"

"Placido liked to tell that story. How the tank was going by, and a Jap standing in the turret—Toro reaching for his rifle, laying there, aiming—"

"Couldn't have missed. But Chief stopped him. They'd have wiped everyone of us out if he hadn't." Joe pointed his pipe toward the grave. "Not the only time Chief saved our asses." He drew again on the pipe and looked a long moment at the mountain. "I guess when your buddy dies he pulls some of you in there with him. But—" He curled his lips about his pipe. "You're glad he died here instead of some stinking prison camp."

The other man nodded. "In his own pueblo." His nostrils flared, as Chief's used to do when things were very right, or very wrong.

"I should have kept in touch. But, there were reasons."

"He knew that."

How in hell's outhouse does this guy know so much? Who is he, anyhow? Joe glanced puzzled at the man beside him. *Or is he just putting on this mystic-Indian crap?* The man's eyes seemed to crinkle with some secret amusement.

Joe snapped a salute to the grave and they started back. Past pueblo people going about their business they walked, and past the Kodak-clickers, thinning now with the threat of storm. They walked quietly, each in the privacy of thought, until a little man with a baseball cap, a beer belly, and a smile like a Halloween pumpkin's stepped in their path.

"You." He pointed at the bronze man. "You speak English?"

"No."

"Well, tell me. What in tarnation is that thing sticking up over there?" He pointed at a ladder rising from a kiva.

"That," said the Indian solemnly, "is our TV antenna." They walked on still grinning until they reached the bridge. A cool gust lifted Joe's sweat-damp collar and riffled his hair.

"Many thanks." He gave a quick two-fingered touch to his brow. "I'll head back now. Got to find a room."

"And Toro."

"Yes." Joe squinted his eyes a little, looked hard at the tall angular man. "Yes. Toro." *Who is this man?* He shrugged. Chief had doubtless talked about the war, and this guy, whoever he was, must have listened a lot—even adopted Chief's gestures.

"Know how to find Toro?" the Indian asked.

"He has a phone."

"He won't be home."

"You know him well?"

"Better than he knows me."

Joe stared at the sculpted face, at the eyes in whose dark depths golden flecks moved. Eyes like an eagle's. Like Chief's.

The strange man began to tell him how to find a certain lane that wound west from the village plaza to a blue-painted door. "That's the cantina. Look for him there."

He started across the bridge, then stopped. His shadow fell on the stream below, longer and gaunter than he was, and its outline rippled on the water. He looked toward the mountain with its thickening vapor spilling now like white smoke down the slope until it veiled the earthen walls.

Then half smiling at Joe, he raised his arm and pointed skyward. Gliding above, just ahead of the rolling weather, soared a golden eagle.

Joe looked up, let his gaze follow the great bird in its flight, felt the damp mist on his face. "Thanks, Chief," he muttered without thinking. *Chief?* Well, it was as good a name as any. He never had learned the Indian's name.

The man nodded and moved on, until he was enshrouded in white fog. So too, Joe saw, was the eagle.

4

WHEN AN OTHERWISE RATIONAL
man turns knight-errant and crosses the path of another questing fellow of
singular purpose and volatile disposition, it follows that a few windmills may
find themselves fair game. An adventure is almost assured when their paths
cross in a certain village as flammable as the knight who lives there.

That village has a name, but to protect the innocent, and the not so, it
shall be known only as La Mancha. Its ragged western edge straggles
faintheartedly toward the river and peters out in a poor barrio known locally as
Tuceros—a name commonly given to prairie dog colonies.

At the farthest fringe of Tuceros lived Victorio Duran—quixotic of
temperament, charming of manner, cunning of mind, and as stubborn as the
burro who grazed among his apple trees. Toro lived out where the road frays
into dirt paths, where small boys drive their goats each morning and evening
and the land widens down toward the river. Around Toro's house weeds and
sacatone grass elbow each other democratically and a few tough hollyhocks, left
from the days when Toro's wife lived and tended her little plot, still push
blowsily around the doorway like aging whores. His apple trees scent the air
and barn swallows nest beneath the *vigas*.

Through the years Toro's house had settled comfortably into age. He
made no payments, paid no rent, and what he owned was his—which was
more, he liked to say, than most of the *ricos* who called him poor could claim.

It was Toro's custom each evening to pull on his red boots, mount his
ancient pickup, and roar clattering to the cantina. Through spring winds and
summer torpor he bumped his nightly way, through autumn's nostalgia and
winter's icy dark. Inside the cantina was warmth and friendship and light.
Inside abided faith, hope, and cold *cerveza*. His amigos. *Los cuates*. This nightly
junta could almost be called a religion, except that religion always tries to sell its
isms. At the cantina you could ride the horse or leave it in the corral.

On this August night Toro Duran was, as usual, preparing to join his amigos. But this night he had a purpose. This night held more than conviviality: the very destiny of Tuceros was involved. This night Toro girded to fight for justice, to vanquish the evil that had come into their midst.

And from the other end of La Mancha, his Stetson cocked a bit roguishly to one side, strode the lonely, lanky figure of Joe Steele. He had claimed a no-show's motel room, grabbed a quick beer and a pizza, and set out on foot to find the cantina. Walking was easier than negotiating the Olds through the crowds around the plaza. He needed to stretch his legs, and most reaches of La Mancha were within walking distance.

The day was sighing toward late-summer dusk and the piney scent of evening rode above the dusty day. The mist had rolled through the town quickly and hung over the dark mesa beyond the river, half veiling the near-gone sun. It was the hour of the afterglow, betwixt the end of day and the red dawn of neon beer signs. It was that time when tomcats stretch lazily, test their claws, and begin to anticipate the night's amours, not unlike their human counterparts beginning to emerge for their evening's antics.

La Mancha—and by its extension Tuceros—is a fascinating and frustrating village. It is an attitude, a tradition, a transcendence, a pulse or an impulse. It is tonic or toxic, a playing ground or a praying place, a spot to rest or roister, where causes breed like jackrabbits, and most are as soon forgotten.

From fall through spring it is a self-contained village that feeds (often noisily) on its own affairs, happily unconcerned with life beyond its own watershed. But in summer the village swells like a pregnant mouse. The chemical balance of La Mancha in August is roughly eighty percent tourists and forty percent artists, with trace elements of indigenous residents. This mathematical inaccuracy is explainable when one reflects that in late summer the tourists double in mass and money and the artists in importance, while the townsmen crawl back behind their doors like children sent early to bed who peek giggling until the funny grown-up party is over.

Tourists and tradesmen people the village, ski bums and sculptors, mystics, midwives, and musicians, preachers and panhandlers, potters, pawnbrokers and pimps, saddlemakers and social workers, bartenders and booksellers, woodcarvers, weavers, and welfare workers, horsebreeders and whores.

It is a village unique of soul. That is not to say that its individuality has gone unchallenged. But, like a small desert turtle, Joe had once remarked, it plods its own slow path through the fast lane, gobbles the fruits of the new age, and retreats into its medieval shell without so much as a thank you.

One shopkeeper, a true La Manchan of inspired method, ran his business from two cigar boxes. One held the previous day's profits, and from it he paid the present day's expenditures. Into the other went that day's take. If by closing time (which might be day's end or whenever he thought the trout might be biting) the second box held more than the first, he marked it a good day. If not, he shrugged and waited for the next.

His youngest son, on vacation from the university, walked into the shop one morning. Glad to see him showing some interest in the business, the old man began to explain its complexities. Then came the cigar boxes. The boy looked amazed. Appalled. He gaped and then he took the floor. He lectured long on the gospel of proper accounting. He grew eloquent on double-entry bookkeeping and orderly filing and the necessity for duplicate copies of all transactions. He cited government mandates and the IRS. His father listened with patient and tolerant heart.

"Dad—for a man who can read Homer in Greek and do calculus with one eye shut, surely simple business arithmetic—"

His father shrugged.

"You just can't run a business this way, Dad. It won't work. I mean— cigar boxes?"

The old man tipped his chair back on two legs and looked thoughtfully up at his offspring. "You're right, son," he said softly. "I'm impressed. Nothing beats solid, state-of-the-art education." A hint of a smile tugged at his lips. "But you know—these cigar boxes paid for your education."

Besides the tourist shops and art galleries, La Mancha boasts a sewage plant, a weekly newspaper, a post office, a dentist, and three banks. Even these latter sometimes abandon their traditional sobriety. A pert young teller named Lisa was once approached by a new arrival with a beer belly and a golf-course tan. He needed to exchange his American currency for pesos, he told her.

She looked at him blankly.

He tried again. "You take A-meri-can dol-lar?"

She stared back.

"American money for your pesos."

Lisa smiled enchantingly. "*No hablo inglés, Señor.*" It was the only Spanish she knew, so she said it again. "*No hablo inglés.*"

He took a deep breath and tried again, louder. People began to look his way amused. Lisa smiled sweetly, shrugged eloquently, and looked stupid. So did the next teller, and the next, each repeating the litany. "*No hablo inglés.*" Customers joined in. "Hey Billy, you *hablo inglés?*" "Hell no, *no comprendo.*"

A portly bank officer stepped through his door.

"All I want," said the frustrated tourist, "is some of your currency. Could you direct this young woman—?"

The officer shook his head. "No, *señor*," he answered. "I *no hablo inglés* either!"

La Mancha is shaped roughly like a hand, with the plaza centered in the palm, surrounded by shops and restaurants and galleries. Beyond this small but bustling hub fan the more sedate businesses, museums, and homes that nestle in small enclaves screened by cottonwood copses, making La Mancha a patchwork of contrasting communities, each moving to its own heartbeat.

Angling roughly toward the river spread the fingers of the hand, and it was along one of these that Joe Steele was walking this August evening, down a crooked lane where, if he followed the Indian's directions, he would find the cantina. And Toro. He smiled again at the absurdity. For forty years he hadn't known—or particularly cared, if he examined the truth of it—whether Toro still lived. He had let the thing between them lie like a spent ember until suddenly it flamed into a compulsion. A mission: he must find Toro Duran.

He passed the plaza, through the greasy smells of fast-food joints and the red-chile aromas of enchiladas, and the loud canned music that rushed through doors as they opened, and he had thought in passing how even this little village had been hit by the vulgarization of America, the Madison Avenue hype that had ground once-proud communities into cogs in a network of interchangeable parts. He watched the crowds pushing in and out of the doors and he thought how much alike so many faces looked, all fed by the same government agencies, the same television shows and doctored news and brand names and politically correct causes, so that they too grew standardized and interchangeable.

The stereotyped face of a *politico* smiled charmingly at Joe from a poster on a telephone pole, a leftover from a past election, like the epitaph on a weathered tombstone. Joe grinned remembering his own brief stint in the state legislature. Persuaded by some fellow ranchers, he had run and won, suffered through a single term in Santa Fé, and refused to run again. He got enough hot wind at High Lonesome, he said, the difference being that the wind on the ranch pumped something useful.

A short distance past the plaza Joe crossed an irrigation ditch, the *acequia* that marks the beginning of Tuceros. Although the barrio is part of the greater whole that is La Mancha—and a poor section at that—it enjoys a greater part of La Mancha's political process than its rather seedy condition might indicate. The politicians court Tuceros during election years, and try to keep it happy in between, for Tuceros votes as a solid bloc, as witnessed by the year-after-year reelection of their own Tuceros locals as sheriff and magistrate judge for all La Mancha—namely, Chico and Rico.

Tuceros perches like a ragged mustache over the lip of the river. In its bristles the cantina burrows like a flea. And like the flea the cantina is the source of many an irritation. For it is here that its congregation spin many a puckish plot. Here centers the political life of Tuceros. Here is its social and philosophical home. Here all significant ideas generate, all important decisions, all major plans for the barrio and its citizenry.

Though only a ditch separates Tuceros from the rest of La Mancha, the separation marks a change less in scene than in character, subtle but distinct. For beyond the *acequia* lies the happy insouciant soul of those who have little, covet less, and live exactly as they please, unfettered by social dictates, material trappings, financial obligations, or the world's opinion. The rest of the world can tend to its business. Tuceros minds its own.

Past the ditch Joe turned into an adobe-lined alley, which gave onto a narrow lane winding through a stretch of ground-hugging earthen houses with squat chimneys like fat complacent matrons. It was an area of red geraniums and patchy grass like the hair of a mangy terrier. The air smelled of piñons and dust and manure and baking bread—on the outside much like the rest of La Mancha. The difference lay in personality.

Lupe and Epifanio Cataño lived in one of the houses Joe passed. It was an old house, and small, and they could have afforded a better one, especially after Epifanio won five thousand dollars in a contest by naming a new brand of extra-sour pickles. (His winning name was "Mother-in-Law.")

The social worker—a skinny pop-eyed lady of many smugnesses named Mrs. Muddler—kept telling Lupe she needed a new place. She had even found a modest house for her. But Lupe wouldn't move. *Sí*, the pipes they kept freezing every winter; and *sí*, when the snow it begin to melt in the spring her flat roof leaked; and *sí*, one wall had a long wide crack going all the way through it. But she and Epifanio had grown old here. The house was part of them. And besides, she couldn't leave her mother.

Her mother? An acquisitive glint lit Mrs. Muddler's eyes. She hadn't heard there was a mother too.

Sí. Her mother she was buried in the yard.

The lady's eyes bugged and she gave a yelp. In the yard? Buried? In the yard?

Sí. Next to the bird bath.

Mrs. Muddler forgot to ask where Lupe's father might be. Or maybe she didn't want to know.

Near most of the houses Joe saw *jacals* or corrals housing a burro or so, and remembered how Toro had always nursed a special fondness for the big-eared little beasts. One stabled a good looking horse, a sturdy pinto. Beth liked pintos. She was one helluva good horsewoman too, he thought smiling.

Tuceros is untidy. Yards are cluttered with pickup seats whose stuffing oozes out. Sprawled across one was a boy engrossed in plucking a guitar. He grinned at Joe's two-fingered salute and kept on making chords. Orange marigolds and purple petunias blossomed brightly in old toilet bowls. A plastic Virgin surrounded by artificial flowers stood enshrined in an upended bathtub in one yard. Another held masses of car parts marked by a hand-lettered sign reading "Pedro's Garage—you bend we mend." Children played shrill-voiced and burros brayed and dogs barked.

Houses grew fewer, empty spaces larger. A big money-green sign marked one empty stretch of sand as the property of the JD Emmenthaler Realty and Development Company. Joe wondered again who in hell's outhouse this Emmenthaler might be who seemed to have invaded La Mancha. The white letters shone arrogantly in the late light. But three holes pierced Emmenthaler's name. Someone, it seemed, had been having a little target practice.

A few paces beyond he saw the cantina.

It was a long low building, flat roofed, some of the adobes crumbling, with a single window from which a neon Coors sign glowed redly. A faded blue door beckoned the thirsty.

The cantina had stood so long it was again almost fashionable—or might have been with a different clientele. But then it would not have been the cantina. Inside Joe would see a singer on a high stool at the end of a long bar. A *guitarristo*. The cantina had a juke box, but it had been broken for years. No one missed it, though, not with such a fine singer. He came every night to enrich their lives with myth and music. A Cervantes awaiting a Quixote, a Homer seeking a Troy.

He would not have long to wait. Toro Duran would soon chug noisily up the lane in the name of justice, to plot darkly with his cohorts against the threat that now hung over Tuceros.

And outside, though none inside knew it, stood Joe Steele. He paused a moment, straightened his Stetson, hitched his jeans, and stepped toward the blue door.

5

LET IT NEVER BE SAID THAT
Arabela and Ysidro fail to patronize the arts. Without judgment or restriction
they harbor in their cantina the creators, be they painter, poet, or the singer of
songs. For theirs is the open spirit that fosters civilization itself.

The fruits of their patronage smote Joe Steele head-on as he stepped into
the world beyond the faded blue door. *¡Eeeee-yay-hoooo!* Past a forest of
Stetsoned heads rolled the sound of music, a guitar-thumping *Rancho Grande*,
sweeping toward him like a prairie gale, and with it the stamping feet and
bravos that testified to a music-loving clientele.

"Alla en el rancho grande . . ."

"Eeeee-yay-hoooo!"
"Brrrrrrrrrr-aah-hah!"
Joe's mind flashed back to the image of moon-washed nights in the
jungles of Bataan as the regiment of New Mexicans waited for the final
Japanese thrust they knew would come, and knowing they couldn't last much
longer without food or ammunition, and the homesick chords of *El Rancho
Grande* flooded those last long nights.

". . . alla donde vi-vi-aaa-ha!"

And then he thought again of Toro, and of those last gut-tearing
accusations he had lobbed at his old buddy, and he wondered what sort of
meeting this would be. But he'd headed for this stream. He'd ford it. Make
contact tonight, size up the situation, deliver that damned box tomorrow. And
in the transaction he'd face whatever answers he got—lay some ghosts maybe—
and then head out.

Then he saw the paintings. The brilliant primary colors leaped from the plastered surface of every wall. Large detailed portraits—he guessed of the clientele—peered and leered at him. Caricatures of others danced across the periphery. And behind them all vibrated a landscape of cacti and purple mountains, and in the exact center of the far wall, dominating the panorama, loomed a black mesa, through which a low door opened.

Every inch of space quivered with life and color. What the cantina lacked in finesse it made up for in gusto. The red glow of the neon Coors sign issued from the window by the door in which Joe stood. It lit the room and gave a lurid life to the painted walls. In the air hung, not too subtly in the August air, the incense of stale beer.

Joe glanced about the room. He recognized the portly man with whom Toro had been arguing in the street earlier sitting beneath the red-lit window. The *mustachioed* man called Rico—the magistrate judge. With him was a somewhat smaller look-alike, undoubtedly the brother who had gone fishing. Chico, they had called him. The sheriff. The two were concentrating seriously on their evening's business, which seemed to be the amassing of dead beer cans beside the live ones they were working to dispatch. Both lowered theirs to watch Joe walk to the bar.

A lone Anglo couple was laughing with the darker occupants of a neighboring table. The man was beginning to bald on top—prematurely, to judge by his young face—looking as if his long yellow hair had slid down and implanted itself on his chin in the form of a long untidy beard. His unkempt look was heightened by the woman's white-bloused neatness. In contrast to the fetish hanging from a leather thong around his neck and the rows of bracelets on his arm, she was as primly unadorned as a medieval nun.

Toro was not among the clientele.

Behind the wooden counter that ran the length of the far wall, a woman of grand proportions chewing vigorously a large wad of gum stopped pushing her bar rag along its surface to watch Joe's approach. She wore a gauzy orange blouse and a large fake poppy drooped over one ear that matched the small tattoo on a muscular arm a sculptor might envy.

Every eye in the room seemed to follow him, like those of bright-eyed prairie dogs who sit on their little haunches, ready to protest the entrance of a strange species to their honeycombed village. Joe sensed a tension beyond casual curiosity. The *guitarristo* who sat at the end of the bar on its only stool stopped playing to contemplate Joe through the hooded eyes of a wise old bird of prey.

Joe nodded. "*¿Qué tal, señor?*" and when the gaunt old man nodded he walked toward him. "You play a mean guitar."

The old man nodded again, warily.

"I'm Joe Steele." From behind the beaded curtain back of the bar came the sweet aroma of green chile stew.

"You from that building company?" Dark suspicion peered from beneath the hooded lids.

"No."

"One of them artists come slumming?"

"Not by a long mile." Joe's voice was dry, sanded by many desert winds. "I ranch. Run cattle."

"Not around here I think." The old man's politeness was colder than hostility.

"Place called High Lonesome. Down in the plains country where you breathe good air. Get a fair wind and you can piss clear into Texas." Joe turned to the dark goddess behind the bar. "*Una cerveza, por favor.* Bud."

"Got no Bud." Her voice was low for a woman, almost masculine. "Coors or Carta Blanca." She popped her gum loudly and stooped to lift a puppy that had strayed from a penned-off corner behind the cooler. "Coors?"

"Make it Carta Blanca."

"Costs more." She scooped up another puppy. "Out-growing their pen."

He laid a ten on the bar. She fished a bottle from the cooler—an old washing-machine tub that sat next to a refrigerator nearly as old—popped the cap, and set it dripping before him. "You want change? Or more beer?"

"Maybe both." He took a long swig. She shrugged.

"Eh Arabela," someone yelled. "My throat's dry!"

"Come get your own *cerveza, panzón*." She sent two cans sliding down the bar. Arabela was a large loose woman—large of bone, large of flesh, and her laugh was large and loose too. Her eyebrows were thick and black and they flared satanically toward her temples. Her hair was piled high like the waves of an incoming tide, with loose ripples that never stayed in place.

The musician plucked his guitar softly, still sizing up Joe. "You come a long way for a *cerveza.*"

"I'm looking for someone. Thought he might be here."

"You a bill collector?"

"No. And I'm not a fed or a plainclothesman. Just a rancher, looking for someone I knew a long time ago. Maybe you know Victorio Duran?"

"Ahhh." It was a long soft sound. "Toro!" His hooded eyes grew wary. "He owe you money?"

"No, I knew Toro in the army, forty years ago. We were National Guardsmen, all from New Mexico, and we were amigos, at Fort Bliss, and later on Bataan—"

"Ahhh!" Suddenly the *guitaristo* smiled. His eyes turned up into wrinkles at the corners. They pulled his cheekbones higher in his gaunt face, and then the mouth followed, and a thousand little chasms deepened like the arroyos that seam the mesa, and his down-drooping moustache worked hard to make his face look sober again, but didn't succeed. "You fought in the war? With Toro?"

"We fought all right. And not always against the Japs." Joe remembered some grand free-for-alls and grinned. "See this crooked nose? I got Toro to thank for that!"

It was before they shipped overseas. They'd gone to Juarez for an evening's fun, he told the *guitaristo*. In the bar they ended up in, a corporal from a rival battery made a comment Toro failed to appreciate. He came only to the shoulder of the vulgar one but size did not deter Toro. "Up yours," he graciously suggested.

The corporal took a swing. Others joined in. The melee surged into the street. No one knew what it was about. No one cared. It was a glorious fight until the MPs arrived and broke it up, and one they recalled with pleasure later when they were hunkering in a foxhole on Bataan.

"Remember that fight in Juarez?" Toro had smiled nostalgically. "When I smeared your fuckin' nose?"

"And I knocked out your two prize molars?"

"Ah, *compañero*!"

"Old buddy!"

Joe told this story, and he told about some other fights, too—fights that had cost Toro his corporal's stripes many times over, a sacrifice he made willingly, Joe said, for each noble cause for which he fought. Toro always found a noble cause to fight for, Joe said in his dry sandy way, and they grew nobler as he neared the bottom of whatever libation they found cheapest in Juarez. Even then, he said, the seeds of heroism spouted in Toro Duran.

He swallowed the last of his Carta Blanca and signaled for another. "Join me, *señor?*"

"*No, gracias.*" The *guitarristo* hesitated for a moment and then a puckish glint lit his eyes. "But—maybe I drink a little *vino*—"

As many furrows, Joe guessed, had been plowed into that face by laughter as by tears and time. "*Vino* for my friend, Arabela!"

"It makes for me the lubrication."

Arabela leaned over the bar to pour the red wine into a chipped glass. She smelled of beer and garlic and dandelions, all blended into a piquant perfume. The old man took the nectar gently in his long calloused fingers, held it aloft, and a true *aficionado*, gazed through the glass at the neon Coors sign. *Gracias, señor.*"

"*De nada, amigo.* But I'd guess you have a name?"

"They call me Tecolote."

Tecolote: the owl. No one knew much about him, except that he came from Mexico, by legal, or—more likely—illegal means. He had no family. His parentage was obscure, though he must have had a remote childhood somewhere below the border and he seemed to retain something of the dark soul of Mexico in his brooding eyes. He once had a wife, it was said, but that was a long time ago, before he came to Tuceros.

He had simply wandered in, a strolling bard to lighten their nights and chronicle for the generations the mishaps and miracles of those who gathered behind the blue door. But if he had come a wandering minstrel, he became artist-in-residence. The wise old fowl had nested.

Tecolote resembled the round-faced bird of his name only in his hooded eyes and wise expression, for his face was bony and his body gaunt. He could have posed for El Greco. He asked many questions, answered few, and spoke in a round full voice that enriched even the weakest argument with the deep-belled tones of wisdom.

By day he made adobe bricks. He was as earthy, as solid, as sun-baked, and as fundamental as the bricks he made. With his slender hands he hammered the wooden molds and mixed the clay and water with just the right amount of straw and poured it in the frames to bake in the sun. Heavy earthen bricks he made, which, laid into thick walls, kept out the winter cold and the summer heat, nourished the souls they guarded with something of the earth mother's own soul, and when their time was up they melted gracefully back into the soil that bore them.

He was a master adobe maker and a steady worker when he chose to work, though he hired out only to those who would take him on a handshake, for Tecolote signed no papers. He attended mass on Sundays and as faithfully he joined the communion at the cantina each evening and made his own contribution to the fellowship within. Music and poetry, he knew, transform a simple rite into a high mass, and Tecolote was in these fields divinely gifted.

With a tapping foot and a glint in his eye, he cast his spell each night. He sang the tarnished old songs as if they were newly minted silver; he extemporized with glee or gravity; he sang of the weak, the wild, or the wayward; he could spin a web of human wiles, a ballad for the humble, an anthem to the heroic. Tecolote sang of his people and to his people, and his music held the passion of their dreams and therefore the meaning of their lives.

Tecolote's hands were his manhood. With their grasp he pledged his word and his honor. With their sturdiness he caressed the earth and molded her flesh into shelter for her people. With their delicate touch he freed the songs that linked his soul and the souls of his people with God.

Once when stacking the heavy adobes, one fell on his hand so that he had to stop working. Someone must have told Mrs. Muddler because she came with bandages and bound it tightly, with a stiff splint on the swollen middle finger— a finger, she murmured lovingly, that they told her made beautiful music, and must be protected. She seemed mesmerized by a hand so godlike in its artistry, and she touched lovingly the stiff-splinted member.

He thanked her for her kindness and told her it felt much better. That night at the cantina, drinking the red wine, he felt a song rising inside him, and, unable to play so tightly bound, he declared the price for charity too high, pulled off the splint and bandages, and canceled the debt. Pain was a small price for freedom.

It was rumored he had once been offered professional training, but refused it. All those rules, he is said to have retorted, would ruin the sweetness of the music he made with his friends. Besides, he was a 'dobe maker. He always had been. He liked the feel of it, he said.

44

Tecolote was a Cervantes who saw the heroic in the trappings of the humble, and the humbug in those of the mighty. He had yet to compose his *opus magnus*, his great *corrido*, but he had no doubt it would come when God wished it. And so he sought, from the great turmoil of life, to catch one quick moment of eternity, which may be all we have; to add one small comma to the journal of Man; to cause one twinkle in the eye of God.

These things Joe Steele learned later.

Now he stood at the bar by the *guitarristo's* stool and they drank another round. Arabela returned another puppy to the little pen. There were five. "Their mother got run over," she said. She tilted a can of Coors into her own thickly painted lips and left a stain like blood on the can. The others in the cantina, seeing Tecolote quaffing amiably with the gringo, turned back to their own affairs, though it seemed to Joe there was an underlying grimness in many faces, and the tenseness he had sensed in them earlier remained.

A man with gray hair hanging from beneath a squashed-in Stetson touched Joe's arm. He sure could use a *cerveza* himself, he said, and Joe signaled Arabela to put it on his tab. His name was Félix, the man said with a pudgy chuckle. Everything about him was pudgy—his large tummy that ballooned above his swollen legs, the fingers with which he clasped his beer can, even the grin of thanks he gave to Joe.

Tecolote asked about the war, and about Toro in the war. Arabela flashed her buck-toothed grin and threw in a couple of stories of Toro's great exploits in that war. The damned little bull, Joe thought, seemed to have laid it on thick in colors like those on the walls.

Tecolote thumped out a tune.

> "With his buddy he crept through the jungle one day,
> A bullet flew right by his ear.
> The sniper he chased with his rifle in hand,
> El Toro, the man with no fear."

Joe cocked an eyebrow. "As I remember it, that 'man without fear' dove into a carabao wallow. Fast."

Tecolote looked hurt. "That's how he told it."

"Well, you're the song maker, not me."

Tecolote asked again about the war.

Joe told about the Saturday night Toro tied a goat under the drill sergeant's cot at Fort Bliss, and how the sergeant came in drunk, and every time he tried to sit or lie down the goat began to buck. And about the time, before the war started, when Toro had bought a monkey from a Chinaman in Manila and turned it loose in the barracks, and about the sergeant's fury when he found all the mosquito nets shredded and the barracks a mess.

But those, Joe said, were minor skirmishes in the great sergeant war. Toro's greatest victory was the result of brilliant strategy and careful tactics.

"From the first he hated that sergeant. We all did—a real bastard he was—voice like a jackhammer, hard drinker. Toro's number one enemy."

Toro began to watch his enemy's habits closely, Joe said, and he stored this intelligence for future combat. No man breathes, he knew, who couldn't be penned inside his own corral.

It chanced that on a certain windy weekend in March the sergeant drew a two-day pass, and Toro drew KP. Every artist, he pronounced later, should be offered the salutary benefits of KP. Demanding little concentration, it marvelously frees the mind to ascend the airy realms of true creativity.

Washing pots on Sunday, he cursed his own ill luck. Mopping floors, he cursed the sergeant. From here he began to contemplate the sadistic possibilities of that one's baleful, blood-shot return, and the pure hell he would dole at Monday's drill. At some point into his second barrel of potatoes, Toro crossed into the realm of pure inspiration.

Ideas piled with potato peels. One possibility particularly intrigued Toro, and his mind kept sniffing at it like a poodle at a fire plug.

Off duty, he pushed his way through the high Texas gale to the tent-covered framework of two-by-fours that were the barracks. After Taps, with the single-minded dedication of true genius, Toro set to work.

Sometime before dawn the sergeant stumbled in.

Toro smiled in innocent slumber until reveille blasted him into morning. Covertly he watched the enemy who, he smiled to note, followed his usual pattern and kept to his sack until the last possible moment to throw on his uniform and make formation. It was a habit Toro had counted on.

The sergeant's snores metamorphosed into strangles, and then he opened a bleary eye, struggled upright, belched, and, gathering sudden energy, thrust his feet into his shoes for a forward lunge.

The shoes failed to lunge with him. The sergeant pitched forward. A curse worthy of Zeus filled the tent, followed by round epithets for whichever son-of-a-Juarez whore had nailed down his shoes.

Smiles cracked the corners of a few mouths.

The sergeant leaped up, grabbed furiously for his neatly hung pants. They too were immobile, nailed to the upright from which they hung. Larger, rounder curses filled the barracks. Scattered titters escaped the less stoic.

Then the sergeant saw his shirt. It too was secured to the two-by-four frame; and, neatly buttoned, tie in place, it swelled pompously, stuffed with the sergeant's skivvies.

Smiles expanded. Titters grew to guffaws as the men raced for formation. Behind them descended the lashes of vile threats. The sergeant was not amused.

Not knowing who the felon was, he spread his fury democratically to every man in the battery; but each, armored with the delicious aftertaste of that apple-pie scene, grinned and marked one up for Toro.

It was his first rung to heroism.

His friends called him a genius, a tiger, a hot tamale.

Joe called him an asshole.

"Our good Lord teaches us humility," Toro intoned. "That's why He invented KP."

"Bullshit," said Joe (who wished he'd thought of it first).

"So he sent me this beautiful vision of shoes, and pants—"

"Cram it."

"—and then I saw a shirt—"

"Stuff it!"

A radiant smile beautified Toro's face. "Ah, *amiguito*," he said, "that's just what I did!"

Arabela laughed loudly and so did several others who had gathered to hear the story.

But what about the war? And how Toro became a hero?

Hell, Toro was a hero before the war started, Joe said. "After taming that sergeant, why worry about the Japanese army? Being a hero had gotten to be a habit." A habit, Joe thought, Toro still had. "He was also good at starting fights—that was before the war too —and then letting me finish them."

Tecolote nodded. That was Toro! But—what about the war?

Joe shrugged. "His version's better than mine."

An hour ticked by, and part of another, and every time the door opened Joe looked toward it. So did everyone else, and the edginess seemed to increase. Occasionally someone opened the low door cut through the black-painted mesa. (That led to the outhouse, Tecolote told him. "But you got to cross the *acequia* first. There's boards across it. Don't fall in.")

By then the puppies were yelping, loudly and continually, and Arabela poured milk in their pan. The sounds of noisy lapping replaced the yelps, until one by one they fell asleep.

Joe yawned. He could use some sleep himself. "Doesn't look like Toro's coming."

"He'll come," said Tecolote.

Arabela leaned on the bar. "He's plotting. He's just before busting loose with one of his half-ass ideas. And then try to rope us all in." She turned to Joe. "He'll try to corral you too. You better sleep with one eye open."

Joe put down another ten and they settled to another round. Periodically the old one's long fingers fondled the strings, thrummed a few chords. From a curtained door behind the bar Ysidro appeared from time to time, leaned against the jamb, picked his teeth, and ducked back again. "To his TV," Tecolote explained. "Him and Arabela live back there." Arabela kept polishing the bar. A tiger-striped cat slipped through the beaded curtain, finished off the remainder of the puppies' milk, and disappeared back through the curtain. Intermittently the blue door swung open and new arrivals walked in. Chico and Rico, expanding with drink, were entertaining their end of the room, Chico with fish stories, Rico with his adventures of the day. "*Turistas* and Toro—don't know which is more trouble."

"Where the hell is he?" yelled someone. "We got to settle that damn bi'ness."

Heads nodded in vigorous agreement and the silence of waiting lit for a moment like a bee on a hollyhock. Tecolote's strings hushed as he reached for another quaff. In that moment of quiet the roar of an unmuffled engine came from beyond the blue door. It sputtered out with a final protest, a pickup door slammed, the blue door burst open, and a red-booted, red-shirted Toro shot in like a meteor.

In the doorway he stamped a booted foot, struck a wide-armed pose, grabbed the rim of his black Stetson and sent it arcing through the room. Bathed in the red Coors light he stood like Mephistopheles, and he twirled a non-existent Pancho Villa moustache he might once have had.

"El Toro!" someone yelled and like a prairie-dog village the room came alive cheering, Chico and Rico in the lead, and Toro yelled back:

"Ride, Vaquero!"

Joe remembered that cry. After they were surrendered and became Japanese prisoners, they sometimes had to herd carabao, those lumbering Philippine water buffalo that lay in pools of mud and pulled from it with a sucking sound. They could get mean, but Toro had a way of jumping astride with a loud yell, and what was more, he hung on.

"Ride, Vaquero!" He'd show those slant-eyed bastards how a man could ride, he'd boasted.

"You'll break your skinny neck," Joe had answered. But he had to admit, Toro was one hell of a horseman.

"Sure," said Toro. "*Mi papa* was a cowboy. When I was 'bout four years old he put me on a bronc—wild as hell. He say he'd break boy and horse together, 'cause that's how you make a cowboy. A *vaquero*. He told me, 'Just hang on.' And I did."

Toro became a *vaquero*, and when he joined the regiment he became a cavalryman, until Washington changed the outfit to artillery. He griped, but he still hung on, then and later in the war and then in prison camp. And on the carabao.

"Ride, Vaquero!"

"*¡Vaquero!*" yelled Félix.

Joe felt a rising tension in the cantina, sensed that something had the assemblage worked up, and saw that Toro was in the middle of it. Watching the little bull prance like fire from one table to another, pausing in his dance to light a friend's cigarette with his Zippo, sharing a quick "*hola*" here, a clap on the shoulder there, Joe noted an energy of determination that confirmed his feelings. Well, at least here was one fracas in the making that Joe had no part in.

Toro, caught up in whatever it was that was sticking in the collective craws in the cantina, hadn't noticed Joe.

"So what happened?" someone yelled.

"What did he say?"

"You tell him?"

"You even get in to see him?"

Toro jumped onto a table. (Pretty spry for sixty years, thought Joe.) He cast his long eyes about the room. "Okay, *compañeros!*" His voice was like rough burlap, frayed from long and violent use. "Shut up and listen." A relative quiet began to settle around the room. "I saw him—but not 'til after I had to straighten out a traffic jam for the judge!" Toro grinned whitely at Rico. "Wouldn't nobody let me in his office," he yelled, "so I wait around behind some cars 'til he came out, and I got between him and his big green Continental. I flatter him—told him I knew he was a man who would listen—"

"We know what you said—what did he say?"

"I told him a man as charitable as him would want to hear our side. That we love La Mancha, and Tuceros, and our cantina. I told him I was elected by *mis amigos* that I love, to speak for them—"

Toro was giving quite a performance. Joe grinned, watching his quick gestures that sprang from a quick mind—some might say shifty—the same darting-fire hands Joe remembered from the old war days. They were hard tough hands that had come in contact with their share of jaws, and yet they were strangely graceful.

"Get on with it." "What did he say?" "Will he come talk?"

"I told him these things, and I pled with him, and the tears they came in my eyes—"

"But what did he say?"

"*Mis compañeros*—" Toro paused and a full-bodied moment of silence hovered in the hot air as the congregation held its collective breath. Toro opened his mouth and made an exaggerated mime of spitting in disgust. "*Compañeros*—he said *no!*"

Like air from a punctured tire was the sound of exhaling lungs. "*¡Piojo!*" "*¡Utá!*" "*¡Adió!*" "*¡Chite!*"

"The sidewinding sonofabitch said no! No, he wouldn't listen. No, he wouldn't stop his plans. No, no, no! An' then—then the lying bastard said he was doing it all for our good—our good, he says—like he hadn't even heard me. So then—I told him go to hell!"

50

A volley of rage-red shouts filled the room, with calls for *mas cerveza, mas vino*, for their fury fed their thirst. "Go to hell!" cried Félix happily to the ceiling.

Glancing about the room Joe sensed a oneness of purpose in their ranks. Something in the cantina, some warmth—the brotherhood of the humble, maybe—pulled them togther, sticking like flies to flypaper. And somehow every man, whatever his sorrows or deprivations might be, seemed somehow whole, one with himself. Watching, Joe felt his own empty spot more keenly, that missing chunk of himself he had left behind in a tangled war-torn jungle. That part maybe Toro could help him find. If he would.

Toro began to roar again. "I go to him in peace, in good will, with love in my heart. I talk to him friendly. And what does he say? He says he gots money in this thing, and God done told him to do this thing for us, and the guv'ment love him so much they giving him more money. I ask him would he rather have a guv'ment he can't even see for a friend, or us that's got faces and hearts inside us? I tell him we gots smiles and love—

"And then I tell him we got fight too, if that's what he wants!"

Heads nodded and growls rose to howls and howls to threats.

"So now," shouted Toro, riding the crest, "now is the time for action! Amigos!" he roared. "That gutless bastard ain't no fighter. He's a plotter—a jelly-faced spaghetti-spined son-of-a-Bible-quoting bitch in love with his own ass and his own lies! He don't even plot smart. I can look in that snake-eyed face and know everything that's going on in his cow-chip brain! And I don't got to go very damn deep before I stub my toe on the only thing he has got—his stinking money and his apple-polishing Bible quotes and his guv'ment laws. But when he sees a hard-nose fight coming—like you and me are going show him—then all his money bags and his law papers and his fake pretend religion gonna be *no bueno por chite!*"

Cheers, *olés*, and maledictions filled the air.

But Toro wasn't through. "It got to be all of us!" He glared redly at a couple of men who looked at each other and then at the floor, and at a deep-breathing Rico gathering himself for a rebuttal. "There got to be no sonofabitch caving in—like getting on that money-flinging bastard's payroll!" He glanced again at the floor-gazing pair.

"We got to make a living—"

"So make it somewhere else! You are one dumb *mexicano*, Onofre!" Toro appealed to his audience. "We got to take care of dummies like Onofre!" The answering guffaw spurred Toro further. "Remember old Seferino Guttierez? Went off to the university and got hisself educated—and when he came home he was still a dumb *mexicano*."

Rico had had enough. He heaved himself from his chair, pushed his hat back on his head, wiped the sweat from his forehead, and began pounding two beer cans together for silence. Chico banged his own against the table.

"You better listen to me," Rico yelled. "You better not do nothing like you're talking about. You better stay inside the law!" He belched loudly.

"Stay inside the law!" bellowed Félix.

"We done tried that," Toro shot back.

"You cause trouble," said Rico, "and all you do is get the law on his side. You want Chico have to come and arrest his own friends? You want me have to sentence my amigos to the jail?"

"You done it plenty times before!"

"This man—he is powerful. He has got money and he has got friends in the government—"

"It's our cantina—"

"We didn't send him no invitation!"

Rico clapped his cans together. "You got to use some reason—"

Toro exploded. "You ever try to use reason with a sidewinder? Hell no!"

"We could all of us talk to him" said Rico, and there was deep sadness in his voice. "If only he'd come here."

"Well, he won't. He's coming in Tuceros grabbing up our territory. We won't have none left. We'll lose our cantina—"

"Ysidro ain't sellin'!" someone yelled.

"You know what he told me?" Rico looked in the man's direction. "He told me if Ysidro keep on refusing to sell the cantina he'll have it condemned!"

"Let him try!" "We'll show him!" "He can't do that!"

"He damn sure can!" Rico's voice rode over the rest. "I keep telling you—he has got the law on his side!"

Toro routed the noise. "Okay, then. One, we got to get rid of him. Clear him out. You with me?"

"¡Andale!" "¡Bravo!" "¡No bueno por chite!"

"!No bueno por chite!" roared Félix.

"Only one way to get a sidewinder out," yelled Toro. "We fire his hole! Smoke him out!"

Cacophony erupted.

"It is time," said Tecolote with a white-flashed grin, "to quiet down some tempers." A loud thrum of strings, a crack of his hand against the sound box, and a lively tune burst into life. A favorite.

> "*Las mujeres son el diablo,*
> *Parientes de Lucifer . . .*"

A few feet began to stomp. "Eeeee-yay-hoooo!" "Brrrrr-aaa-hah!"

Toro had sewn the seeds. He had flung the gauntlet. He had captured his audience. And he knew his exit line. Grinning widely, he flashed the old V-for-Victory sign, as they'd always flashed it during the war, jumped from the table and headed for the bar.

> "*Se visten por la cabeza,*
> *Se desnudan por los pies!*
> *La cucaracha, la cucaracha . . .*"

Joe inhaled deeply and wondered again if his old buddy and antagonist would recognize him. And if he did, would he still remember those last bitter words?

> "*Ya no puede caminar,*
> *porque no tiene, porque la falta . . .*"

"Fish me out a cold one, Arabela!" Toro turned to Tecolote. "Amigo!"

> "*Marijuana que fumar!*"

Tecolote banged his guitar at the finale. "Toro! Here is come somebody you know when you were the young man. When all of us were a young man."

Toro reached for his Coors, raised it to touch his breast and then his forehead before he guzzled the first long satisfying swig. It was a ritual he had initiated in Juarez—some sort of heart-and-head pledge to the great god of booze, presumably—and the Fearsome Foursome had adopted it as a pledge to each other. Joe smiled remembering.

Then Toro turned toward where Tecolote was pointing.

He stopped short, squinted his long eyes at Joe not quite recognizing him, and while his memory groped, Tecolote slid gracefully into a plaintive song, a gringo song to honor the gringo guest.

> "Come all you *compañeros*
> And listen all to me . . ."

A flame of recognition spurted in Toro's eyes, and the fire of old memory caught and kindled as Tecolote sang softly in three-quarter rhythm, vibrantly, heartbreakingly, no longer man, but the song itself.

> "I'll tell you a story
> Of a bold company . . . "

The two old sons of the regiment looked long at each other. Toro seemed bursting with the enormity of the moment.

> "*Envejeco*—I grow older,
> *Mis momentos* are not long,
> Ooooooh—
> You may forget the singer
> But don't forget the song."

Then, as Joe waited, wordless, his own thoughts searing his brain, the tears began to flood Toro's eyes and his arms flung open for embrace.

"Amigo!" He cried in his hoarse ragged voice. "Amigo!"

6

OUR LIVES ARE PEPPERED WITH
moments wherein we involve ourselves, consciously or not, in an idea, only to
wonder later, when the idea poises at the gate of action, how we got there. But
by then we're in the arena and the bull is charging.

Joe never did figure out how it happened to him; but facing Toro Duran
that night in the cantina was such a moment.

"Amigo!" Toro clasped his old buddy in a strangling *abrazo*. *"¡Mi
amiguito viejo!"*

A tear-spurting shock hit Joe, like biting into a raw jalapeño, and he
almost returned the hug. But another image flashed, and he saw Toro again,
diving for cover in the splatter of bullets, Toro dropping the limp Cholly who
shouldn't have been allowed to come with them on that mission in the first
place, Toro dropping him and running.

But Joe had remembered that only in flashes before, and even those
didn't come to him until months after the action, when he awakened
sometimes in the hot nights in that Jap prison camp and caught the quick
glimpses of Toro in a sudden brilliance like lightning, running. Then all he
could remember was stumbling through the jungle, crawling, tugging at the
heavy weight that was the millstone they had stolen from right under the Japs'
noses, because theirs was broken and they had to have one to hull their rice or
starve.

It had been Toro's idea. When some Filipinos told them where they
could find the stone in a little barrio the Japs had taken over, Toro had
volunteered the Fearsome Foursome. But Tomcat, in the throes of a malaria
attack, had been dragged to the row of cots on a hillside they called a hospital;
Chief had been ordered on another foray—an officer-ordered one—and Toro
had drawn guard duty, but he conned someone into covering for him, which
left Toro and Joe and the kid Cholly who was never cut out for soldiering but
insisted on going.

Joe remembered pushing stealthily through the jungle night, crawling toward the barrio with little else but their rifles, a machete, and the wire cutters Toro always hung from his belt in case of a barbed-wire booby trap, finally sighting the thing in a clearing. Vaguely he remembered unhooking the coveted stone, and crouching low and covered by night pulling the heavy thing toward the jungle thickness.

But by then he was fading in and out of reality as the malarial fever swept through him. The details were smoky, though he seemed to remember a stretch of barbed wire, a flash of light, and all hell breaking loose as the Japs opened fire. And then the spate of bullets as the malarial chills closed over him.

He remembered crawling in and out of the fevered mists, remembered coming somehow in that long night back to their own camp—he and Toro, for they were only two by then—and Chief running out in the pre-dawn dark to help them drag the stone inside camp.

For a long time that was all he could remember. Because almost on the heels of that mission the Japs opened the final mass offensive, and Joe's memory of that night was swallowed in dark smoke and after that came the wrenching word that they were being surrendered, the heartbreaking orders to stack arms, and the beginning of what was later called the Death March, when buddy sought buddy and all tried to stick together.

Tomcat, Chief, Joe, and Toro. If one stumbled, the others held him up and made him walk, because the Japs bayoneted those who fell. When Toro, crazed with thirst, tried to dash toward a flowing artesian well alongside the trail, Joe jerked him back. "You want to get shot like those other poor bastards you see lying there?"

Once when Joe started to scoop water from a trailside pool, thick with scum and blood and the bloated bodies of the dead, it was Toro who stopped him. "Go on, you stupid sonofabitch, drink it and die" and Joe, jolted to sensibility, limped on past the water.

And when nearing the end of the march he'd collapsed, it was Chief who carried him the last few miles, while Toro and Tomcat staggered along on bloody feet bolstering each other with insults. Buddies became brothers on that march.

During the immediacy of survival Joe remembered little of the millstone raid. It wasn't until months later, after Toro and Tomcat escaped into the jungle, that brief moments of memory began to flash in the long nights as he lay on wooden slats in the verminous prison camp at Cabanatuan. Until then those troubling visions streaked like distant comets, unseen beyond the clouds of his mind, and he and his brothers were one.

Still they looked after one another as the months dragged by. Chief stole food for them all, and Tomcat kept them laughing through the grim nights with blown-up tales of his prowess with women, seasoned with Joe's irreverent comments. So that each owed his life to his comrades, and each held a part of the others in an interweaving mesh that none could tear.

Always Toro clowned. He mocked he Jap guards behind their backs. He played mind games with them to confuse them. He lost or damaged irreplaceable equipment and nodded in agreement when they screamed he was a "dumb Amelicano." He sang bawdy songs. He kept his prison mates laughing.

And herding carabao, he flashed a V-for-Victory and jumped astride. "Ride Vaquero!"

These things flashed through Joe's mind as he stood looking at Toro Duran.

"Amigo!" shouted Toro again. "You cadgin' drinks like always, you old cockroach!" He punched Joe's shoulder laughing.

But Joe couldn't drop into the old camaraderie. He opened his mouth and nothing came out. The reunion of two old war buddies was supposed to be nostalgic, he thought drily. This one promised to be just plain disgusting.

Ysidro appeared in the curtained door picking his teeth.

With a grand sweeping gesture that embraced the whole cantina, Toro cried out that here was his *amigo viejo*, his oldest best buddy that fought the by-god war with him, his own Anglo *hermano* that he thought was dead for all these years. His lifted his Coors in the old bosom-to-head ritual and stamped a red boot, and his eyes boiled over again.

Joe yo-yoed between amusement and annoyance as he always had. He growled a little and grinned a little and shook his head. It was the same old Toro, seeming not much older except for a few fine furrows around his eyes. A thick thatch of hair still topped his head in the same lawless disorder, though now it was white like a heap of ashes.

Tecolote strummed softly and watched from his hooded eyes. Other eyes, that had watched Joe narrowly on his entrance now widened in curiosity, or maybe relief, and a few drifted closer.

Sudden inspiration seemed to infuse Toro. As if he were drinking a *cerveza* with God, his face took on a glow. Joe had learned to read that face long ago—a face that could change like a flash of lightning from craggy devilment to shaggy sainthood. A face that grew more saintly as he grew more devious. And when he assumed his crucified-Christ expression, someone would be the loser. Now it sparked with creative genius.

"*Compañeros,*" he bellowed. "We have done been sent a by-god sign!" He pulled a Marlboro from his pocket, lit it, took one puff, snuffed it in an ashtray, and jumped into an elated spiel. "Always before, from the time we first was in our Uncle Sam's army, and when the war came and those yellow bastards had us all outnumbered, always the Lord and my own special saint, they sent *mi amiguito* here, my one by-god friend Joe"—he pronounced it Choe—"and always we fight together and save each other! My buddy Choe. He is one fighting *hombre!*"

Rico ambled up to the bar, signaled for two more *cervezas*, ignored Toro, and eyed Joe judiciously. Other eyes crackled amiably as Toro warmed to his subject.

"And now the good Lord sends me again *mi amiguito, mi hermano,* to fight at my by-god side again!"

This saintly inspiration triggered a signal in Joe's brain, a warning of impending battle into which Toro had always dragged him. Damned if he was going to get maneuvered into this one. "Hold your horses, Duran."

But Toro was crackling like a blazing piñon forest. "Rico, you say stay inside the law. You say get that sidewinder here to talk with us. So I tried. I talk reasonable." He turned to Rico, threw an arm around his shoulder, and his voice warmed with hoarse fellowship. "Rico, *mi amigo,* you are right! We got to get him here, drink a *copita,* tell him our side. We got to show him we ain't a bunch of *paisanos* he can fool. Then—if he still won't back down—to hell with the law!"

Arabela stopped her mopping motion. "Watch out, Toro. Emmenthaler hear you he'll lock up your dogs again." She laughed.

"Who told you 'bout that?"

"His cook."

"When?"

"Before you found out!" She laughed again.

"Why you didn't tell me?"

"You didn't ask." She attacked the counter again.

Toro resumed his monologue. "Rico—you know all that law shit—tell the smirking scoundrel about how it protects *los pobres*. Even a sidewinder got to respect the law."

"*¡Chale!*" Rico's eyes sidled toward the door below the black painted mesa. "I don't see you had no luck getting him here."

"Ah, but amigo—that's where my old buddy Choe comes in! I told you the good Lord sent him!"

Joe's eyes tightened a little and he hitched at his jeans.

Toro rattled on happily. "Texas sonofabitch thinks we're bunch of *paisanos*. Won't talk to us. So—we send Choe in—gringo smart as him. My buddy, sent by my own special saint. He ain't no sidewinder going give him no runaround, I good-and-guarantee! Old Choe will lasso him and tie him and drag him in! The one thing Choe Steele ain't is scared of a fight!"

"*¡Olé!*"

Rico looked dubious.

Joe smiled but it had a sardonic twist. "Just out of curiosity," he asked, "who is this Texas critter you think I'm going to lasso?" He could guess the answer.

"That sidewinding critter," said Toro, "is name of JD Emmenthaler!" He punctuated the name with a long stroke of his invisible moustache.

"Ah." Joe took a long pull on his Carta Blanca. "Let me guess the rest. He's buying up land."

A gale of explanations hit him like a spring sandstorm. Through a front man, or men, Emmenthaler had, Joe gathered, quietly bought large chunks of property in Tuceros with promises and prices these people couldn't resist. Except for Ysidro, who refused to sell the cantina, which now sat like a hostile island in the middle of JD's proposed development.

Culling this information from a counterpoint of outraged voices, Joe concentrated on filling his pipe. Arabela was wiping the bar vigorously, chewing her gum in rhythm.

"Tell him what the sonofabitch did next!"

"¡Uta!" "¡Chite!" "¡Piojo!"

Toro took a deep angry breath. "Started making threats. Said no dumb gin-mill owner of no 'dobe dump was goin' louse up his plans." He banged his fist on the bar as the noise mounted. "Amigos!" he bellowed. "Shut up and let me tell it!" He turned to Joe. "Said he'd have this property no matter what—that he'd offered more money'n Ysidro'd ever see again, and if he didn't take it, it would be Ysidro's bad luck, because he'd get this old piece of junk condemned."

Another round of epithets erupted.

"The one thing Emmenthaler ain't," Toro yelled, "is nice. Here, amigo." He aimed his Zippo at Joe's pipe, leaned against the bar and swigged his Coors while the fulminations of his outraged friends rose and diminished. Then he wiped his large mouth with the back of his hand and delivered his punch line. "Well, *compañeros*, let him by-god try! Because he can't! It's the law. He can't do that!"

"¡*Quítate!*" Rico took a swill from the nearly full can, gestured widely with it, and in the doing slopped a healthy wash of still-foaming brew down Joe's chest. "Listen to me!" he roared. "Listen!" Chico, who had by now joined the group at the bar, grabbed the can from his brother's raised hand and lowered its contents into his own parched gullet.

Joe puffed his tobacco thoughtfully. Whatever Toro did, he remembered, he had always done intensely, and expected everyone else—and God too—to pitch in as enthusiastically.

"Listen to me," Rico yelled again. "I am trying to tell you—that piece of Texas garbage can do that! He can get this property condemned. And he will! This dude has got money, and he knows whose hand to grease with it. He is doing this with a federal grant. From Washington dee-cee."

"What does Wash'ton know about our business?"

"They don't need to know nothing about it. He's put in that he's a good guy that's putting up low-cost housing for people like us that couldn't afford such good living as he's going to give us in cheap rent, and they have financed him with government funds which he ain't about to let hisself lose.

"You think we can fight that? I tell you, amigos, he got the damn law on his side and if we go outside it like you are thinking, and make him mad, he'll use that law—he'll use anything we do outside the law against us and give us a double whammy. We got to try and find out just what he is up to, and then we move first—legal, with the law on our side!"

Ysidro, still picking his teeth, looked at Rico as if he didn't quite believe him.

Toro took over. "What Rico says is true," he cried. "He knows the law, and he is right!" He flashed a wide white brotherly grin at Rico and his long eyes smiled too. Toro always smiled so sweetly—like a saint or a salesman, Joe though—when he was plotting most deviously.

"Rico, he ain't no dumb Mes'can. Even if he acts like one sometimes. Our only chance is to make Emmenthaler understand we don't want his fine big complex, and ain't nobody going rent his damn apartments—that we love our little houses he calls huts, that our grandfathers' ghosts live in them."

"Gringos don't know about ghosts."

"Gringos don't hear nothin' but cash registers."

"Amigos," said Toro, "you are right. But so is Rico. We got to talk to him. We can't get in his office, so we got to get him here. Then Rico can tell that asshole what the by-god law says! Hell, Rico can make up some law, like he does all the time to them *turistas*, and they never know the difference.

"But we got to get him here. He won't come for me, 'cause I am one dumb Mes'can. But," and he paused significantly, "my good friend Choe can make him come!" Then, flashing his wide white smile, Toro delivered his clinching argument:

"Else why, just now, after all these years, would the Lord and my own special saint send him here?"

Joe tapped his pipe sharply into the ashtray. It was time to cut this scene. "Just a goddamned minute." He tapped it again. "I was not bridled and saddled by your saint or anybody else's. Any saint worth his halo has better things to do."

Ysidro threw down his toothpick and started toward the beaded curtain. This discussion was all gobbledegook, and the Dodgers were playing. Arabela kept swiping at the bar.

"God moves in mysterious ways," intoned Toro.

"I'm sure He does. But I'm not His agent, or any saint's. Unless you want to call Tomcat Little a saint."

"Tomcat! Tomcat Little!"

"Yeah. Remember?"

"Tomcat by-god Little! He send you?"

"You might say so."

"*¡Ay, compadres!* What do I tell you? Not one, but two, my oldest friends." Toro was darting about like a prairie fire.

"He gave me a box to deliver," said Joe quietly.

"Where'd you see Tomcat?"

"Manila. Forty years ago." He stuffed his pipe in his pocket and picked up his hat. "Took me a while. I'll get it to you in the morning."

"*Bueno*. We'll talk about Emmenthaler then."

"No. I'm heading out after I deliver that box."

Toro turned to his friends and laughed loudly. "*Ay, compañeros*, always Choe, he says no at first. But my good amigo, he never deserts his old buddy. We fight together always! Anybody got a smoke?" Someone tossed him a cigarette. "*Ay*, amigo—you remember that big fight on Angel Island?"

But Joe wasn't going to be drawn into any nostalgic reminiscences and then into another of Toro's quarrels. They could talk about the war in the morning, maybe, he said. He wished their cause well, he told the listeners, but he had to get back to the ranch.

Tecolote strummed softly. Toro's Zippo flared, and he blew the smoke toward the ceiling.

"Just one more day." Toro inhaled again, and gestured widely with his cigarette. He held it like a piece of chalk between his thumb and forefinger. "Just one more fuckin' day," he said almost dreamily drawing pictures in the air with his cigarette. "After forty years! And when you hear what that side-winding bastard is doing—"

"No way, Toro," said Joe softly. "No way." He swallowed one last taste, tossed another ten on the bar for whomever it could cover, and turned to leave. He hitched his jeans, threw Tecolote a two-fingered salute, nodded to Toro, and headed for the door.

"Amigo."

"*Mañana*," said Joe.

Félix lifted his head from the bar. "*Mañana*," he bleated weakly, and slid lumpily to the floor.

Tecolote's song followed Joe through the room, and his strong voice rose—the gringo song for the gringo guest.

Joe paused at the door and stared again at the figures on the walls. He recognized Rico in his judge's robes, and Chico wearing a badge that covered his entire chest. He saw Tecolote, or at least his hooded eyes peering from behind an oversized guitar painted in shades of blue, and his hands, also oversized, delicately mastering the strings.

Slithering among the painted populace was a serpent of enormous size, with a human face, a pampered, pink-cheeked, baby face with crafty blue eyes and a small pinched mouth, and he wondered if this serpent in the desert Eden was Emmenthaler.

Toro was not among them.

Joe stood like an art critic in a museum and Tecolote's voice throbbed in the air.

"You may forget the singer,
But don't forget the song."

The yellow-haired Anglo he had noticed earlier pushed back his chair and slouched toward Joe. He seemed a pulled-down man with his down-pulling beard and sagging pants, and even the pheasant feather in his droopy-brimmed hat trailed down. "You like the murals?"

"They're—unusual."

"There's more out back." He pointed to the low door leading through the black painted mesa to the outhouse. "Step outside and at first you only see that mesa—the real one—in the distance, but if you follow the little path to the right you'll see the rest of the paintings."

"Who's the artist?"

The yellow-haired man blinked his pale blue eyes like shutters and pulled at his beard, and Joe saw his hands were paint-stained.

"You're lookin' at him," he said. "I am Wesley Wetherford Jones."

7

HIS NAME HAD NOT ALWAYS BEEN
Jones. Wesley Wetherford III had, after half a semester, quit the small
fundamentalist seminary in the east Tennessee mountains that his parents had
insisted he attend. Gravitating west, he came at last to La Mancha, to breathe
with others of sensitive psyche the spring-wine air that quickens the artistic
soul.

But sharp stones lie in the path to aesthetic greatness. The way is steep
and hard to climb; and Wesley became first frustrated, then despairing, and
finally hungry. It was in such a state that he drifted to the cantina one windy
March evening looking as thin and blue as skim milk, opened the faded door,
a down-and-out artist in need of beer and consolation, and crossed the
threshold of fulfillment.

Arabela served him beer, sized him up, and, knowing a hungry man when
she saw one, disappeared through the beaded curtain behind the bar. She
emerged, a high priestess bearing a bowl of green chile stew, and placed it like
a chalice before him.

"Eat," she commanded.

Arabela recognized that his was more than hunger of the belly, and with
a few leading questions and a buck-toothed smile, she began to warm his soul.
For the arms of the blue cantina, like those of Mother Church, are wide.

Wesley Wetherford was a classic gringo. Pale and blond, he lit like a
white turkey in a barnyard of darker fowl and, like Tecolote before him, stayed
to roost. He became a happy man. He regained confidence. Wesley was not a
great artist, probably not even a good one by critical standards. But his art
pleased himself and his followers in the cantina.

He couldn't afford to pay a model, so he painted a series of cockroaches,
which came free at his place, and gave one of the pictures proudly to Arabela.

"Oh Jesus," she said.

From his new friends he learned the practical reality that those lacking in worldly goods must exercise. He also learned a few necessary subterfuges. He could be sly with the tourists in the plaza. He set his prices according to the seeming finances of his clientele. He dropped the names of well known artists as if they were his intimates, and the names of galleries as if they had hung his work. But is not such creativity part of the artist's craft? And do not these small deceptions fall unnoticed like dry leaves in the wake of true art?

If he often seemed brooding, it was part of the role he learned to play, and it pleased him as an artistic accomplishment, for it helped him charm the tourists to whom he began to sell enough sidewalk sketches to keep him in paints and shabby comfort.

But it was in the cantina that his true artistry took wings. Arabela, knowing his need (for he had no studio) and believing it good business, gave him bare walls to brighten with his genius; and after each work session she led him through the curtained door to the quarters where she and Ysidro lived, and fed him green chile stew.

He painted mountains and mesas, sands and cacti, sky and cloud and the river's gorge, and beyond it on the west wall he painted the distant black mesa that was the first thing one saw on entering the room. A low door on that same wall opened onto a view of the real mesa rising in the distance, the first thing one saw en route to the privy. On the east wall he painted the pueblo beneath the mountain, for it too stood as part of the land. With these scenes Wesley expanded the cantina's periphery, so that what had once been solid walls now flowed out into the infinity of the land surrounding them.

Next he began to populate his scenes, for an earth unpeopled lies dead as the moon. His models were his friends of the evening, in solemn mood or merry, and upon seeing themselves so immortalized, they acquired an importance they had not known before, and they began to come earlier and stay later. Sometimes they brought friends new to the cantina who, anticipating their own canonization in brilliant color, soon became regulars. Arabela was filled with deep satisfaction.

Ars longa, vita brevis. So spins the earth.

Then the time came when there was no space left. Wesley proposed to cover the old scenes, a section at a time, with plaster, upon which he would paint new ones. Everyone thought it a fine idea at first, for it excited them to watch, to comment, to suggest, and thus to participate in the process of creation. But when it came time to begin the project, dissension arose. No one wanted his own image removed, and after many evenings of argument as to where he should begin, the idea was abandoned.

Arabela nixed the suggestion that he paint the cantina's exterior: she preferred not to court too much attention from the tax collectors.

Then one evening, on his way to the outhouse, Wesley stopped, contemplated the ugly bareness of its walls, and was immediately consumed with creative fire. Here was canvas from heaven!

Arabela's kindling was slower to catch. How could paintings outside the cantina lure patrons inside? But Ysidro threw his toothpick on the floor and said that no man lived who could linger long outside any saloon without going in to refresh his soul and cool his throat. To that reasoning, Wesley added that the art lover, lured by what he saw outside, would inevitably come inside to see more.

Arabela conceded the wisdom of both observations and Wesley took brush in hand.

The walls were soon covered. Theirs became the most popular privy in all La Mancha. It added a richness to their lives, and those proceeding to perform the more mundane functions could view themselves in a fuller dignity. The increased traffic, and the need for more walls to cover, necessitated an addition. The two-holer became a three-holer, then a four, and eventually a five. The possibilities for future growth were limited only by the availability of real estate.

For in the interim the JD Emmenthaler Realty and Development Company had quietly bought up the surrounding land. Ysidro's outhouse, JD informed them, had already expanded over the line into his property, and would have to be removed.

Wesley Wetherford gasped. Such a razing would destroy a museum full of art! He struck back. A reptile of giant size began to slither around the ankles of the inside mural's subjects. Around all four walls the serpent crawled, and the face, which looked toward the mesa, was the baby pink countenance of JD Emmenthaler.

But before Eden was invaded, Adam met Eve.

Her name was Serenity Jones, and though she was not a regular, she came on her nights off work, or when business was slow. Her manner was easy, her humor loud and lively, her friendliness puppylike. Her spotty reputation stood out as boldly as the freckles on her face, and she tried to cover neither. Because she was treated as a true lady at the cantina, she liked to go there, and the clientele were always glad to see her. They could tell jokes to Serenity they dared not tell their wives, and they warmed to her large red laugh. She drank gin and tonic and paid in cash. She did not solicit business and, respecting her right to professional leave, they did not proposition.

Serenity, like Wesley, loved Arabela's green chile stew. Though Arabela hoarsely proclaimed that the cantina was a bar, not a diner, the truth was she fed many in her back quarters, for in diagnosing human needs she found few ills that a hot bowl and a warm word would not cure.

So it was that Wesley Wetherford III met Serenity Jones in a back room, over an oilcloth-covered table and two bowls of green chile stew.

Wesley fell in love. And Serenity found in Wesley something she had never known. The rich world of art spread before her, a world of beauty, a world beyond the world, its horizons stretching toward infinity. A garden began to bloom in the desert where both lives met.

"Honey," she pronounced, "you are the cutest thing since pink lace panties!"

Sometimes, when Wesley could afford a canvas, Serenity posed for him. It was easier work than her usual profession, though the pay was minimal, ranging from a couple of gin-and-tonics (when he'd had a profitable day among the tourists) to nothing more than the artist's heart-brimming gratitude. And as a model, he avowed, Serenity beat the hell out of cockroaches!

Spring ripened to summer. Wesley explained the techniques of portraiture, the subtleties of symbolism, the messages of color. Some of it she vaguely understood, or pretended to, and they were happy together. An artist's wife, she began to muse, would certainly merit the status of lady.

The courtship was of short duration.

In May they announced their intent quietly to Arabela, who said she'd known it all along and announced it raucously to the cantina. Cheers resounded and bawdy jokes ricocheted from the painted walls. Everyone had suggestions for the wedding. Wesley, contrasting the merriment to his narrow fundamentalist upbringing, delighted in the irreverent fun.

Serenity gave notice at Lily's establishment and went shopping for a virginally white wedding dress. The nuptials would take place in the cantina. Ysidro would give the bride away, Arabela would prepare the wedding feast, and the regulars, volunteered by Toro Duran, would provide the decorations.

The groom bought (on sale) a bright green suit. Then, deciding that Serenity should not have to change her name, he sought out the district attorney about changing his instead. So was born Wesley Wetherford Jones. Serenity hadn't asked for this wedding gift, but the gesture touched her.

Rico offered to officiate. But Serenity wanted a preacher. To do it up right, she said. Like a lady. That stymied them for a time, for the parish priest could perform no ceremonies outside his faith, the clientele knew no other minister, and the couple to be married knew none at all.

At length they found a parson recently arrived in La Mancha, a missioner from New Jersey who had come west to bring the Lord to the heathen. The Reverend Mr. Tobias Greenleaf agreed to marry them and the date was set for the first of June.

When the madam wailed that she'd be three girls short that week, Serenity agreed to work until the night before the wedding. She couldn't let Lily down on such short notice.

The nuptial evening arrived. The guests began to congregate, some in coats and string ties. Their wives wore flowered dresses. The air grew heavy with perfume. Arabela was resplendent, exuding the musty smell of old-gold velvet long packed in a chest of mothballs.

Never had the cantina looked so festive, for in the night Toro and his carefully chosen crew had visited the most exclusive gardens in all La Mancha, and even some in Taos. If their owners were dismayed to find their gardens stripped of their loveliest blossoms when morning dawned, Toro reasoned that more blooms would replace them. Was that not why God caused them to bloom again and again? Foliage lined the painted walls, bouquets graced the tables, and the perfume-laden air was made heavier by the aroma of hundreds of roses. Toro had erected an arch in front of the door to the outhouse path for the wedding party to stand before, and his crew had covered it with trailing vines.

Arabela had loaded the bar with beans and tortillas, enchiladas and green chile stew. A roast *cabrito* shared center stage with a three-tiered wedding cake that rose in pink-flowered majesty.

Close by stood the popcorn machine from the Geronimo movie house. Toro borrowed it from his *primo* whose daughter operated the machine on movie nights. It made a festive touch. No one had consulted the theater manager. Why waste such an important man's time over such a small matter? And too, the manager had taken a dim view of Toro ever since the last time he'd borrowed it for another big party. The problem had arisen when, in returning it, Toro came face to face with the manager who at that moment was coming out the door. He asked for an explanation. With his saintliest expression Toro explained, pointing out his own reliability in seeing to its prompt return.

The manager, an insensitive type, asked how the glass cage came to be broken. Toro's saintliness grew and he shook his head in sad sympathy. "Cheap glass at that factory," he said, "and scroungy work—*¿como no?*"

This time Toro vowed to return the thing whole. If any sonofabitch picked a fight, he by-god better not punch nobody into the popcorn machine.

The appointed hour arrived. Two self-styled acolytes lit the candles that graced the room, and expectancy rose like a fountain. But the preacher had not arrived. Toro, in his best red boots, turquoise shirt, and bola tie, ducked outside to wave the parson down in case he missed the building.

Half an hour passed. The acolytes snuffed the candles. No use letting them burn down before the wedding even began.

Suddenly the door flew open and Toro pranced in. The congregation cheered.

But instead of the preacher, Toro led in a bevy of Serenity's erstwhile fellow workers, dressed in colors that rivaled the paintings on the wall, led by the madam. If anyone present knew Lily or any of her girls, they covered it well. They had brought champagne, Lily announced, plenty of the stuff, and she ordered the nearest guests to unload it from her van parked just outside.

The party, everyone agreed, could start. Corks began to pop and so did the popcorn machine and those who didn't already have *vino* or *cerveza*, and some who did, began to pass Lily's bottles around, and when the first were emptied they opened more.

Ties and coats were soon discarded. Was not a party to be enjoyed in comfort? Tecolote played lively music. Some joined him in song, and a number of couples pushed tables aside and began to dance.

The festivities were gaining momentum when the old blue door suddenly flew open and Toro ushered in a small pale man in clerical collar, looking as anemic as a winter tomato.

"Ride Vaquero!" Toro tossed his sombrero arcing. "Let the wedding begin!"

"¡Olé!"

A look of terror squeezed the little man's white face as he surveyed the guests, and he might at that moment have fled, had not a dozen hands reached out to hoist him onto the nearest strong shoulder, which happened to be Rico's. Tecolote struck a grand chord, the music resumed, and the Reverend Mr. Greenleaf, clutching his prayer book in one hand and Rico's head with the other, was paraded around the room three times.

The acolytes relit the candles. The popcorn machine popped busily.

Toro jumped onto a table, upsetting candle and flowers. "*Señores y Señoras*," he yelled. "The wedding is now goin' to begin so all you shut up!"

The silence of piety, broken only by the sound of popping corn, settled over the room as the quaking Mr. Greenleaf was deposited beneath the vine-covered arch. The plaintive strains of *Lohengrin* began to throb from Tecolote's commanding fingers. Then the tremulous notes of fiddle and tenor sax joined in, and through the curtain marched the musicians. Led by Tecolote, they paraded the length of the bar and pushed a path through the crowd toward the arch and the trembling Mr. Greenleaf.

Behind them came Serenity, her hand resting softly on Ysidro's arm. The men couldn't believe the Serenity they saw, buxom in snow-white satin and gauzy veil, her eyes demurely focused on her large bouquet of the town dowager's prized pink roses. What, they wondered uncomfortably, had happened to their friend of high spirits and loud humor? Was this a wedding or a funeral for the Serenity they knew?

The musicians reached the arch and parted to stand on either side of Serenity and Ysidro. Chico, stationed by the low door behind the arch, gave it a kick. The groom emerged in his new green suit, and as he joined his bride the crowd cheered again.

The Reverend Greenleaf dropped his prayer book. Ysidro, stooping to retrieve it, felt the suspenders he wore for special occasions snap and smite him on the back of his neck. Grabbing pants and missal in one coordinated gesture, he handed the book to its owner.

Toro's shaggy voice again quieted the congregation.

Mr. Greenleaf found his place. "Dearly beloved," he quavered, and his slightly popped eyes swept the room fearfully, "we are gathered together . . ." A gallery of dark faces and darker eyes met his pale ones, but except for the popcorn machine, the room was silent.

". . . if any man can now show just cause . . ." Here he hesitated, and Lily, playing mother of the bride, began to sniffle. ". . . let him now speak . . ." Lily now burst into loud sobs. " . . . or forever hold his peace."

The pale minister turned suddenly paler and began to gasp for air, whereupon Rico, standing respectfully behind the arch, leaped forward to steady him. The little man, feeling his arms pinioned from behind, gave a yelp and again dropped his missal. Ysidro was still wrestling with his pants and the bride was no longer able to stifle an explosive laugh that rang once more of the brassy Serenity the regulars loved. Everyone relaxed and felt better.

Serenity regained her dignity while Wesley, stiff as a saguaro cactus, croaked his responses. Then she began hers, repeating softly and properly after Mr. Greenleaf.

". . . to love and to cherish," he prompted.

"No!" She looked up from her bouquet. A few gasps escaped from the ladies, a few stifled laughs from the men. "No," she corrected softly. "Not cherish. It should be obey! Love and obey!" Tobias Greenleaf's eyes sought heaven and he returned to his prayer book breathing deeply. "To love and—obey . . . ."

As he neared the end of the ritual he seemed to feel some divine assurance. His voice gained strength and, filled with gratitude, he closed his book, ready to finish the ceremony without its aid. Sensing his final gallop for the finish line, the congregation began to cheer. The musicians lifted their instruments. Arabela prepared to clang the cowbell for the feast to begin and Lily, tears of repressed laughter streaking her plump rouged cheeks with mascara, began to pass bottles of the fast-warming champagne to any who would take them. Most preferred *cerveza*.

The Reverend Tobias Greenleaf, release in sight, lifted his arms for the final pronouncement. The *olés* hushed. The musicians poised for the triumphant march.

But the sudden silence unbalanced the minister, as a man leaning heavily into a raging gale will lose his equilibrium in a sudden lull, and as he opened his tight little mouth the words left him like dandelion puff. As he groped to find them, the sudden grasp of muscular arms assailed him and in a rush of rising altitude he was heaved helplessly onto Rico's waiting shoulders.

He sought desperately for the words. "I now pronounce you man and wife," he gabbled quickly before the words flew away again. And then, above the hearty *olés* and the first crashing sounds of guitar, fiddle, and tenor sax, he blurted loudly ". . . to be joyfully loined together!"

8

"NICE PAINTINGS," SAID JOE.
"Original. But I don't see Toro."

Wesley pulled at his beard. "Cain't get him to stand still long enough. Like trying to paint a comet—gone before you can see it." He pointed to the opposite wall. "Besides that, he wants me to put him on that mesa, big as the people in the foreground."

"That's Toro."

"Throw the whole thing out of perspective."

"He's good at that too."

"I asked him how could I put a big close-up figure on that far-off mesa." Wesley pointed again. "And all he said was that was my problem, he wasn't the artist."

"Well, nice talking to you. Enjoyed the paintings."

Toro reached Joe at the door. "Amigo—wait for me. We go to my house."

He had a room, Joe explained, already paid for. He'd see Toro in the morning. Toro kept protesting that they were amigos, and *mi casa es su casa* and his wife had died and his children were grown and flown and he was lonesome for his amigo, and his eyes widened with deep and abiding tragedy.

Joe had seen that look before. It was a good maneuver, but it wasn't going to work this time. He wasn't about to get roped into Toro's latest cause. Then he remembered the same look in Toro's eyes when their captain had announced that he'd put Joe in for a Silver Star for heroic actions in the millstone raid.

"Oh hell," he said, "let's go get my gear."

So they roared to the motel in the beat-up red pickup which Toro parked at an angle taking up two spaces while they threw Joe's few effects into the Olds, and headed back in tandem. *¡BORACHOS ABORDO!* Toro's bumper sticker read: Drunks Aboard.

Following, Joe wondered why he'd agreed. Then he shrugged. Why not?

He was forewarned. He'd give Toro the box first thing in the morning, and maybe—if he really wanted to know—he'd learn the truth of what had happened. The old anger had dulled, and maybe he'd been wrong all along about it. Because in all honesty—and Joe had always tried to be honest—he needed to uncover his own actions before he condemned the man who had once been his best buddy.

But the image returned of Toro dropping Cholly, falling flat behind him as the bullets tore through the air. And Cholly hadn't come back. The vision always left Joe with a knot balled in his stomach like something undigested.

As long as you sit on a coiled rattler he can't strike you, Joe reflected. But you can't sit forever. Time comes when you've got to move and take your chances. And whatever had happened, and whatever his own actions may have been, Joe had sat on it long enough.

They left the plaza behind, and the late-night restaurants and bars with their spurts of noise whenever a door flew open, past the construction and the tall fence around it where Joe had halted in the morning's traffic jam, out past JD Emmenthaler's big sign with the bullet holes in it. Past the cantina a deep quiet blessed the adobe houses that straggled toward the river's deep gorge and the mesa beyond. Moon-washed, they looked like ghost dwellings. An occasional yellow-lit window looked onto the night from a house not yet abed. On the fringe of the thinning houses they passed a small *grocería*, marked by a single sign, and beyond it a stretch of bare ground.

And then, ahead on the left rose a large adobe home, an hacienda with enough age to be stately. A high wall encircled the big house, and around it clustered a number of small outbuildings. Barbed wire guarded the entire compound. Toro slammed on his brakes, cut his roaring engine, and jumped from the cab. Joe pulled up behind him. "What's the problem?"

"That!" Toro jerked his head toward the house.

"What about it?"

"Come on." Toro started toward the fence. "I'll show you."

"And get us shot for prowling," Joe muttered. But he followed.

The big house reared pale in the night, and one square of golden light shone from an upstairs window. A small breeze brought the cool damp smell of a well irrigated lawn.

"See that little house over there?"

Joe nodded. A small adobe hut on the far edge of the compound sat close by a stable and a corral. Toro pulled the barbed wire strands apart and they climbed silently through and approached the outbuildings, whose shadows seemed more tangible than the moonwashed walls that cast them.

"That little house—I live there once." Toro spoke softly, though they were still some distance from the big house, and the outlying buildings seemed unoccupied. "When I was a little kid." They stood a moment in the deep quiet. "When I was gone, in the war, always I was thinking of this."

"I thought you grew up on a ranch over Mora way."

"That was before I went to live with my grandma—*mi abuela*. My papa took off rodeoing. So I live with *abuela*. She worked for the people in the big house."

"So what's the problem?"

"Abuela, she died. Long time ago. And the people she work for, they ain't there no more. They was good people." He was silent for a few moments. "I had me a little burro—they let me keep him in the corral. I called him Panchito. He was my best friend."

Toro loved animals, Joe remembered. In the Philippines, before the war, he had found a baby monkey in the jungle, brought him into camp, and made a pet of him. And later, in prison camp, Toro had flamed in rage seeing the Jap soldiers beating wounded horses, forcing them to work until they collapsed, dead.

"Abuela, she wasn't so happy when I brought Panchito home. We were very poor, and he was something else we had to feed. And always—" Toro chucked softly. "Always he was getting into trouble."

"I used to ride him to school. It was a little school and I staked him outside. But he raised hell out there and the teacher she didn't like the noise. One day she told me go make him shut up. So—I brought him inside. She told me I couldn't bring Panchito to school no more."

"Teachers are like that." Joe chuckled. "I got some flak too on occasion. But—would you mind telling me what we're doing here?"

"I was telling about Panchito." Toro's long eyes seemed to look inward, dark in the silvery light, with an almost haunted look, a look Joe remembered from the long waiting nights in the jungles of Bataan. But now, as then, a quick-kindled passion burned short any long thoughts that may have been brooding in Toro's mind.

"Them people here now—in this big house—you know what they going do?" Toro sputtered like a lit fuse. "They going get some burros, and little ponies—pen 'em up behind a by-god barb-wire fence—oh God, I hate fences—hitch 'em to a by-god turnstile, make 'em walk round and round and carry tourists' brats." His voice shook. "That ain't no way to treat a burro."

Joe's warning signal buzzed. Toro was maneuvering him toward something, and he began to see the direction. "Who?" he asked shortly.

Toro spat on the ground and his voice rose. "Mr. Devil's Bastard JD Emmenthaler. That's who."

"Well, let's get out of here before he wakes up and hitches us to a turnstile. We are trespassing, you know."

Toro was gazing at the lighted window. "I could shoot that light out easy," he whispered, and he raised his arm as if aiming and pulled his trigger finger on an imaginary pistol. "Pow!"

Joe remembered Toro aiming a Springfield rifle at a lit window in Manila. Immediately after the Japanese attack part of the regiment was ordered to Manila, he and Toro among them. Standing guard duty outside Malacañang Palace during a blackout a lone window suddenly blazed. Toro aimed and fired in quick fury, the light went out, and Toro assumed his innocent look when the sergeant came searching for who had fired without orders.

"Pow!" Toro grinned and aimed his finger again at the big house of Mr. JD Emmenthaler. "Pow!"

"Okay, *vaquero*, you got your rustlers. Now let's vamoose."

They gained the road quietly and climbed into their vehicles. Toro's door slammed sharply like a shot and the roar of his engine filled the night. Joe followed quietly, with only the crunch of gravel under his tires. In his headlights Toro's bumper sticker danced happily. *¡BORACHOS ABORDOS!*

Past a short stretch Toro turned onto a rutted path to his small house. The enormous dog Joe had seen in Toro's pick-up that morning bounded from a clump of trees, followed by an erupting little fury that seemed predominantly terrier. (Strangers, Toro told him later, were always afraid of the big dog, but he was interested in love not war. No one was afraid of the little one, though many later wished they had been.)

"*¡Mis niños!*" Toro shouted, jumping from his pickup as Joe pulled up. "These are name Grande and Poco—Big Dog and Little Dog." Still yapping their greetings, the dogs raced for the door as Toro gestured widely. "*Mi casa es su casa.*"

The warm smell of manure and ripening apples floated from the little copse with a breath of piney air from the mountain. Joe inhaled these odors of the earth. To the west the fat waxing moon was setting—it would be full in a night or two—and against its light rose the distant mesa, stark and black.

"That mesa," said Toro softly, "that's where I found Panchito."

9

JOE AWAKENED EARLY. IT HAD been one of those ragged nights of half sleep, with kaleidoscopic images from the previous day flashing through his consciousness. He saw again the baked desert floor of his drought-plagued ranch, and the face of God in the great river gorge, and the pueblo floating in the mountain-bred mist, and the sun-baked plaza, and through all the scenes marched an invading army of billboards in money-green uniforms.

He saw the painted walls of the cantina and the neon sign's red glow, and the hooded eyes of the *guitarristo*, dark and deep-seeing above a strange guitar that turned a throbbing blue as he watched, and began to expand until it covered the gaunt face and the hooded eyes and all he could see of the player were his fingers on the instrument's deep blue neck.

And again the image flashed as it always did of Toro with Cholly in his arms, and Toro dropping Cholly in a rain of gunfire, Toro falling behind him, Toro dashing low to the ground away from Cholly, and then the blackout and the old question that vibrated through Joe's head like a dentist's drill.

Through his half-sleep he heard the late-summer bugs that buzzed in the night and sometimes hit against the window screen; and once the far-off horn of an impatient tourist rode the air from La Mancha.

Dawn was graying the air when he awoke to the first sleepy calls of stirring birds. He lay a moment listening and then stretched. Sooner up, sooner gone, and sooner home to Beth and High Lonesome. And maybe, with luck and some cooperation from Toro, with his old snake scotched.

Hearing no sound from Toro, he decided to drive in search of a newspaper. Outside, he threw a few sticks for the dogs to chase, and squinted past the river to the mesa gleaming darkly in the early sun. The hoarse bray of a burro shredded the air and walking toward it Joe saw the shaggy little beast, huge ears erect, staring from among the apple trees. Joe called and after a moment the burro, satisfied or bored, resumed his grazing.

Beneath the covering of Toro's small patio, swallows darted from their earthen nests that clung to his earthen house and seemed one with it. They flew now in clusters, circling, forming groups for their coming journey south, to leave before summer did.

The morning now gleamed white and amber, air clean and cool, and tendrils of coming autumn wound softly against his face. He decided to walk. Maybe the little *grocería* they'd passed the night before sold papers.

It didn't, but the owner, just opening the store, offered him a cup of coffee and a *bolillo*, which, Joe decided, was more pertinent to life than any newspaper anyhow.

He was Patricio Lopez, the storekeeper said, and Joe recognized him from among the cantina's congregation the night before, a squat, square, busy little man.

"You going see that JD Emmenthaler for us today?"

Joe shook his head. "I've got to head out."

"Ah." A small sadness perhaps tugged Patricio's eyes down at the corners. He poured two cups of coffee and motioned Joe to a small corner table. "*Siéntese, señor.*" He moved with the gentle dignity of those who know who they are.

"*Gracias.* It wouldn't do any good anyhow—going to see the man." He sipped the coffee. It was fragrant, strong, scalding. "If Toro couldn't get the guy to talk, I couldn't either."

Patricio grinned. "*Sí*, that Toro, he get fired up. Then he stir up ever'body, and Rico he try always to put out the fire. It's their regular routine." He chuckled, turned the sign in his window to *ABIERTO*, and sat at the table.

"Toro seems to be the burr under Rico's saddle."

"Well—it's like a game them two play. Them and Chico. But they're all amigos. We're all amigos. But Rico—well, see, Toro, he get wild sometime. Like to fight—fights with ever'body. Even hisself. And Rico, being he's the judge you know, he don't like to spook nobody's horses. Tries to keep things quiet. I remember one time—

"It started in the cantina on a lazy sort of evening. September it was, most of the *turistas* gone. We was just relaxing over a few beers when this big lardy gringo from Los Angeles, what had no business in our cantina in the first place, pushed through the door and started looking around. Then he spotted Serenity—this was before Wesley ever had come."

At this point Patricio interrupted his story to wait on a man he called Garcia who bought a cigar and scratched his head trying to remember what it was his wife had sent him to get for breakfast. "She was needing eggs, I think," said Patricio. Señor Garcia bought a dozen and would have stayed for coffee had not Patricio reminded him his wife was waiting.

"Well," he continued, "we couldn't hear what he said to Serenity. But we sure heard what she said to him! Toro, he heard from clear across the room, and he blazed toward that guy like a prairie fire in spring wind. Told him he could apologize to the lady or move his fat ass out. So the gringo told him to butt out and yelled to Arabela to bring him a whiskey."

Patricio laughed. "Arabela, she just said she *no comprendo*, and kept on mopping the bar, and then Ysidro came and bounced him out.

"That would have been the end of it except for Toro. He thought Chico should of arrested him, and when he didn't, Toro said he'd do it hisself. Nobody paid him any mind when he rushed out the door. Toro, he always popping off. We just settled down to like we was before.

"But Toro, he springs for the patrol car—Chico never did take the keys out, or his pistol either—and flies after that gringo's Cadillac, flashing his red lights and blowing the siren, and finally pulls the guy over. Only that *californio* recognizes him and drives off.

"So then Toro, he grabs Chico's pistol and fires straight at that Cadillac's right rear tire and watches it go limping down the street. Well, he cruises around awhile, just enjoying the evening and that purring engine, and the next morning he takes the patrol car to Chico at the station. Only the *californio* had got there first demanding Toro get arrested and buy him a new tire. Chico is plenty mad and says he guesses he gots to lock Toro up.

"Toro never minded getting locked up. He and Chico always had a good poker game. But he liked a good chase first, just to make it sporting. So he lights out towards the mesa, with a couple deputies on his tail, and they play for oh maybe an hour, until a sudden cloudburst ruined the fun.

"They was hauling him back in the patrol car, all of 'em wet as drowned cats, and mud up to the hub caps, until a big mud-sucker stops them dead still.

So Toro leaves them trying to get unstuck, ducks out, and starts on foot back to the mesa. Figured it would all be forgot by morning."

"Was it?" asked Joe.

"Oh, sure." Patricio poured more coffee.

"Did Toro pay for the tire?"

"That," said Patricio guffawing, "is the best part. Rico, he sat there in his judge's robes looking all stern, with Toro and that California dude in front of him, and a lot of people in court to watch the fun. And he gabbed on about the law for awhile and allowed as how the *californio* asked for that ruined tire when he drove off from Toro. Which, he said, was resisting arrest.

"So then the guy said Toro wasn't no law officer and couldn't be arresting him. But Rico said he was so, he'd done deputized him. 'Since when?' that dude asks, and Rico, he'd had enough by then, 'Since right now,' he says. And fines the *californio* three hundred dollars. For contempt of court."

10

"YEAH, IT HAPPENED SOMETHING like that." Toro scraped eggs onto their plates, clattered the skillet into the sink, and sat down. He was naked to the waist, and Joe saw and remembered the tattoo Toro had gotten in Juarez—probably the only guy in Uncle Sam's army to have a tattoo of a burro on his biceps. "Rico done his duty and I done mine. Salsa?" He pushed the jar across the table. "Now—you was asking about this JD Emmenthaler—"

"No, pal. I've got to shove off."

Toro found this funny. "You drive all this way. So what's another by-god hour?"

"As soon as we do these dishes—hand over the box—tell you what I know about Tomcat—ask a couple of questions. And head south."

"What questions?"

"About the raid."

"That was long time ago, my friend." Toro's voice was soft.

"About what really happened."

"So you can blame me again?"

"Maybe. Maybe blame myself some too."

A quick flame blazed in Toro's face and then he shrugged. "Choe—we got the millstone. The bastards opened fire. And they got Cholly. But we brought the stone back."

"For which I got a goddamned medal. And you didn't."

Toro shrugged, pushed from the table, and carried his plate to the sink. He grinned. "You remember, there was that little matter—"

"I know." Toro had pulled guard duty the night of the raid. Chief was ordered elsewhere; and Toro, not about to miss the fun, got someone to cover for him and walked off. Sneaked back to his post on returning so no one knew he'd been on the foray. Better miss the accolades than risk getting busted again.

Toro was laughing now but Joe remembered his face when their captain announced he'd put Joe in for that decoration. Sort of sardonic. A little sad maybe. "Some parts I can't remember."

Toro was still grinning. "You remembered enough to give me a bucketful of holy hell. Long time after." He turned the faucet full force onto an overdose of Ivory. Bubbles rose like butterflies.

"So here's your chance to get back."

Through the open window the drone of heavy equipment roared and then dimmed.

"What the hell's that?"

"That is one of Mr. JD Emmenthaler's earthmovers."

"Sounds like another war."

"It is." The flame flared again in Toro's eyes and he smiled grimly. "They started yesterday."

"He's got land out there too?"

"Sonofabitch ain't content with his apartments out by the cantina. Wants to build a goddam nursing home between here and the river. Done bought up that land past me. See, Choe—always he talks like one of them Baptist preachers—and all the time swindling his own grandma probably. He's one of those *hombres* who goes around acting good to hide the fact that they ain't good."

"I know the type."

"Only—he ain't built nothin' yet." Toro grinned. "And he ain't by-god going to."

"Looks like it's out of your hands. Where's a dish towel?"

"In that drawer." Toro clattered the dishes in the sink. "There's ways."

"Look, a stray woman-chasing Californian's one thing. A slick Dallas developer armed with government subsidies is another. You better play it cool—and inside the law. All he needs is one illegal move by you—"

"Ah, amigo, you are so right! You and Rico. That's why I hope you would go talk to this man. Just get him to talk to us. That's straight-up legal enough."

"He'd tell me it was none of my business." Joe went to fetch the box.

The living room was piled with catalogues and unopened envelopes. He never bothered with mail, Toro said, except for his government checks. He lifted a stack off an overstuffed chair, deposited it on the floor beside a like stack, and motioned Joe to sit. A small desk was covered with little wooden animals—mostly burros, Joe noted, and birds. Yes, he'd carved them all, Toro said. He walked to the desk, and picked one up. "You get back over there behind that jackrabbit," he told it, and rearranged a couple more, talking to each in turn.

But Joe's gaze was drawn to the walls. Apparently Arabela and Ysidro weren't the only art lovers in Tuceros. Pictures framed and hung, or thumb-tacked, adorned every wall in close profusion. It was an eclectic array. A Daumier print was tacked beside a primitive charcoal of a charging bull. A framed Corot landscape reproduction tilted a bit unevenly beside an old, somewhat frayed Betty Grable pinup. Another print, a large Georgia O'Keefe flower, passionately colored, was tacked above the red plush sofa. From the flower's center protruded a dart, and small holes stippling the surface attested to other dart activity. "Makes a good board," said Toro. "Nobody never seen any flower like that thing anyways."

Another earthmover roared by. The windows shook. Toro's eyes blazed. "That by-god nursing home going rise up like that by-god Tower of Babel. Between us and our mesa, which we won't see no more. Choe—he wants to build that thing three stories high. On one side of me is his big house where he lives and the little house which I live once with my *abuela*, and the little *jacal* where I keep Panchito. And on the other side of me he wants his big tall nursing home. And I am in between, like a little piece of cheese between his big fat tortillas.

"And he is all around our cantina. On all sides he pushes and squeezes at it for his big old apartment buildings. To shove us all out. And nobody even talk to him for us." Toro looked at Joe from the corner of his long eyes and sighed. "But I understand, amigo. You got to get back at your ranch. I understand. And I am happy for you that you ain't got no JD Emmenthaler going squeeze you out of your home."

"Look, I hate these damned developers as bad as you do, coming in from outside, parceling out our land—"

"What we fought for, Choe."

"—and our water. Ruin our land, bring in more people to suck us dry, collect their geetus and move on." Joe walked to the window, watched the dust churn behind another lumbering machine.

"Choe—a good man I respect, and even a bad man. But this lying *hombre*, he ain't either. He's just disgusting."

"I know. And I might even go see the sonofabitch if it would do any good. But it wouldn't."

Toro nodded, sighed, and conceded. Joe, wary from old experience, waited and wondered where the next siege would resume. He handed the small package to Toro, who placed it on a table between two chairs and gestured to a larger box—pictures, he said, from their early army days. His little old *abuela* had saved up all her spare pennies to buy him a Kodak camera when he went off to Fort Bliss, so he could send her pictures to look at and show her friends and save for when he came home.

Another truck rumbled by.

"You're in them pictures. And Tomcat, and Chief. And Cholly. Then we see what Tomcat send in the little box. And talk about your questions."

What the hell. Joe shrugged. Who knew—maybe these might jog some memory. "But I've got a three-hundred-mile stretch ahead."

"It won't stretch no longer *mañana*. Choe, it's only you and me we got left. My kids all gone. Make good livings, got good boots. Closest one is in Taos. Good kids, but they don't understand, Choe. And my grandkids. I try to tell them about the war. But they rather watch the TV."

Joe could relate to that.

"And Chief." Toro sighed. "Gone now."

Joe asked about the strange Indian at the pueblo.

"I don't know who he is. Comes to the cantina sometimes. Ain't any of Chief's clan. Yes." He looked obliquely at Joe. "I miss old Chief. Just you and me now."

So there they were in glossy prints, the old Fearsome Foursome, or at least three of them, because Toro was behind the camera clicking the others into black-and-white immortality. And some included Cholly, who had early on attached himself to Joe and was forever tagging along, when they couldn't ditch him. Even now Joe could feel a rise of the old annoyance, and then of self-censure for feeling it.

The kid had latched on to Joe during high-school days, when he'd arrived at the military academy in Roswell, young and green and scared, and Joe, a couple of years older, had shown him some kindness. Later, learning that Joe was in the Guard, Cholly joined too, got himself assigned to Joe's battery, and began dogging him on duty and off.

Just like he'd tagged along on the raid for the grinding stone. And got himself killed.

Toro had tried to nix his going, but Cholly kept insisting, and it was Joe, annoyed, who had said to let him come if he wanted to be a damn fool.

Another roar grew, rolled past, diminished.

"Look at this one!" Toro laughed. There stood Joe in a posed shot looking a little rueful, flanked by Tomcat and Chief each pointing in mock shock at Joe's nose swathed in tape and bandage. That had been taken after that first big fight. He and Toro had creamed each other mightily, gained a healthy respect for each other, and after that fought side by side.

Joe remembered another big fight later on Angel Island, which was their port of embarkation for the Philippines. Some of the other units made fun of their regiment and the fight began. Joe, trying to pull Toro out before it got well started, found himself pulled in instead, and Tomcat joined in gleefully, until Chief came in punching, put their immediate assailants out of commission, and dragged all three of them out just ahead of the MPs.

It wasn't long before they met the real enemy, and the flag of the Rising Sun.

They sat talking of their days at Fort Bliss, of Toro's running feud with the sergeant and the hell they raised in Juarez and the fights they fought, and the mornings after in camp. They talked of the early days in the Philippines, their occasional passes to Manila, and their frequent nights at the barrio they called Sloppy Bottom, of their exploring the jungle to trade with the little Negrito natives, and of the adventures they had before the real adventure began with the Japanese attack, and of exploring the jungle again, this time not to trade with the friendly natives, but to search for food when the rations ran low—and snipers.

They talked of the surrender and the March and the prison camps, and of the escape from a work detail that Toro and Tomcat made.

But neither spoke of Cholly, or the raid for the millstone, and when Joe motioned toward the little box, hoping to lead into the subject they were both thinking of, Toro flashed his wide white grin, crinkled his long eyes, and pulled more pictures.

Another truck rolled by. The windows rattled and Joe paced the small room and Toro kept passing snapshots. There stood Joe with Chief and Tomcat by a *calesa*—one of the little donkey-drawn carts the soldiers rented whenever they wangled a pass. He remembered when this one was taken, because it was their last junket before the war. It was also the last of the pictures, because they went on alert after that and, sensing a war brewing, Toro had mailed camera, film, and a bundle of cheap mementos to Abuela. He remembered how just as Cholly snapped the shutter Toro had jumped aside, so there was only a light streak, like a white flame, where Toro had stood.

"Aren't you in any picture?"

Toro lit a Marlboro. Holding it delicately with thumb and forefinger, he puffed happily, inhaled deeply, enjoyed, and remembered.

When he was small, he recounted, and used to ride Panchito into town, he caught some artists' eyes. They found him small and appealing, imp-eyed and mischief-making. They found in him a model and he found in them a source of wealth. He collected a quarter for an afternoon of posing. He and Panchito were soon trekking every day to the artists' places to become the popular subjects of dozens of scenes. Boy and burro.

It lasted until his little old *abuela* found out and lit into him like a small fury. It wasn't honest, she scolded, taking money for doing no work. The sin was doubly compounded, she learned further, by his sometimes skipping school to do so. She forbade him to continue.

But, Toro added grinning, those quarters sure had bought lots of things—hay for Panchito, beans for him and Abuela. Sometimes a little candy. But never enough for the boots he'd always yearned for. Boots were power. "I got me eighteen by-god pairs in my closet right now," said Toro. The aside seemed irrelevant and overly casual, and Joe smiled. If Christ had been wearing a good pair of boots, Toro had once said to him in prison camp, he would never of got Hisself crucified. Nobody would of dared.

"Are any of those artists' pictures still around?"

Toro shrugged. "*No se.*"

"And you're not in Wesley's mural. Or any of these snapshots. No pictures of you anywhere."

"Ain't none of Jesus Christ either!" Toro grinned.

"Or Jack the Ripper. Which are you, Duran—saint or rogue?"

Toro blew a smoke ring at the ceiling. "I'm a man with boots."

Noting a number of Toro's little carvings on the television set, Joe stopped, idly picked up one and another, and then his eye fell on another small object, a familiar one. He began to laugh, and Toro began to laugh too as they both remembered the night when Toro had acquired it.

The Foursome had gone to a Juarez whorehouse, not so much to sample the merchandise as to sate their curiosity while testing the watered rotgut at the bar. Toro had first fingered, and then lifted, the object Joe now held. It was a tiny ceramic cup the bartender used as a jigger, fashioned into the exaggerated shape of a balloon-breasted, balloon-hipped nude, gaudily painted. Riding back to camp in the trolley, he produced it.

"Why you want that thing?" Tomcat asked, and Joe mumbled something about Toro trying to land them into the Juarez hoosegow. But Toro as usual had his reasons. "Ain't even a full jigger. Sonofabitch been cheating us honest red-blooded American soldier boys. I am protecting the rights of the US of A!"

Another truck thundered past.

Joe watched the dust rise and hang in the air and as it began to settle a large green Lincoln Continental swung into Toro's lane and braked screeching.

"Looks like you've got company."

A large loose baby-faced man with orange hair leaped from the car and slammed his door, and the dogs raced toward him barking. A black-booted kick stunned Grande, whereupon Toro erupted yelling. Poco, seeing Grande attacked, leaped for the man's wrist. Grande retreated whimpering to his master as the man aimed another boot at the snarling little dog but failed to make contact.

"You touch my dog and I'll by-god strangle you!"

"Then call him off!"

"And you can by-god get off my property, Mr. JD Emmenthaler!"

"Hey, buddy, I came here on a friendly visit," the man whined, and his soft pink face had a puzzled look as if he couldn't understand what these people had against him. He was grasping his wrist.

Joe handed him a handkerchief and tried not to grin at the expanse of flesh puddling above the collar of an expensive western shirt, or at the clean tan Stetson that had obviously never seen the inside of a corral, or the boots that had never kicked a cow chip. A Nieman-Marcus cowboy.

Toro looked up from consoling his dogs. "I told you to vamoose."

"Yesterday you were beggin' me to come talk." He had a prim pinched-in mouth, too small for the rest of his face.

"Yesterday you weren't attacking my dogs."

"Well," snapped Emmenthaler, "yesterday they weren't assaultin' me."

From his right index finger, still nursing his left wrist, a large diamond-encircled emerald glinted in the sunlight.

"So what do you want?"

"I'm fixin' to make you a jack-dandy offer." JD fingered the emerald ring in an unconscious habitual sort of way, turning it to refract the sun's rays, and stared at it as if in contemplation.

"I done told you—this is my house, what I fought a by-god war for, and it ain't for by-god sale to no asshole moneybags. You ain't going run me out."

Emmenthaler looked up from his emerald and his puzzled face grew pinker. "Mr. Duran, I ain't tryin' to run you out."

"Yeah, I'm Mr. Duran today. Yesterday I was that dumb Mes'can!"

"Could we maybe just set down and talk reasonable?"

Toro stood glowering.

"I got a proposal I think you'll find pretty attractive. A real jack-dandy!"

Still Toro stood, his hard craggy face glaring into JD's fleshy one.

Seeing no sign of an invitation to the house, the developer began his spiel. He had come to La Mancha only to bring progress. His factory would create jobs, bring money to the village. His apartments would house the poor cheaply. His nursing home would care for the elderly. He was a God-fearing citizen doing his Christian duty for his fellow men.

Sure, thought Joe, the butter-voiced bastard spread his philanthropy on thick. Santa Claus with a bag full of rattlesnakes. Saint Francis strewing bird poison. The leprechaun luring the gullible toward a pot of nothing.

Better homes to live in, JD continued, with modern conveniences. And surely no one could criticize a nursing home.

"As shoddy as that thing you're building in town?" Joe spoke before he considered, and it was a wild shot. He hadn't seen the project in town. But he knew his type.

Toro smirked and Joe, feeling himself being pulled into the affair, walked away before JD could answer. Should've kept quiet, but oh god how he hated developers, and he hated hypocrites even worse. He didn't much care for professional Texans either. Poco, having done his duty and sensing an ally, sniffed happily at his heels. Grande followed, found an old bone and a cool spot, and flopped. Close by a flock of sparrows pecked at grain Toro had scattered around a plaster Saint Francis.

Joe looked west, saw the dusty activity where the treeless land sloped gently toward the bluff overlooking the river. Scraping, filling, leveling, the earthmovers crawled like giant red ants whose cement-block construction would soon rise as unwelcome as the hills the ants built. He looked beyond and saw the mesa, dark and solid in the yellow air, beyond the reaches of JD Emmenthaler. The bastard could never despoil the mesa.

But he could block it from view.

Suddenly Toro's voice exploded. "No, I ain't going sell you my house and my land even if you say you let me live here still. I don't care if it was part of your property way back when. My old *patrón's* family done deeded it to me and my *abuela* before they sold it or ever hear of you."

JD's voice was rising too. He'd have it appraised, pay that and then some.

"I done had it appraised. At two hundred and fifty thousand by-god dollars!"

JD smiled. "That's pretty hard to believe."

"You calling me a liar? Because the one thing I ain't is no liar. Except when I got to be, like when some ass-hole wants to know what's none of his by-god business! And no, I ain't going work for you neither or have nothing to do with you ever! And I don't give a good by-god if I am obstructing your project."

"Mr. Duran, try to think of your community. It's them you're obstructin'."

"I'll tell you about my community, Mr. JD Emmenthaler. My community, not yours, and it never will be yours, even if you buy all by-god Tuceros and La Mancha too, and all the land around. Because you can't buy people's souls.

"We don't want your fancy do-good charity. We don't want any by-god thing you got. And we don't want you on our land."

Ready to back his master again, Poco raced toward JD, and Joe ran behind, scooped up the feisty little guardian before he could add another wound to JD's anatomy, or before JD could inflict one on Poco. Grande lay gnawing his bone, unconcerned.

Once safe, Emmenthaler recovered his calm. "I'm trying to talk reasonable, approach you fair and square, offer you good money, let you stay and live on this property."

"Yeah, until you're ready to use it. Well, I am staying on it, mister, and I am by-god keeping it!"

JD shook his head like a preacher beholding sin. "I'm mighty sorry to find you so unreasonable," he said in sweet tones. "It's awful sad to see a man working against himself." He sighed heavily. "Another man, not so tolerant as me, might have your property condemned. I could, you know." He turned toward the Continental. "Think about it."

Joe hitched his jeans impatiently. Toro spat. Poco wriggled snarling from Joe's arm. The burro brayed.

JD pulled his eyes back to the company. "That jackass yours?"

"He is his own man. My friend. And he ain't in no by-god pen like you been talking about putting little burros in."

JD shrugged, started for his car, then turned back. "One more thing," he said softly. "I think you should know. Your dog got into my compound last night. He dug up my wife's prize peonies." He accented the second syllable. Pee-YON-ees. "Just tore up her beds. She is real upset, too, I can tell you. Been crying over it all day. Ruined her garden she loved so." His voice trailed off sadly. "I'm a kind man. I'd hate to have to shoot your dog."

"Well, I sure wouldn't hate to shoot you if you did."

"Unless you fence those dogs, immediate, I'm going to file charges for destruction of property. And for bodily injury." He pointed toward his arm, still wrapped in Joe's handkerchief, and opened his door. "Think about it."

But Toro's sizzling fuse had burned its length and his powder blew. He lunged. Emmenthaler jumped back.

"You file all the by-god charges you want, you low-down, side-winding, rattle-shaking belly-crawler." He lowered his head, jabbed a sharp shoulder into JD's midsection. Emmenthaler's air expelled like that of a punctured tire. He flung up his hands in defense.

Joe leaped for Toro, pulled him off. "Cool it, you stupid ass. Lost your mind?" Before the startled Toro could charge again, Joe, still holding him, stepped between them. The mounting din of another truck rose above Toro's bellows, and the three stood glowering in arrested movement like statues awaiting the pigeons. JD's face flushed red as a baby's bottom.

By the time the roar receded, Joe was in charge. "Okay, you yahoos, grow up. Both of you," he added as JD's small mouth opened. "Toro, you want

Emmenthaler to come talk with your people—here's your chance. He wants to talk with you. If either of you had half the sense of that little burro over there, you'd quit braying and arrange a meeting, try to act like civilized adults and iron things out."

"Okay," said Toro. "Let him come to the cantina."

"To that dive they all flock to? Meet with that Anglo-hating mob?"

"No they aren't," said Joe. "They just want to be heard."

Toro bunched his muscles, but Joe's grip tightened and he went slack. His eyes, looking as if they hadn't grown up with the rest of him, slanted craftily toward each in turn. A sweet smile lit his face like a moon coming out of the clouds, and it shone on JD Emmenthaler. "My friend is right, señor. You come. Listen to us. We listen to you. All friendly. Ysidro and Arabela, they listen. I listen. Chico and Rico, they listen." Joe let go of Toro.

"What's wrong with they come to my office?"

"I believe Duran tried that," said Joe. "And got booted out. It's your turn now to talk on his turf."

"A crummy Mes'can bar ain't a place to talk business."

Joe shrugged. "You want to shoe a horse, you go to his stable."

"You, whoever you are, you seem to be sane. You be there too?"

"What for?" Joe hitched his jeans. "It's not my affair."

"Sure he'll be there!" Toro's grin cast a radiance. "He'll come. Keep ever'body calm." Joe opened his mouth but Toro added quickly. "He got to stay over anyhow. To discuss some private things. Things he need to know. So much I have to tell him."

Oh hell, thought Joe, the day was already shot. Beth didn't expect him till she saw him. He'd give her a call. And there were those questions curling like snakes in the back of his brain. He sighed. "Okay. Tonight?"

"Make it tomorrow," said JD, "and I'll come." He climbed into the Lincoln. "But," he added before he shot down the drive, "I still mean it about the dogs."

"I hate fences," Toro growled after the departing car. He looked heavenward. "God," he said fervently, "if you will send my old sergeant's ghost to scare that mother away, I promise I'll say fifty Hail Marys. After he's gone." He crossed himself and turned toward Joe grinning. "We got him, amigo! I knew you could."

11

WHEN JD EMMENTHALER HAD first roared into La Mancha in his private Lear Jet, nobody thought much about it. People like him were always coming—businessmen sensing money to be made in the town's barely tapped potential, star-eyed do-gooders to uplift the native inhabitants through government agencies, pleasure-seekers envisioning a desert oasis of grass-hilled golfing and poolside daiquiris. And most left when their mirages faded, as desert mirages do.

Those few who stayed did nothing to upset the close communion of the cantina. They didn't know it existed. Neither the businessmen nor the rich pleasure-seekers were interested in Tuceros, and even the do-good government agencies planted their offices in the better sections of La Mancha and did more paper work than leg work.

So when JD Emmenthaler lit from Dallas with ginger hair, black boots, tan Stetson, and wads of long green money, no one on either side of the village took much notice of him, his blonde-mopped wife Narcissa with her red Corvette she sashayed all over La Mancha in, or his small son Travis, except to note that the latter was a snotty little ass. JD was just another Texas jiggle-butt, puffy with self-righteousness and a lifetime of good Jack Daniels, well heeled and well jowled, flying importantly in and out on his private plane with his private pilot.

They regarded Narcissa as a bubble-brain—those who thought of her at all—and a laugh went around about the time she'd sideswiped a garbage truck in that Corvette she liked to floorboard, and wouldn't even get out and look until she'd tilted her rear-view mirror, primped up her hair, and retouched her lipstick. And a few people had seen her fling one of her snits when something displeased her. But for the most part she kept her temper wrapped in a thick cloak of sticky sweetness.

The Emmenthalers, most agreed, would soon leave. Those types always did.

JD became a regular at some of La Mancha's better bars and restaurants. He was expensively casual, jovial, greeting anyone who sat near him or looked his way. His usual order, four fingers of JD, prompted some to guess that JD was a nickname standing for Jack Daniels. Others said no, they reckoned he acquired it from the jack-dandy with which he labeled object, place, event, or person that met his fancy. Maybe, said others, it stood for a real name. Jefferson Davis? (He flew a small Confederate flag from the aerial of his Continental.) Or John D, like that other rich man? But the speculation was desultory, because no one really cared. To most he was just another John Doe, with thick hair combed back like a Baptist preacher's. Dull. Typical. Harmless.

Until it came to the attention of certain citizens of the business community that JD Emmenthaler had acquired an unsettling amount of real estate. He had moved quietly (unusual, all agreed, for a Texan), the negotiating and purchasing having been accomplished by a mousy little man in JD's employ with thin lips, a moustache, and dark-circled eyes. A few scattered residential lots, an office building, a couple of vacant commercial structures, a glitzy motel—these purchases caused some tremors, which grew to serious shakes when the JD Emmenthaler family took possession of the gracious old Vanderkraat home and grounds (vacated by the death of the last Vanderkraat), the twenty-acre remnant of what had once been an old Spanish land-grant *estancia*. It was the one imposing home in Tuceros and, like a feudal castle, it dominated the small adobes that straggled toward the river gorge.

It seemed the JD Emmenthaler family intended to stay.

Then one morning the villagers saw a tall wire-and-wooden fence encircling a row of stores just a block below the plaza, fronted by a large green and white sign proclaiming it the property of the JD Emmenthaler Realty and Development Company. Heavy machinery moved in and the din of razing and rebuilding soon invaded the plaza's peace and the tourists' pace. More big green signs began to appear like loco weeds along the highway and through the town.

But that was in La Mancha's business district. Tuceros, all felt, was by its very poverty safe from such as JD. True, he had moved into the big house and compound, but the poor area surrounding it could hold no interest for such as him.

The mousy little man with the dark-rimmed eyes and the moustache disappeared into the office complex now housing the JD Emmenthaler company's headquarters, and a series of smooth-faced young men (JD saw to it that the same ones weren't seen too often) began making offers for the poor lands and little houses on the west side—offers many of those who lived there could not turn down. Quietly the serpent slithered into Eden.

Toro was the first to become suspicious, the first to spot the puff of smoke on the horizon of their lives, to hunt out the tiny blaze and ignite his own. "Stop a fire with backfire," he muttered.

He'd caught his first warning signal when two strange Anglo men bought a house in Tuceros, and then a third bought another. These were not houses such well-dressed gringos as these would live in. But the plots (and several more that followed) all put together made a sizeable chunk of acreage that soon crowded toward the cantina. And, he and his friends learned when the sign went up, that acreage formed a contiguous unit and now belonged to the JD Emmenthaler Realty and Development Company.

The smoke of suspicion leaped into flame when, after the project off the plaza got under way and Emmenthaler began to hire workers, some of Toro's friends hired on. "A job's a job," they shrugged when Toro chided them. Toro, they agreed, was an alarmist.

But it wasn't long before they began to suspect something wasn't right and, like a village of alerted prairie dogs, they sat up and began to chatter. They weren't getting paid on time, or their wages were being cut for reporting to work a little late, or losing a tool, for mishandling a piece of equipment, or for allegedly violating some sort of piddly-ass rule.

Toro, after a furious round of I-told-you-sos, leaped to do battle. "Somebody got to take care of the dumb shits," he growled, raced his battered pickup to the company headquarters, and burst past the mousy little man into JD's private office. He was Victorio Duran, he announced furiously, and he demanded to know why his friends were being cheated of their wages.

JD's innocent blue eyes widened, his baby face flushed pinker, and from his small mouth sputtered a few surprised syllables. Then pained dignity steadied him. "I have never," he said in slow dark tones like a funeral knell, "cheated anyone in any way. I am an honest, upright, God-fearing Christian gentleman, sir!" His eyes lit up like sun-pierced stained glass. "And I think you'd better explain yourself."

Toro did. At length.

JD raised his hand. "That's enough," he commanded.

But Toro wasn't through. He enumerated who had been cheated, when, and of how much. "And," he finally finished, "you sit there like some fat old gold-plated Buddha statue like I seen while I was a Jap POW and tell me you ain't a low-down by-god cheater?"

"I'm a Christian, sir," Emmenthaler snapped. "And I never cheated nobody in my life." His baby face grew petulant. "You make me very sad, Duran, if you believe these things." His colorless lips grew thinner.

"You look in your by-god books, man, and you'll see what they ain't been paid."

Emmenthaler ran his hand through his thick brushed-back thatch. "It costs money to run a business—a business that gives jack-dandy jobs to your friends, that they ought to be grateful for. They're grown men. They're responsible for the equipment they handle. If they damage or lose it, certainly it comes out of their pay." His voice softened and he began idly to twist his emerald ring. "The good Lord knows I don't like to dock their wages. But right is right."

"You think it's your by-god right to charge them three times what you paid for your damn tools? Or dock an hour's pay if they're five minutes late?"

"I'd say your friends incline toward considerable exaggeratin'."

"You calling my friends liars?"

"That's your word."

Toro balled his fist. JD raised his hand again, conciliatory. "I am a man of justice. I'll check into the matter with my paymaster, make sure ever'thing's jack-dandy. Okay?"

Toro's eyes shot fire. "You by-god better start treating my amigos honest. Because if it happen one more time, I'll be back. With the sheriff."

From behind his desk JD watched Toro storm out, and for a moment a puzzled look sat on his flushed face. Then he summoned the mousy little man from the front office. "Stevie," he commanded softly, "that man is never again to be allowed inside this office. You will see to it."

Which may explain why Toro was unable later to arrange a proper business meeting in the office of the JD Emmenthaler Realty and Development Company.

But the cantina was threatened. The red-headed dragon loomed at the gates. He already abutted the outhouse, pushed at its painted walls, endangered its immortal art. The communicants met. And even when JD came to the cantina himself and made generous offers ("I'm a God-fearin' Christian and I want to be fair") Ysidro and Arabela refused to sell.

JD left with the hurt puzzled look on his face.

"But," Rico warned dolefully, "rich men speak with dollars and the law listens."

Another doom approached like purple clouds in the west, though the innocents in Tuceros didn't know it. Preoccupied with the encroachment on their cantina, they paid scant attention when several men, JD among them, churned out the rutted little road past Toro's. The businessmen on the other side of La Mancha, focusing on Emmenthaler's incursions into their turf, were unconcerned, or unaware of his dealings in the periphery of Tuceros.

The only questions raised were in JD's own camp. He was proceeding too fast, his lawyer warned. The nursing home project had yet to be approved. He'd better wait until he had the documents in hand. He was premature, agreed the mousy little man, and his moustache bristled and the circles around his eyes grew darker. There could still be a glitch. JD paused to reconsider.

"So what's happened?" Narcissa demanded when he came home that evening. "There wasn't one machine out there leveling today." She'd raced out in her Corvette to check (he did wish she wouldn't drive so fast) and there was no sign of any activity whatever. Why not? She followed him into the bedroom, handed him a tall highball, well iced, the way he liked it.

"We don't want to move too fast." He sat on the edge of the bed, eased off his boots, took a long drag of Jack Daniels. "Smooth drink, pet."

She looked into her dressing-table mirror, pushed a yellow curl into place, squinted at what looked like the prelude to a wrinkle. "So what's the hang-up?"

He took another long swig, tossed his shirt on the bed. "Still waiting for approval. And our grant."

She shrugged, intent on her reflection. "You've as good as got 'em. And you're wasting time."

He took another sip and slipped off his jeans. "Stevie says—"

"Stevie says," she mocked, turned from her mirror, cast her mascara-lashed blue stare on him, and thought how flabby he looked in his underwear. "And don't put that wet glass on the dresser!"

He stopped in mid-motion. "Sorry, pet."

She turned back to her mirror and wondered, as she sometimes did, just why she'd married JD. As a matter of fact, she remembered, training an eyebrow to lie right, she nearly hadn't. When she'd marched into her father's office one day to ask for some money, and said casually that she might marry JD Emmenthaler, she wasn't at all sure she intended to. But when her father began to bluster, red-faced and outraged and tie-tugging, she said it again in a more positive way. "I'm going to marry JD, Daddy." And she'd walked out the door and told her father's secretary to call JD and tell him she would.

"The land's yours." She picked up a lipstick. "I can't see what's wrong with a little leveling. I mean, it's only a preliminary." She retouched her lips.

He started toward the bathroom, glass in hand. "Stevie thinks—"

"Stevie, Stevie, Stevie!" She turned back toward him and her eyes were brewing blue thunder. "Stevie, shmeevie! Stevie Prissybritches Naramore is nothing but a twitchy little pimp. A nobody. A hired hand. You're the boss. You're JD Emmenthaler. Are you going to let that whining little snot tell you when to go potty?" Her nostrils flared like those of an angry horse. "And after you promised me."

Then she smiled and softened, began stroking his neck and shoulders. "You're just tired, honey. Tense." She took his empty glass to refill. "But you're strong. You won't let Stevie Naramore dictate to you." She followed him to the bathroom door. "All you need is a good hot shower and another drink."

He sighed. But she was right, he thought as the water cascaded over his shoulders. All he needed was a good shower and a shot of JD. The project hadn't cleared yet, but it would. He'd greased the right palms, donated to the campaigns of certain elected officials. The right ones were beholden to him—in Santa Fé, Austin, Washington too—and even some city officials in La Mancha.

There were times when a small pang of doubt darkened his world. But it was momentary. These little puffs of worry were easily dispelled, especially on a Sunday morning listening to a good sermon on other people's sins. And when the hymn began, JD would pull his chin in sternly and sing with fervor and enough volume to persuade God, the preacher, and all the congregation that even if sometimes his methods seemed questionable, they were excusable because of the purity of his motive. And wasn't philanthropy the purest of motives?

Besides, these projects meant so much to Narcissa. She'd wanted that little nursing home for a long time. And the apartments for the poor. Always trying to better people's lives, Narcissa was. Too, as she always reminded him, there was money in these charitable projects—government money for financing, and huge profits for the JD Emmenthaler Realty and Development Company. Why not? He did the work. Why shouldn't the government fund it?

He did wish Narcissa wouldn't push him so hard. Not that he didn't adore her—so pretty with her puffy golden curls and skin like a pale peach rose—though JD had learned early on, she could be as thorny to handle. She ran a good home. Was a good mother to Travis, though she was inclined to overindulge him. Well, she spoiled JD too he reckoned. Though she did like to have her way. But when things were to her liking, she laughed, and her laugh was like bubbles rising. When Narcissa laughed, JD laughed too.

12

JOE DECIDED AS LONG AS HE WAS
roped into this meeting—and, it seemed, committed to keep it from
exploding—he might as well do a little nosing around. Might keep him from
making an ass of himself. Though he had no intention of fighting Toro's battle.
But what the hell, these were decent people. Arabela and Ysidro. Patricio who
ran the little *grocería*. Chico and Rico. Tecolote.

And—he had to admit it—Toro. Maybe he had burdened his old
comrade with a blame that might be partly his own. Besides, damn it all, they'd
faced Japs together, risked their necks to get the millstone and keep their outfit
eating. At any rate, whatever had happened was a long way past.

Anyhow, he'd get the lay of the land. He guessed he owed Toro that
much, as long as he was here and stuck with the meeting. And for the moment
he had nothing better to do. Toro had gone bursting off into La Mancha on
some mission or other right after JD had driven off.

First he called Beth. He'd be a couple more days, and don't let Mike
forget to pick up that harness when he went to town. He'd already done so, she
said, and not to worry, everything was under control. He might have known.
So, feeling a little useless, he drove to the site.

It was noon and the earthmovers were quiet, massed down on the far end.
Joe cut his engine and stepped out to a coterie of prairie dogs, upright on their
little haunches, shrill and protesting. Looked like a sizeable village. He
reckoned they wouldn't have their hills and holes long—not after JD's
earthmovers got good and started. Well, the little fellows weren't alone in
losing out to a goddamned developer.

Funny he should meet this guy—the kind of despoiler Joe hated most—
just as he was determined not to be drawn into Toro's antics. Ironic really. His
Presbyterian mother would have said it was predestined, as if God had nothing
better to do than schedule the trivia in each man's life, like setting traps for
coyotes.

Quite an expanse here. The river bluff dropped sheer ahead and the mesa shimmered dark and still in the distance.

A car pulled up behind him. "Looks like we meet again," said JD Emmenthaler.

Joe pushed his hat to the back of his head, which he knew gave him a bumpkin look, and drawled, "Howdy." When he'd served in the legislature a colleague had once warned that when Joe Steele started his country-boy act, it was time to guard your hole card and put your hand on your wallet.

"Like my spread?"

"Depends," said Joe, "on your intentions. Are they honorable?"

The Texan laughed. "That's a good 'un!" He slapped his thigh and the big emerald on his finger caught the sunlight. "Like 'do you intend to marry it?'"

"Yeah, or rape it," said Joe. "You got it, buddy."

"Don't know what them Mes'cans told you, Mister."

"Joe Steele. Well, Mr. Emmenthaler . . ." He was still affecting his bumpkin persona; he wasn't sure why, but certain people brought out the worst in him. "I'd say first off, they're not Mexicans. They're real live American citizens, just trying to keep what's theirs."

"I'm workin' entirely for their benefit."

"Sure." Joe hooked his thumbs over his belt. "The welfare crap. Politically correct, I think they call it. Easier than thinking with your own brain." But JD wasn't listening.

"Decent housing."

"They already have homes. Better ones than you'll build."

"And right here where we're standin', a nursing home. Charitable works. Tell you what, Joe Steele. Come on over to my house. We'll have us a cold beer and I'll show you some pictures of projects I've built other places. Show you the plans for this one, since you're goin' to be refereein' this pow-wow."

Joe was tired of playing the country boy and started to decline the invitation, then decided not to. What the hell. He might even learn something. He shrugged.

"Lead the way."

The first thing JD showed Joe was his wife's wrecked flower bed. "Prize pee-YON-ees they were. Cost me enough. Broke Narcissa's heart."

Joe nodded. The bed was a mess, all right.

"Damned Mes'can dog." JD pointed past the wall-enclosed lawn toward the compound beyond. Joe smiled, remembering his and Toro's foray the night before.

"Got some burros comin' in today," said JD. "Narcissa got a jack-dandy idea. Wants to set up a little amusement park next to the motel I bought. Have a little petting zoo, hitch the burros up to one of those wheels. You've seen 'em. Sell rides to kids. Keep 'em here till it gets built. Meanwhile, they'll amuse my kid. Come on in, let's get a couple beers."

"Looks like you're elbowing in for a big slice of La Mancha's pie."

JD laughed. They passed through a heavy carved door into a large entrance hall. It was a graciously built adobe house, cool, solid, amply proportioned. The builder had been a man of taste, though now a dozen chrome-framed mirrors intruded, giving the hall a schizophrenic tone. Varying in size and contour, they hung in groups. From every side Joe saw fragments of himself. Up the stairway wall the mirrors climbed, and from the living and dining rooms opening off the hall Joe glimpsed more mirrored walls, visions of vanity.

JD led him into a large, sky-lit atrium—a late addition by its appearance—and extracted two Lone Star beers from the refrigerated depths beneath a black leather chrome-trimmed bar. A single mirror covered one entire wall, unadorned except for an enormous Texas Lone Star of red-and-blue cut glass in its center. Cowhides covered the overstuffed sofa onto which JD sprawled and the chair into which he motioned Joe.

"Yeah, like you said, I'm gettin' in on some La Mancha pie." His pink face grew solemn. His voice rounded with sincerity. "Kinda town I like to help—poor people, 'specially over here in Tuceros—cryin' out for good housin' and a nursin' home they can afford. Place I can do good Christian charity."

"Subsidized by your doting Uncle Sam?"

"Man's got to make a livin'. And it's a good cause, ain't it? We got a benevolent government." He took a long pull on his beer, wiped his lips with the back of his hand. "And for the tourists that support this town, a wholesome motel with a kiddy park.

"And then," JD's enthusiasm was mounting, "with all the arty types they got around here—man, what a sellin' point—this is confidential, Joe, just between us, because I know you can see the business potential for a big development! Expensive homes—town houses, condos, retirement community. It'll draw the rich classes in like flies. Money, people. The population could double!"

"And when the water dries up. What then?"

JD shrugged. "Worry about that when it happens."

"What's your big project off the plaza?"

"Offices. To rent out. Got my own big office complex on the north side. Come out later, I'll show you my headquarters. Yep." He took another long swig. "I do good for the poor, improve the downtown, bring in big business to this chicken-shit little burg. And make enough profit to invest in the next community that can use some improvin'."

"Seems to me," drawled Joe, "if a man keeps his own fence mended he won't have time to make mischief with other people's."

JD belched loudly.

A phone rang somewhere and in a few minutes a sandy-haired kid Joe judged to be about nine or ten years old ran into the room. "Mom's lookin' for you." He eyed Joe briefly. "Stevie called."

JD rose. "Fetch Mr. Steele another beer. No, no, set still, Joe, I'll be back before you can miss me." He moved fast for a fat man, Joe thought.

"I'm Travis," the boy said. "That your car in the drive?"

"Sure is. And don't bother with the beer. I've got to leave."

"No. Daddy said wait." He ducked behind the bar and returned with another Lone Star. "I gotta go. We got some jackasses comin' in." He grinned. "The four-legged kind."

Joe sipped his beer, eyed the Texas star, and wondered how he could gracefully leave.

A woman's voice rose from somewhere down the hall. "I am sick and tired of Stevie's everlasting whining," she screamed. "Stevie or no Stevie, we are going to start that building!"

JD's voice was a blur, and then hers mounted. "Then get the damn government grant settled! You know the ropes. I know it takes time, and I also know it's coming, which is why I say let's get started anyway. And you can either shut Stevie up or get rid of the whining little pimp."

The voices came closer. "Relax, pet," JD was saying. "We're leveling like you wanted. But the rest has got to wait for clearance. Because—"

"Because Stevie says," she snapped.

"Please, pet, we've got company." Their voices dropped for a moment before the door opened. Joe glimpsed the woman patting her hair in place at one of the mirrors before she continued down the hall. JD looked petulant, but quickly altered his expression and entered the atrium pink-faced and genial. He opened another beer and made small talk while his shallow eyes stabbed at Joe's. Wondering how much I heard, Joe thought, and kept his own face bland.

JD led him to the den. Photographs replaced mirrors in this room. He began to point out pictures of apartment complexes, plaques, framed certificates and letters—civic-club and chamber-of-commerce types—commemorating his services to the community of mankind. He throve, it appeared, on accolades. Or perhaps he planned to submit them at the pearly gates as documentation for admission. A letter of appreciation from his Sunday school class in Dallas, of which he seemed inordinately proud, hung between a contrived photo of the banal Texas jackalope and an oil painting of the Alamo. Wherever JD might reside, he obviously lived in a mental set that was Dallas.

"I take pride in these buildin's," he said, "and I thank the Lord every day that He chose me to be His instrument and help the unfortunate lead a better life." He picked up a photo from his desk and looked at it in that slightly puzzled way Joe had noticed earlier. "I just can't understand what those Mes'cans at that crummy bar are so suspicious about."

"Could be they don't like you plowing into their lives too much. Their cantina—it's sort of sanctified, I guess you'd say. It's their church-away-from-church. Their center. And—it's theirs."

"Well, hell's catoot, there'll be a jack-dandy rec room in my complex!" His small mouth pursed. "I just can't understand it."

"No." Joe looked into the pale eyes. "I guess you can't."

"That fallin' down wreck. And would you believe—an outdoor privy?"

"That privy's a sort of gallery, you know."

JD snorted.

104

"That you threatened to raze."

"It runs across my property line. Looka here, Joe, I don't want to wrong nobody. But right is right. And I can't have that thing so close to my housin'."

"And the cantina?"

"What I'm gonna build them's a sight better'n that thing."

"So you plan to level it too."

"Just between us, confidential—I wouldn't say this, Joe, but I know you can understand. You can see why—that thing has got to go."

"So've I." Joe stood. "Thanks for the beer."

As they stepped outside, a line of burros was trotting up the drive beyond the wall, and from the compound came Travis's high voice. "They're here!" Dust rose and hoarse brays shredded the air.

"Well!" JD's voice was dry. "For once one of them greasers delivered somethin' on time."

The procession headed toward the barbed-wire pen where Travis was motioning to the driver and giving orders. The woman Joe had seen earlier was crossing the lawn.

JD waved at her. "Come meet Narcissa." She wafted toward the compound, a small southern breeze in an eddy of blue denim dirndl, white cowboy boots (silver-tooled and tasseled), and a long fringed vest. Blue-tinted sun glasses in silver frames gave her an airy innocent blue-hued look. A silver butterfly perched on yellow curls that poufed high like sun-gilt clouds. Only the weight of heavy Navajo jewelry—concho belt, squash blossom necklace, massive bracelets—seemed to keep her earthbound.

"Travis!" she called shrilly. "Get back from that wild herd," and when he ignored her she yelled that the dust would stir his allergies. He retreated a few yards and she gusted toward Joe and JD. "I am soo glad to meet you!"

Joe hadn't noticed the southern accent inside, but she was working it overtime now. When the rose smelled that sweet, Joe always watched for the wasp in the blossom.

"Travis, baby," she shrilled, "don't get too close!"

"Been acquaintin' Joe here with our buildin' plans. He's gonna try and talk some sense in those bar-room pests."

"Now, now, honey," she chided softly, "they just don't understand that it's all for them." A tiny sigh puffed from her pouty red lips. "We mustn't be intolerant. Even of that Toro Duran." She turned toward Joe. "Have you met Toro Duran yet? He's the trouble maker. Just last night he deliberately turned his dogs loose in my peony bed!"

"I doubt it was deliberate. Careless, maybe."

"Oh, you don't know Toro Duran. We've had trouble with him before. I loved my peonies so." She dabbed at a tear before it could smear her mascara. "We're very forgiving people, Mr. Steele. But we've caught him prowling more than once." Joe tried not to let a smile show. "And he has actually threatened my husband!"

Travis's voice rose from beyond the compound above those of the burros. "You put 'em where I said," he was yelling. The drover, pointing toward a more commodious wooden corral, seemed to have his own stubborn streak, and as he saw JD striding toward him he pointed. "Corral!" He nodded passionately. "In the corral! Better place for burros!"

"Don't you forget you promised me a horse, Daddy," yelled Travis. "I don't want burro shit in his corral!"

"Travis!" Narcissa dragged the name into three syllables. "Tray-a-vis! You watch your language!"

"Burro poop. That bob-wire pen's good enough for burros. Tell him, Daddy!"

"Well, goddam."

"Honey," warned Narcissa.

"God bless," amended JD, and Joe thought, what the hell, if his developments fall through there's always TV evangelism.

"Put 'em in the wire pen," JD ordered.

"Too little."

"I said put 'em in the wire pen!"

The drover shrugged and spat in dark disapproval. "I guess you the big boss. When you pay?"

"Come by the office end of the month."

"*Señor.* I got to buy the beans! You said—"

"You want paid, you get it on pay day." JD turned to follow Joe to his car. "Hate to sound so hard," he said, "but you got to keep 'em in line. And sometimes you just got to kick a little ass!"

13

JUSTICE, THEY SAY, IS BLIND. Which is why judges shouldn't be. For a judge—at least as Rico saw it—is something like a seeing-eye dog who must steer his charge through the traffic of human error into the ordered halls of law.

But halls and judges vary greatly in style, especially in the villages of the great American Southwest. Here strange remnants of medieval Spanish law—high-flown, pious, and convoluted—mingle and marry with those of Yankee frontier realism—blunt, immediate, and practical. And into the stew modern bureaucracy is forever poking its finger to confuse everyone. Local variations on the theme of justice are therefore many, wide, and often creative. Unique among the village courts shines that of La Mancha.

Rico's magistrate court was no sudden institution. Its character had ripened over the twenty-three years he had run it. Practices once considered innovative had, like old silver, acquired the patina of use. Philosophies once deemed outrageous were now dignified by tradition. And he had an air.

"Like a damn *rico*," someone had grumbled back in 1962 when he first took office as JP, and the epithet stuck. Used first in derision, it had by the time the office became a magistracy grown to a friendly handle, and finally to one of admiration. His slightly younger brother became affectionately known as Chico, and soon no one even remembered their real names. A dedicated bloc from the Tuceros district, combined with passive acceptance by the La Manchan merchant-Anglos whose boat he didn't rock and a lack of any concerted opposition, had managed to reelect Rico repeatedly and even overwhelmingly, despite or because of his unorthodox methods, and they likewise kept reelecting Chico their sheriff.

When humanity was wanted, Rico supplied it. When discipline was needed, his was quick and stern. When humor could melt a sticky situation, Rico injected it. When a misdemeanor was best left unobserved, Rico knew when to turn his back.

Nor did he (or Chico either) ever abandon a chase in favor of paperwork. As a result, a lot of paperwork remained unwritten. It often irritated the hierarchy, but his friends and his mirror always grinned back. He listened to everything, remembered what he chose to, and when large problems seemed insoluble, he went fishing.

In Rico's court the law was malleable. It bent to the circumstances encaging it. For Rico—no coyote to be trapped in a cage of government regulations—entertained a strong belief that justice was often served best by dismissing petty rules entirely. And if he artistically varnished (some said tarnished) the rules, he considered it his moral duty. For his was a mission. His credo was simple. Do it legal, or make it seem so, don't step on the toes of the powerful, and when the rules fail, let ingenuity take over. His was a mind that yeasted quietly with innovation. He also believed autocratic action was usually more effective than board-meeting palaver. Always a realist, Rico admitted with a slow smile (designed to drag those about him into the conspiracy) that a bit of humbuggery from time to time, used judiciously, could be a very useful tool. Big words, hundred-dollar words, served their purpose too, when inserted into an argument. It did not signify that he was often innocent of their meaning. His audience didn't know their meaning either.

This philosophy had served him, and the community, well for twenty-three years.

The two legs Joe saw extending from a battered Ford in front of the magistrate's office proved, as their owner emerged behind them, to belong to Rico.

"It's none of my damned business," said Joe, "but I just learned something you might want to hear. About Emmenthaler's government subsidy."

"Yeah?" Rico wiped a streak of grease from his chin with a once-white undershirt. "What about it?"

"There isn't one. Not for these Tuceros projects. Not yet anyhow."

Rico pondered this a moment, wiping his hands. "Where'd you hear that?"

"His place. It may be coming, but as of about an hour ago it was not a done deal."

Rico let out a long low whistle and polished the wrench he held on his jeans. "That ain't what he told us."

"That's why I thought you'd be interested."

A slow grin widened Rico's lips. "Let's go inside."

A deputy intercepted them in the hall. "You're late. You got a court hearing."

"Oh hell," said Rico. "I forgot." He beckoned to Joe. "Come on, this'n won't take long." He turned to the deputy and winked. "You know what to do. Soon's I get my gear."

In the black robes of justice Rico stood transformed. His expression grew wise, benevolent. He was, quite clearly, a man who believed deeply in the trappings of legality, if not always in its provisions. The folds of judicial dignity hung protectively, like the all-enfolding law they symbolized, concealing the greasy jeans beneath. Motioning Joe to follow, he strode solemnly down the hall, clutching his wrench like a scepter, and swept into the anteroom.

Joe slipped inside the courtroom and sat quietly in a back corner. An obviously unhappy tourist, with his wife and two pre-teen daughters in tow, turned to him and began to protest that he'd been falsely accused of speeding, that he was going to stand his ground, that he refused to be railroaded. The wife and daughters punctuated his assertions with vehement nods. "So what did they accuse you of?" the man asked Joe.

But before Joe could frame an answer a ruckus in the hall grew louder, the door flew open, and down the aisle two uniformed deputies escorted a pulled-down surly looking man with wild eyes and a yellow beard.

From the anteroom Rico stepped majestically, seated himself behind the bench, and looked inquiringly at the three who stood before him.

While the oaths were being administered and the charges read (forty-two miles in a thirty-mile zone, no seat belt, resisting arrest) Joe began to smile. The deputy speaking was the same one at whom Rico had winked just minutes ago. ("You know what to do.") Joe looked at the defendant with the paint-stained hands and the yellow beard and knew him from the night before. It was the Michelangelo of the holy cantina, the artist of the outhouse whose threatened murals all Tuceros was poised to defend.

And from the pale lips of Wesley Wetherford Jones resounded two firm words: "Not guilty!"

"You deny you were driving forty-two miles per hour in a thirty-mile zone?"

"I dang sure do."

"You will not use profanity in this courtroom."

"You call that profanity? You want to hear some real cussin'—"

"You heard me."

"And I wasn't drivin' no forty miles."

"How fast do you think you were going?"

"Under thirty."

"How much under thirty?"

"Lots. Maybe twenty-nine."

"I suppose your ad hoc contentionary estimate is more accurate than the speed guns?"

"Well, I know what I was goin'."

"So does the arresting officer," pronounced Rico. "If he says you were speeding, I say you were speeding. And if I say you were speeding, you were. And if you dispute my judgment, that's obstructionary hogwashicus. Which means contempt of court."

The mouth of the tourist awaiting his own hearing dropped open and an incredulous look spread over his face.

"What about the seat belt?" continued Rico.

"Judge, I done told you last time, I don't hold with them danged things."

"I just warned you about profanity," said Rico. "And I'm not interested in what you hold with. The law is the law," he pronounced grandly. He looked at the papers on his desk. "You are also charged with resisting arrest."

"I didn't resist nothin'," asserted Wesley. "This here's a free country, and I told the lyin' sonofabitch—"

"This court," roared Rico, "will not tolerate your language."

"Well, that's what he is, your honor," insisted the defendant. "I am only tellin' 'the whole truth' like I sweared to do."

"I've heard enough," the judge declared. "Guilty on all counts."

But Wesley Wetherford Jones was just warming up, and, Joe guessed, he was having a wonderful time. "I was drivin' twenty-nine miles an hour, mindin' my own business, in my own car." (Did Wesley even own a car? Joe wondered.)

"With my own seat belt that you're accusin' me of not having, layin' there beside me, where I wanted it, and I told this lyin' sonofabitch to go stuff it."

"Speeding, one hundred dollars and two weeks in jail. No seat belt, another hundred and another two weeks. Resistin' arrest, two hundred dollars and three months in jail. Contempt, compounded with contumicity, five hundred dollars and six months. Not to be served concurrently. That's—" He punched a palm-sized computer and then counted on his fingers. "That's nine hundred dollars and ten months in jail. Without bail."

"All that for drivin' twelve miles over the limit?"

"Oh, now you're admitting to forty-two? You lied about the twenty-nine?"

"No, dang-it, I'm just—"

"Add perjury to the charges. In flagrante delicto! Another hundred dollars and another two months."

"That's a thousand dollars—and a year," quavered Wesley. "Just for drivin' forty-two stinkin' miles a hour!"

"Case dismissed. Adeste fideles. Take him away!" Rico banged his wrench on the desk. "Next case."

Joe looked at the tourist. He was gasping, open-mouthed like a hooked trout, his look of incredulity now changed to one of terror, a man about to go under the knife. Or the wrench. A tamed man.

"No contest," he mumbled, and when Rico fined him three hundred dollars ("since this is your first offense") he paid it without demur, thanked the judge for his leniency, gathered his family, and fled.

Rico swept back to his office, motioned Joe inside, shucked his robes, and chuckled. He wiped the wrench on his grimy jeans, threw it on his desk, and turned to his waiting friends. Wesley and the deputies were laughing. "Good show," said Rico. "Not a peep out of that last one! Now you sonsabitches clear out. Me and Joe Steele got business."

Still laughing, he closed the door behind them.

"You run some courtroom."

Rico crossed to his desk, sat tilting his chair back, and scratched his head. "I sometimes shoot 'em some shit," he admitted.

"That's what makes the alfalfa grow."

"Now—you sure about that subsidy? Emmenthaler wasn't just telling you this?"

"His wife was yammering at him. She got a little loud."

"So you think—"

"That at this moment JD Emmenthaler's funding is zilch. All foam and no beer. And without the federal green light, can he even get state and local nods?"

"Shouldn't. But hell, he buttered their corn. Promised he'd bring in some big business if they'd waive his local taxes. And the chicken shits caved in." Rico shook his head from side to side. "'You can't keep all the outcasts from hell and Texas out,' I told 'em, 'but you damn sure don't got to pay the scumbags to come.' But—" He spread his hands wide.

"Well, you know more about that than I do, but I'd guess he still has no authority to proceed. And if he's acting under false pretenses, isn't that fraud?"

Rico scratched his head. His was a spiderweb mind that fed its owner whatever items it entrapped. "Maybe." He stood by his desk, toyed with a paperweight. "Way I see it, there's right, and there's wrong, and there's loopholes." He walked to a window, stared outside. "But we got to find 'em. And keep him quiet while we hunt. Act like we don't suspect nothing wrong, like we believe it's a done deal. Mustn't scare him into any tearing down or getting buildings condemned."

Rico paced, then stopped. "You don't think he'd just quietly start anyhow?"

"I wouldn't think he'd dare."

"Well, he's bought lots of drinks for the bigwigs. I'd sure like to know how much money's passed under the table, and who to. And if his wife's pushing him—women can make men do some half-assed things.

"Course, there's always Toro's way. Butt head-on and scare the shit out of him." Rico grinned. "Caught us a thief one day. Guy ran two roadblocks, headed for the mesa, and—well, nobody knows that mesa like Toro. Plus he's a number one shot."

"Yep." Joe was fiddling with his pipe. "Best marksman in the regiment next to Chief."

"Well, we were setting in my office having a good game of poker—couple of deputies and Toro and me—when the call came on this guy, and the chase was on. Toro knowing the mesa, we were up there faster'n the thief—closed in on him, and Toro began shooting his forty-five. Fired in front of him, and on each side, and right behind. Kicking up dirt all around him, and each shot moving in a little closer till the guy stopped running and gave up!"

"Takes an outlaw to catch one."

"Best fun we had all week. Broke up the poker game though. But—" Rico grew serious again. "That was an honest chase after an honest thief. This Emmenthaler's another breed of coyote. We need facts, not bullets. Proof. And—that'll take some time."

"That's what you may not have."

"Not if he gets mad tomorrow at that meeting. That'll just spur him on—more money in the pot, more palms to grease, hurry it through. And then, there's no stopping him."

He sat again, leaned forward on his elbows. "Our game is act like a bunch of dumb Mes'cans, calm him down." He sighed loudly. "Which brings us to Toro."

"Don't look at me."

"Going to the meeting, ain't you? Look. Mr. Steele—"

"Joe."

"Joe. This is—this is to save Tuceros. Just a little barrio, but it's important to us."

"And I wish you luck. I really do. That's why I came to you. But hell, man, I've got a ranch to run."

Rico toyed with the wrench on his desk. "Sure. You already done us a great favor and I ain't like them outfits that you give 'em a donation and next thing you know they're hitting you up for another one. All I'm asking is—since you're going to be at the cantina anyways—is just keep Toro quiet. Toro could wreck the whole thing. Always ready to go charging."

"All we need is Sancho Panza."

"Don't know him. But Toro—if he ticks Emmenthaler off—you challenge that kind of arrogant ass, Emmenthaler I mean, and he'll go into high and get his money or start without it. Before we can do any groundwork. I know his kind. We got to approach it legal, without Toro setting off a powder keg. All you got to do is keep him quiet."

Joe laughed. "Ever try to sit on a smoking volcano?"

But Rico's eyes looked like a hurt burro's. Or a doomed prairie dog's. And Joe felt like a man walking his right foot into quicksand just to follow his left one in. He sighed and shrugged and then he grinned.

"Okay. I'll try."

Rico's sly smile followed him out.

The first thing Joe saw as he drove up Toro's lane was the parked patrol car. The second was Toro charging from the house yelling, and Chico right behind him. Joe had barely stepped from his car before Toro aimed his rage-red tirade at him.

"Know what that sonofabitch done now? That slimy sidewinder done file a complaint—sic my friend Chico here on me on account of his wife's petunia patch got dug up!"

Chico nodded unhappily. "Wants the dogs locked up. Or Toro."

"Then for god's sake calm down, Duran, and cooperate. You have a corral—just string some wire over the wood."

"I ain't penning nothing up!"

Chico tried. "Look, we're amigos. I don't want to have to come with a warrant. All you got to do—"

"I have told you fifty-five times already that I ain't going to pen my dogs."

Chico's melancholy face grew sadder. "Better that than him shooting them."

It was the wrong thing to say, and with it went any hope Joe could see of quieting Toro down. No one better trample on Toro's dogs. Joe remembered the wretched little mutt Toro had adopted in prison camp, at a time when starving men were eating dogs. But Toro fended off his fellow prisoners, divided his own scant hoarded rations with the bony little beast until someone captured and killed it for food. Joe remembered Toro's dark sobbing fury that burned for days.

He'd have hell containing Toro now.

"When you calm down, Duran, we can approach this with something resembling horse sense." He gave Chico a sort of leave-it-to-me high sign and Chico signaled back. He'd be glad to leave it to Joe. Toro aimed a large wad of spit in the general direction of the corral.

114

"Look," said Joe, "it's not exactly a high crime, and there's not a hell of a lot Emmenthaler can do. Except shoot at the dogs. But that flower bed is a mess and your dog did it. If you'd show some cooperation—even an apology."

"The one thing I ain't is apologizing!"

Chico started toward the drive. "I warned you. Fair and square. Next call's yours. I got better things to do than mess over a damned posy bed."

"Oh to hell with it." Toro's fury had flared high, burned quickly, and fallen to ashes. A sweet smile spread over his face as if he'd heard the angels sing. "You are my one good friend, Chico," he said gently, "and you done your duty. So now we can forget the whole thing."

Chico cocked a distrustful eyebrow at Joe and headed for his car.

Joe felt the quicksand sensation again. Both feet were in now, ankle deep. If he had half the sense of that little burro scarfing up his oats in the corral, he'd get the hell out at dawn. But he knew he wouldn't. He'd made a promise.

14

BY THE TIME THEY HAD FED AND
watered the animals the morning was hot and yellow. Uncommon hot, Toro said,
a day for cool mountain air and some serious thought. After he fed his birds.

From a small sack hanging from his belt he scattered seed around the
plaster Saint Francis. A flock of sparrows lit quickly and began to peck greedily.
"They don't need feeding in summer, but it makes me their friend." He lifted
his Stetson, wiped sweat from his forehead, and jammed the hat back in place.
The hours until the meeting stretched long.

He looked east toward the solidity of the mountain, dark against the
rising morning. He looked into the rose-hued distance to the west, past the
river, past the mesa, to the space-purpled mountain beyond. He fished a
Marlboro from his breast pocket, lit it inhaling deeply, squinted at the sky, and
made his decision.

"Amigo," he said grandly, and the smoke streamed from his nostrils, "we
are going fishing!"

Joe said they'd be a damned sight smarter to fence the dogs. A little
chicken wire strung around the corral to keep them from squeezing through the
logs—a nice gesture of compromise to present to Emmenthaler at the meeting.

Toro's face started to set like hardening concrete. "I hate fences," he said.

"All asses do," snapped Joe. "Dammit, Duran, use your hard head.
Emmenthaler means business. A little fencing for a few days—"

The roar of passing equipment shattered the morning, the dust rose, and
the day had begun. Toro spat toward the invasion. "I hate fences."

So there it was—a long day ahead, tensions and mercury rising, and Toro
rumbling like a live volcano. "Keep him calm," Rico had said. Joe wanted some
answers of his own and he knew when to concede. "Let's roll."

They headed north through La Mancha and past Taos and turned west,
dogs, fishing gear, and some six-packs on ice in the pickup bed. The little box
lay in the cab between them. "Open it, *amiguito*."

"It's not mine."

They were rattling across the bridge that spanned the great gorge of the river six hundred feet below, and Joe thought it was like the hidden part of his memory, so far beneath his consciousness it seemed static, unmoving, unimportant. Yet the river, cutting through the basalt bastions, carried the stuff of life to the desert dwellers. Often it ran low; sometimes it dried entirely; occasionally it swelled to roiling brown flood. Rio Bravo. Rio Grande.

Was his own life as dependent on a distant river of memory?

"Open the box," Toro was saying. "I already know what's in it."

Joe lifted the little package, looked at it for a moment, shrugged, and pried at the age-brittled tape encasing it. The heat was mounting through the dusty flat land of sagebrush and chamisa and jackrabbits. Toro fiddled with his radio dial until a blast of ranchero music filled the cab. Joe shucked the last of the tape, muttered that the treasure inside better be worth his trip, and lifted the lid.

"Mungo beans?"

Toro's long eyes cut toward the object and his face crinkled remembering. "See that little carved thing hanging at the end?" He pointed to a small figure, just as a semi roared around the pickup. A spray of loose pebbles rained against the already cracked windshield. Hot air and exhaust fumes rolled through the open window. The pickup veered onto the shoulder.

"For god's sake, Duran—watch the road!"

Toro swung back onto the pavement. "See that—"

"I see it. But—mungo beans? Did I drive three hundred frigging miles to delivery a mess of dried beans?"

"Padre made me that. In prison camp. Used it for a rosary. That's Saint Christopher hangin' on it." He laughed. "Reckon he figured I could use some help when I sneaked through the fence." Toro had made a number of midnight sorties, eluded the guards, and returned with food and medicine for sick and starving buddies. Deadly dangerous missions, spurred by—Joe never decided which—genuine heart or the challenge of adventure.

"Always carried Saint Christopher in my pocket."

The radio blared a new song and Toro began to sing with it until Joe snapped it off. "So what about it?"

"That raid we went on—for the millstone. You know—"

Joe noted the over-casual tone, saw the quick look Toro threw at him. "Yeah?"

"*Nada*. Just that I had it with me that night."

"So? And how did Tomcat get it?"

"That, amigo, is what I am fixing to tell you."

They were now driving abreast of the mesa rising off to their left, and Joe saw it was a long spur, a giant basalt stairstep whose far end dipped into a slight declivity worn as if long-trodden by some heavy-booted mountain god. There it began to rise into piñon-stippled hills and then to the purple-veiled mountains.

Joe looked back at the beans on their brittle cord. He dropped them back into the box.

Toro was smiling, rubbing his chin, a little blue-stubbed because he hadn't shaved that morning. "Remember when me and Tomcat escaped?"

Joe remembered. It was shortly after the surrender, and they'd been put on a work detail outside the prison camp. The two had seen their chance. Taking advantage of the thick jungle and native sympathizers, they'd made a break and, helped by guerrilla troops, made their way to the Zambales Mountains, where they eluded capture for some months. Tomcat had told Joe this much after the war.

"But then Tomcat, he got sick. Bad sick. Me and some Filipinos took care of him in their little barrio till he got some better. But they was Japs all around. You know what they did to Filipinos caught hiding Americans. We couldn't put them people in any more danger. Tomcat—he wasn't in no way up to fighting with the guerrillas. About all he could do was turn hisself in. Lie about how he got separated and was so sick and how he been trying to find his detail, and hope he could sell 'em that shit.

"I couldn't talk him out of it. So that's when I give him that little string of beans, that had on it Saint Christopher that takes care of damn fools like me and him, wandering around in a jungle where we ain't got no business. I was going back to the guerrillas.

"I told him if he got through this war alive to send that thing back to me somehow. So I'd know he made it."

"And I kept it all this time." Joe looked out his window. Clouds were gathering over the peaks to the north, a half-stormy sky, like a bratty kid pondering which way to behave. "And you thought Tomcat was dead."

Toro shrugged. "No. Chief saw him after the war. I just reckoned ol' Tomcat was too busy chasing women to remember Saint Christopher."

They turned south now, angled in toward the mesa on a rutted trail, and as they rattled and jumped the dogs yapped their excitement. They stopped to let a herd of goats cross in front of them, their little tails erect like flags.

The clouds were behind them now. The sun was climbing past midmorning, aiming for noon, and dust-grayed sagebrush and chamisa reared stiffly, drought-defying.

Misty pools appeared ahead of them, shimmering like water, dissolving into hard-baked earth as they approached and reappearing farther ahead. The usual tricks of space and light, Joe said. "Or the Holy Ghost. Maybe the desert mirage is the only glimpse of heaven us dry-landers ever get."

But was it promise or taunt? Or just a reminder of what was dying in this land he loved because the real stuff was all being sucked dry by too many wells.

Joe looked back to the storm-draped peaks and toward the proud lonely mesa they were paralleling now, and the piñoned hills rising ahead, and the Jemez beyond to the south, and he felt a slow rage rise from his belly. He thought of the many droughts he had cursed, and thought too that the desert's dryness was its fight for survival, its only protection against the despoilers. It was what kept it safe from the throngs, or had until now, and he cursed all developers.

"So you didn't go back with Tomcat?"

"Hell no. Walk back like a sheep into a pen? No way, Choe, was I going back inside no fence, not 'less I was dragged, and they'd have to kill me doing it."

"So you ran free with the guerrillas."

"We laid low for a while. Orders. Right then old Mac wanted spies, not warriors. Had a network all organized on the islands, radio signals going out from the jungles. But once he landed—man, that's when the fun began. We blew roads and dams and bridges, cut telephone lines. All hell broke loose!" Toro flashed a grin.

Piñons now gave way to pines as they wound up a short incline to where the ruts ended in sharp rocks. They unloaded beer and gear, the dogs yapping and wagging in circles. They walked the last thousand yards to a tiny lake, and this time the water was real. Mountain jays chattered from the branches, and Toro scattered seeds for them.

"Good fishing here?"

"*¡Por Dios!* All fishing is good, man. But do we catch the fish?" Toro shrugged. "*¿Quién sabe?* Only the good Lord can answer that."

They sat on boulders and sorted their gear. Toro tossed Joe a can of Coors and a peanut-butter sandwich, slightly mashed where one of the dogs had sat on it, and put the remaining cans in the cold water at the pond's edge. He touched his can to breast and forehead before he drank, in the old Foursome gesture, and Joe returned it. They baited their lines, attached the beer-can flip-tops to the end of their poles, where they'd bob and flash if a trout nibbled. Settled on the bank they munched their sandwiches, breaking off chunks for the dogs, and lay back to let the peace sink in.

"I bet God gone fishing while He was planning the world." Toro pushed his Stetson low on his forehead.

When he sat still, Toro had the sad long-eyed face of his ancestors. He could be Christ or Mephistopheles, or an El Greco saint if it weren't for the pointed ears. Ears like Pan, and Joe wondered chuckling if he had cloven hooves inside his boots.

"There's all kinds fishin', Choe. Depends on what you're fishing for. Fish? Or thoughts. Like how we are going to nail that side-winding—"

"Or maybe—what happened on that raid?"

"That ain't so hard. We went after that stone. We got it." His chuckle came from deep inside. "Right out from under their dirty Jap noses we got it. And got back with it."

"Cholly didn't."

"No." Toro didn't say anything for a moment. "No. They got Cholly. Dirty yellow bastards." He reeled in again, checked his pop-top tab, and cast furiously.

"How?"

"What do you mean how? You was there."

120

"I told you. I can't remember. I've tried to. Tried to remember—"

He remembered setting out, not any different from other missions. He and Tomcat and Toro and Chief. The Fearsome Foursome in various combinations had set out on a number of jungle nights as their food stores shrank, had pirated rice from fields in the enemy-infested no-man's land to the north. Risky, but what wasn't in a war, and it kept the whole battalion eating, until the grinding stone broke and they couldn't hull their rice. Then, learning from friendly Filipinos of a stone up at Pilar, they planned their heist. And wanting no interference from their officers, they proceeded without authorization.

But the night of the raid Tomcat was in the makeshift hospital with a load of shrapnel in his leg, Chief was on another foray, and Toro had drawn guard duty. That part Joe remembered.

The sound of a roaring pickup punctured his thoughts, grew louder in the silence, and then behind them someone cut a motor. The sound of voices and boots on stone approached. "*Hola*, Toro!" Three men loaded with fishing gear and six-packs walked up and immediately began to jockey for position on the lake edge.

"Guess I'll set by you," one said to Joe, "'f you don't mind."

"Help yourself." Joe didn't recognize any of the three from the cantina, but they obviously knew Toro. "Get too close and we'll neither one catch anything."

The man nodded jovially and agreed, introduced himself as Porfirio, and let it drop that he always had good luck in that particular spot.

"Cheese it, amigo!" Toro gestured to a spot farther down the bank. "Choe here is my old buddy and a by-god war hero and he ain't goin' move!"

The three moved reluctantly but in good humor to another spot, still within calling distance. Fishing among the Tucerans seemed to be a group occupation.

Joe's thoughts wandered back to the raid. Toro had dismissed his guard duty lightly. He'd get someone to cover for him. He wasn't going to miss that raid for a routine dullness like guard duty. But they still needed a third. That stone would be heavy dragging through the jungle. That was when Cholly volunteered, fresh-faced and eager. He'd overheard just enough. "No way,"

Toro snapped. "You couldn't raid a cookie jar without screwing up."

But Cholly kept on whining like a hungry mosquito until Joe said, oh hell, let him come if he was so damned anxious to get himself killed, and Toro shrugged and gave in.

Joe fished another can of Coors from the pond. "He had no business coming. If I hadn't agreed—"

"Horseshit. He volunteered. Get me a beer while you're up. He was grown."

"Not really. Just an annoying kid wanting to play hero."

"Well, he got that want." Toro cocked a bushy eyebrow at Joe. "And I remember you couldn't stand him until after he got hisself killed."

Joe handed Toro his beer, opened his own, and cast his line again. Not a bite yet, but with their talking and the dogs splashing along the water's edge he didn't expect any. The spot was peaceful, though, and he thanked God there were some places still left in this land where a man could be alone. Well, more or less alone. He glanced at Porfirio and his buddies. Seeing his eye, Porfirio smiled broadly. "Any luck?"

"*Nada*," said Toro. "*No bueno por chite.*"

He had some super-good bait, Porfirio called back and offered to share with Joe if he didn't get a bite soon.

Joe settled back.

"They been talking," Toro remarked, "about building a road through here. A paved one. Been some talk—in La Mancha. Up in Taos too I been told."

Joe felt a slow hardening in his gut like cement setting, and his voice was low. "They can't leave anything in peace, can they?" He recast his line. Toro shrugged. "Prob'ly all talk. They'll forget it before the highway department gets its ass in gear." But Toro's long eyes crinkled at the corners and he stroked his lip where the moustache would have been, and he smiled like a rifleman who'd hit his mark.

"You ready for the meetin' tonight, Toro?" yelled one of Porfirio's buddies and Toro called back that he by-god was, and then he importuned heaven. "God, if you'd just blow up the gas tank on that big green Continental, I will say another fifty Hail Marys. I, Victorio Duran promise you that."

Joe forced his mind back to the raid. "I remember going out and coming in—god that stone was heavy—and somehow Chief was suddenly there. Helped drag it the rest of the way." Chief had returned from his own foray, sneaked out again, and followed his buddies' path. About half a mile out he'd met them coming in exhausted and bent his own muscular back to the tow rope. It wasn't quite dawn.

Their captain, grateful they could again hull their rice, said nothing about their unauthorized actions, even put Joe in for his medal, and Cholly too. Posthumously.

"But you got none. No thanks and no medal." Joe reeled in his line.

"*¡Chale!*" Toro laughed. "I wasn't about to stick around for no lollipops. Man—I got back to my duty post like a getaway coyote! Damn sergeant would of bust a gut if he'd knowed!" They laughed remembering.

But Toro had his own script to follow. "What I will do is ask Emmenthaler, nice and polite, to get lost. Leave us alone. Then—"

"You're wasting your time."

"Tha's right. But we will ask nice first. Then when he starts his smooth talk like a *politico* fishing for votes we'll get tough, push him till he feels like he's setting on a cactus—then nail him. Give him two choices. Get out or—"

"Or what?"

Toro arced his hands widely, embraced the lake, the mountain, and god's wide sky. His smile was gentle. "*¿Quién sabe?* But if things happen—"

"They'd better not. He has the law on his side."

"The law is wrong."

"It's still law, and you'd better stay inside it. Keep quiet for once. Let Rico do the talking." He was tempted to tell Toro about their conversation and the plan to lasso Emmenthaler legally. But Toro couldn't keep quiet, would throw it in the Texan's face, show him their hole card, and blow the whole thing.

Joe's rod vibrated. He felt the tug, set the hook, and began to reel. Porfirio and his buddies started to cheer. "*¡Olé!*" "*¡Bueno!*" "*¡Pescado grande!*"

"Not so *grande*," yelled Joe laughing and threw it back. It wasn't three inches long.

Toro returned to his argument. "Choe. We got a right to fight. To keep what's ours."

"But within the law, dammit!"

"Laws ain't nothing but fences. Every law they pass is one more fence around us." Toro aimed a large arc of spit toward the mountain.

"Funny thing—" Joe cast again. "I always looked at laws—and fences—as protecting what I've got."

"God never made any fences."

"Seems to me He made some laws." But fences, or laws, couldn't do it all, he knew, and he thought of High Lonesome whose fences couldn't keep out the feds in Washington who were out to destroy every rancher in the West with higher grazing fees, and along with it the West's economy. And he thought of all the other liberties they were taking from the people, one by one, and he understood Toro's rage.

"This country's still ours," he said slowly. "But the day's coming when it won't be. But until it happens, I'll tend my cattle and ride my fence. And hope for rain in July."

Toro snorted. "The devil makes fences and Wash'ton makes laws which are the same by-god thing." He pulled another Marlboro from his pocket, fumbled for his Zippo and dropped it. Joe lit Toro's cigarette.

The little bull snorted smoke from his nostrils in two streams and cut his eyes toward Joe. "I cut fences. Like that fence on Bataan. That damn Jap fence. But we cut it, amigo! We cut it!" Toro laughed, a wild laugh that bubbled from deep inside him, and Joe remembered—yes, a fence. Somewhere a fence. And that same savage laugh.

Then his memory blacked out again and dissolved into a kaleidoscope of screaming Japanese and exploding firearms. And that deep free laugh, as violent as the barrage around him. And then the crawling. Of Toro running, low to the ground, darting through the fire toward the kid. And then the old image returned, of Toro dropping Cholly, hitting the ground behind him, making Cholly his shield.

He wiped his hand across his eyes, but nothing more came, and he shook off his confused thoughts, looked again at his fired-up companion.

But Toro was absorbed in watching an ant struggle with a straw. After a bit he ground his stub on a rock. "Choe. Did you have nightmares?"

"Sure."

124

"Long time?"

"Long time."

"Have 'em still?"

"Not so much."

"Wondered." Toro took a long swing, wiped the foam from his lips with the back of his hand, and crumpled the can.

A cool stir of air riffled Joe's shirt front as an awakening breeze began tossing clouds about like tumbled bedclothes. But it was blowing toward the storm to the north and the scent of rain was more tease than promise.

"Tell me one thing. What was it about a fence? Where does that fit in? You cut a fence? When? And—why, in god's outhouse? Why?"

Toro's eyes gazed darkly into some sort of private infinity and both men chewed on their own thoughts. Finally Toro spoke. "I had 'em too."

"What?"

"The nightmares." He turned toward Joe and this time his voice was low. "I hate fences."

15

THERE ONCE WERE A BOY AND A burro, and then there was a fence. Here is how it happened.

He was a small boy and he lived with his grandmother, his *abuela*, who was not much larger than he, for she had shrunk with too many years and he was still small with too few. Their house, which was part of the *patrón*'s estate, was small and plain and clean, and a colored picture of the Blessed Virgin hung in a wooden frame on one wall.

Their little hut stood on the grounds of the Big House where Abuela cooked and cleaned, and where the small boy often did odd jobs, or worked in the stable, when he was lucky. He raked manure and tended the horses and after the *patrón* learned that he had ridden wild broncos before he had come to live with Abuela, he was allowed to exercise them. Even the most fractious gentled in the little boy's hands.

He was generally good-natured, though he had a stubborn streak and a temper Abuela could not tame. But he as quickly smiled again, and learned that he could charm those around him with his sweet smile and long pensive eyes.

One summer the *patrón*'s grandson came to visit in the big house, and chose to ride a spirited bay stallion that his grandfather forbade him to go near.

"You let that pukey Mexican kid ride him," the boy objected, and when he failed to get his way, he turned on the boy and began to pelt him with stinging words.

Humiliated, the boy turned toward the mesa. He stood looking through tears and his anger smoldered and then flared, and he filled a burlap bag with what he could find—cold tortillas, a few apples, some cheese, a bottle of water, and an old blanket; then an ancient skillet, a small hatchet, a rope, and a handful of matches. He started for the mesa that rose in the west.

On the highway he caught a ride with a trucker, until, at the foot of the mesa he asked to be let off.

He slung his sack over a thin shoulder, began circling the mesa's high walls until he found an angled ascent, and began to climb. Through sand and rocks he pulled on his strong skinny legs, and sometimes he slipped backward in loose detritus, until finally, on the flat piñon-dotted plateau, he sat to rest.

There he found the burro.

The shaggy little beast stood in a clump of stunted piñons, his huge ears pointed forward, and he looked at the small human. The boy stood quietly letting the burro exercise his natural curiosity, then pulled an apple from his sack and offered it on his flat outstretched palm. After a bit the burro nuzzled it, his ears still forward, then took the gift. The boy began softly to fondle the skin behind the beast's ears, then slowly circled its neck, matted with cockleburrs.

"You all alone up here? You got no amigos? Me, I got none either. I guess we better stick together, you and me."

Their friendship was quick and warm and trusting.

The boy drew the rope from his sack, looped it around the little burro's neck, and together they pushed on. A down-sloping stretch, cut by an arroyo, led to a shallow declivity in which had collected a small pool of run-off water. Here they drank, and in the protection of the basin the boy kindled a fire from juniper bark and piñon cones. He ate some tortillas and cheese, and when the burro nudged at the sack he fed him another apple.

He hobbled the little beast near a clump of tough grass. Then he wrapped himself in the blanket and tried to sleep, but the night grew large around him. In the distance a coyote wailed his eerie song of love or longing, and another answered, and the boy listened. From time to time the burro awakened and sang his own hoarse song.

Morning lit the mesa. The boy ate the last of his cheese and tortillas and fed the rest of the apples to his shaggy friend. "Boy," he said, "there ain't much water here and our food's all gone. I got a home, and I guess you don't, so you come with me. That gringo kid ain't going stay forever." He started pulling the burrs from the burro's neck. They pricked his fingers and drew the blood. "We better think you up a name."

When he trudged in late that night, tired and dirty and leading his burro, Abuela's fear for him turned to anger. "The *patrón's* been out looking for you— all night and all today," she scolded. "And that burro—we can't afford to feed him."

The little boy began to plead. The burro would work for his keep. He would carry the boy into the village to sell the squash and beans Abuela grew. He could haul wood. "And he'll be mine, Abuela. My very own," and his long eyes filled with tears.

The *patrón* said the boy could stable his pet in the small *jacal* behind their hut and do extra chores for hay and grain, and his grandmother relented.

He named his burro Panchito.

For three years the love between them grew. They explored the valley and the mountain behind it, and always they took some of Panchito's grain along to feed the birds. The boy told the burro his joys and his hurts and the secrets of his heart. They went often to the village, and the villagers grew fond of the boy with the impish smile and the patient, shaggy-voiced burro. They bought Abuela's vegetables and cheese and the tamales she made. The artists liked to paint the boy and his burro and paid the boy quarters to pose.

When Abuela learned of this she grew angry. It was wicked to take money for doing no work, she snapped, and besides, the artists were a worthless lot. So after that he hid the quarters he earned. It was easy money, and he loved to look at the artists' paintings. Someday, he vowed, he would have a nice house with many pictures.

The boy and his burro sometimes got in scrapes.

When a tourist's child gave him a dime to ride the burro, he helped the kid up and grinned. Panchito knew what to do. He trotted to a nearby irrigation ditch, stopped suddenly, ducked his head, and dumped the young *turista* in the water. Someone told Abuela.

"That Panchito," she snapped.

But she knew how the boy loved his burro, and once when he fell and hit his head against a rock the little burro returned riderless and led Abuela to where he lay unconscious.

"That Panchito," said Abuela softly.

They were very poor. Their meals were often meager, their clothes many times mended. Panchito was the only thing the boy had ever owned that was all his, and with him he was happy. He never felt poor.

His days were bright.

And then one day in August it ended. For the *patrón* had died in the night. His heart had suddenly stopped, Abuela said.

After that things began to change. The *patrón*'s family stayed on but the horses went, and so did the hay and the chores the boy had performed for Panchito's keep. Abuela was often unable to work because of her arthritis and, though the boy got a job cleaning the schoolhouse each evening, it didn't pay much.

Panchito, Abuela said, cost too much to feed. It was all she could do to buy beans and *masa* for the two of them. But the boy's silent tears moved her and though she grumbled much, she let the burro stay.

In October the circus came to La Mancha.

It came every year at season's end and stayed several days because the village was on the way to their winter base and the rodeo field was a comfortable place to rest and reorganize. The boy had no money, but he dreamed of being among the few who could land circus jobs for admittance. He could wash the elephants or feed the ponies—maybe even the lions.

He told Abuela about the clowns and about the man who flew between trapezes high toward the top of the tent. He told her about the lion tamer and the handsome boots he wore—boots like he would have some day he said. It was more an impossible dream than an active wish, and later he wished achingly that he had not said it.

In the night the circus rolled in, and the boy went in early morning to the grounds, before Abuela was awake. He fed Panchito and told him softly about the circus ponies. Then he scratched Panchito behind his fuzzy ears and started down the road. It was still dark. He wanted to be first in line for a job.

The lion tamer snapped at him and the keepers said he was too small. Two men carried pails of fresh meat by him, newly killed, and it stunk.

He went next to the elephant keepers. A swarthy man stopped. "Whatcha want, kid?" The boy watched the man's bulgy muscles that moved beneath the mermaids tattooed on his giant arms and made them seem to wiggle.

"Can I help with the elephants?"

"What can you do?"

"Anything."

"Haul water?"

"Sure. I could wash 'em too."

"Shovel shit?"

The boy grinned. "I done that all my life, mister."

The swarthy-faced man laughed. "Start shoveling." He put out his hand. "Call me Jim."

With the pass he'd earned the boy stepped that afternoon into the magic of the big tent, but after the elephants had performed he ducked out and reported back to his job. It was nearly dusk when he finished.

"Ever ride one?" Jim asked.

"No."

"Ain't scared?"

"What of?"

"Okay. Up you go."

It was a tame ride, but a higher one than the boy had ever known, and he wished that snotty lion tamer would come by so he could look down on him from his height. But all he saw around the lion cages were the keepers going by with their stinking meat.

The boy trudged home in the darkening day, tired but content in his happiness. Jim had slipped him a dime as he slid off the kneeling elephant and said he reckoned he'd earned it. The boy spent three cents on an apple for Panchito and two on candy for himself. He saved a nickel for Abuela.

He went first to the *jacal*. But—Panchito was gone.

He searched the compound. Panchito was nowhere.

He went back to the empty *jacal* and it still smelled warm with life.

He ran to the hut. "Abuela—"

She looked lined and tired and very small, and she put her arm about his shoulder the way she'd done when the *patrón* died. He knew how poor they were, she said, and how much a burro ate.

He nodded and a little worm of fear began to turn in his stomach.

She couldn't work like she used to. Her eyes were sad. "*Somos los pobres, mi'jito*," she said. "We do what we must." She had ridden the burro to the circus grounds and found the man who ran things.

The fear inside the boy became a large knot as she told him these things, and only two words came out.

"Why, Abuela?"

"Winter is coming," she said, and because she was sad she sounded angry.

"We must eat. You need shoes. Maybe even—" She gave him a smile but it trembled. "I thought about those boots you been wanting so bad."

"Why?"

"Lions have to eat," she answered slowly. "They eat a lot. Circus people pay good for fresh meat." She had tears in her eyes.

"Panchito!" The boy tore out the door. He ran, wild and gasping, falling sometimes to catch his breath, all the way to the village, all the way to the circus grounds. Panting and sobbing he found the fenced enclosure where he thought Panchito must be, where animals were kept when the county fair was held. A chain-link fence surrounded a building, and inside it were pens. Surely Panchito was there. Unless—

Unless somehow he could manage that fence. He didn't think the building would be locked. If only he had some wire cutters. If only he could somehow tear an opening. Or find a weak spot. He grasped the wire. He pried at the lock on the gate. He kicked furiously at the hinges. Nothing gave.

He went to find Jim, but no one knew where he was. He hunted out the keepers. He begged everyone he saw, and finally someone pointed out the big boss's wagon. Surely he would let him have back his burro.

"A deal's a deal, boy," the man said. "A sale's a sale." He went back into his wagon and slammed the door.

The boy ran back to the enclosure. It was tall and strong and there was no way in. He sank to the ground and, still clutching the fence, he sobbed.

While I was in the big tent, he thought. Inside laughing at the clowns and clapping for the elephants. While Panchito—

A man passed by and headed for the lions' cages, and from his beefy hands hung pails of raw, fresh-killed meat, still steaming with hot blood. Stinking red meat.

* * *

Many years later the man who had been the boy told this story to his old friend. "It is a lump inside my soul," he said, and the tears ran down his cheeks. He had never told it before and he would not tell it again.

"I hate fences, Choe," he said.

Joe only nodded. But it made what came after easier to understand.

16

"RIDE, VAQUERO!" A RED-BOOTED stamp, an arcing Stetson, a lusty cheer from the fast filling room. A lively rhythm leaping from Tecolote's strings, Toro prancing like a fractious stallion, and Arabela sliding two *cervezas* in their direction as they headed for the bar.

Joe glanced about. Rico and Chico were stationed at their usual spot beneath the neon sign. From another corner Wesley Wetherford Jones tossed Joe a two-fingered salute. Serenity, dressed demurely in blue, high-necked and virginal, smiled in his direction, every inch a lady. Arabela was decked out for the big meeting in wild shades of pink and orange, her hair piled higher than usual. A heavy odor of perfume emanated from her like a miasma. Night of Passion, she told someone who remarked on it. Patricio from the *grocería* edged up grinning and clapped Joe on the shoulder. "I knew you'd come."

Men chattered in clusters, glancing from time to time at the door, and Joe thought again of the prairie dogs.

People kept drifting into the packed room. Like dry tumbleweeds onto a fence, he thought, ready to blaze from any spark. And Toro had been throwing sparks all the way down the mountain.

"Sonofabitch thinks he can by-god run us out," he'd grumbled as they paralleled the mesa. "Maybe-so he can," he conceded as they rattled across the bridge. "But we'll be back."

By the time they pushed open the old blue door Toro was expanding with great love for his fellow men.

"Ride, Vaquero!"

At the bar he turned and swept his arm in a wide circle. "This is my cantina, Choe. Used to be I got the nightmares." He took a long swig. "Still do sometimes. But here, with my friends, I don't worry no more. Here we got the music and the bright light, and a little *cerveza*, and you hear a good word and you make the joke. And you keep the dark outside."

"And the mesa? You shut it out too?"

132

Toro looked hard at Joe. "*Sí*. For a time I do," he said softly. "Always there is the mesa." A faint shadow passed over his face, and it was the sadness of one who loves the world. Joe had sometimes glimpsed that sadness when the lonely notes of Taps rode the dark jungle nights. "This cantina, our cantina, someday it won't be here no more." He touched his Coors to his heart and his forehead, and he drank and deep thoughts filled his eyes.

Joe didn't answer and Toro swept his arm again. "Look around." His voice was low and serious. "Every man here is come to save our cantina."

"Then they'd better act civilized tonight." But Joe could see the faces, laughing but tense-eyed. The meeting, he sensed, was degenerating before it began.

Arabela kept wiping the bar. "Full moon tonight. Always makes trouble."

Toro was grasshoppering now from table to table. Tecolote perched on his stool, his old straw work hat on the counter. Joe edged toward him. "*Una copita para mi amigo*." Arabela was already pouring the red wine. The old man nodded and raised his glass but before either could speak Félix materialized between them full of good fellowship.

"*¡Señores!*" He'd already had a snootful, but he could still stand. Swaying slightly, he flourished a ten-dollar bill and announced in grandiose terms that he would stand them both a round. "And Toro too!" He grinned. "You see, I am going along this morning and I am thinking. Félix, I think, it is not right that you let Señor Choe buy you the drink when he was here, the guest in your cantina, an' you not buy him the drink next. But I got no money. What can I do?

"Well, I am going along thinking these things, and how you are helping us to keep our cantina, and I say a little prayer about I want to buy my frien' Señor Choe a *cerveza*, and I look down and there where I am walking, right in front of me, lies a ten dollar!" Félix massaged his paunch thoughtfully. "It was give me so I can do the right thing for my frien' Choe. Give me from heaven!"

"From the devil, you mean," said someone they called Antonio. "Somebody's pocket is lighter! Félix," he said turning to Joe, "is the best thief in Tuceros."

Félix acknowledged the compliment with a somewhat unsteady bow. "I thank you, Antonio. But not the best thief! I shall buy two *traguitos* of tequila— one for me, the grand thief, and another for the grander thief than me, that robs them *turistas* ever' day. So. I buy a double for Rico! Best thief of all us!"

"*¡Olé!*"

"*¡Andale!*"

"*¡Bravo!*"

Cheers rose heavenward. Ysidro stepped from behind the curtain picking his teeth and grinning. Félix carefully deposited the ten dollars of uncertain origin on the counter. Then, feeling the bar wet, he removed it more safely to a chipped glass dish where it sat, for once unnoticed by Arabela who was pouring tequila into two dust-clouded shot glasses and grinning at Rico.

He rose and bowed. "*Gracias*, amigo! I accept your fine tequila!" More cheers. "But—" He pointed to his brother. "What about Chico? If he didn't bring them *turistas* in, I wouldn't have nobody to rob!"

"*¡Sí! Tequila para Chico!*"

"*¡Olé!*"

"*¡Andale!*"

"*¡Bravo!*"

A new sound joined the cheers as the now awakened puppies behind the bar began to howl.

Rico, shouting for everyone to "act proper, get serious, before Emmenthaler comes," started for the bar. "If you *pendejos* wanna save Tuceros, we got to have a proper meeting."

"What he means," yelled Toro, "is shut up. What he means is we got to act dignified."

At this unexpected help from Toro, Rico looked questioning at Joe, who shrugged. The clientele quieted somewhat but the yelping grew shriller. Arabela poured Chico's tequila, set the bottle on the bar, and called to Ysidro to get the puppies some milk.

The musician's fingers ran up and down the strings restlessly like cattle sensing a coming quake, and then launched softly into a melody designed to soothe and calm. Ysidro emerged and set a dishpan of milk on the floor by the end of the bar.

Félix emptied his tequila in one gulp, signaled for another and, lifting it high, launched into a speech. "For all my goo' frien's." He paused, looked around and two large tears spilled down his plump cheeks. "For all my goo' frien's." With his glass still aloft and an angelic smile lighting his face, Félix slid

134

gently to the floor, his freshly filled shot glass still clutched in his pudgy hand.

"When that sonofabitch going come?" someone yelled.

Arabela's dark gaze swept the room. "Full moon tonight."

Félix stirred, blinked, and seeing first the puppies at their pan and then his shot glass still full, leaned around the end of the bar. "*Perritos*," he said, "I buy you a *traguita* too! I share with my little brothers. *Aquí, perritos!*" Carefully he poured his tequila into their milk and lapsed into contented sleep. No one paid any attention.

Toro, having completed his tour of the cantina, angled to the bar, stepped over Félix, and ordered another *cerveza*. He clapped Rico's shoulder and grinned whitely. "We do things your way tonight, amigo. Then, if that don't work—"

"Just keep your mouth shut tonight is all I ask."

Toro fished a Marlboro from his pocket, crumpled the empty pack into the glass dish, felt in various pockets for his Zippo, then caught the matchbook Joe tossed him. "Sure, sure." He lit his cigarette and tossed the match toward the dish. "You talk all that law crap you want. Won't work. But I give you this chance to try."

"Look, *hombre*—" Rico grabbed Toro's shirt front. "Whatever happen, *keep your damned mouth shut!*"

At that moment the empty Marlboro pack blazed. So did Felix's ten-dollar bill beneath it. Toro grabbed Tecolote's work-frayed hat from the bar and swatted at the flame. But instead of smothering it, the sun-dried straw caught also, and a plume of fire rose like a jaunty yellow feather.

"*¡Mi sombrero!*" Tecolote's song ended with a thump.

Joe upended his beer on the pyre, handed the soggy remains to Tecolote, and picked up the remaining corner of the heaven-sent bill. "The Lord giveth," he murmured, "and the Lord taketh away."

Arabela mopped up the mess and glared at Toro. "One of these days," she said darkly, "you'll burn down half of La Mancha."

Rico banged the half-empty tequila bottle on the bar. "Let's get some order in here." He lifted it high for another whack and froze. "Goddam!"

There, framed in the doorway in stained-glass rectitude, bathed in red neon light, stood JD Emmenthaler.

17

NARCISSA STOOD BESIDE HIM, bright in hot pink denim, vest and boots black-tasseled, her yellow curls high-bubbled, her lobes weighted with great silver stars.

"The ears of Texas are upon us," muttered Joe.

But it was JD who dominated the scene. Like a Nieman-Marcus version of frontier preacher he stood in black frock coat, black string tie, black boots. In the red neon light he seemed a missionary stepping into hell. He swept his black Stetson from his bushy mane to his bosom, and his emerald ring glinted green. He stared at Rico, who gently lowered the upraised tequila bottle to the counter, flashed a quick smile, and stretched a hand toward the advancing guests.

Toro stood feet wide, knees bent like an alerted samurai, and beside him Joe leaned on the bar beer in hand, and regarded the scene. Like a grade-B oater, he thought.

Every eye in the hushed room watched darkly as JD and Narcissa moved toward Rico. Arabela stopped mopping the bar. Ysidro leaned against the curtained door frame and picked his teeth. At his far table Chico sat stiff and intent.

"Nice evening," said JD cheerfully. He shook Rico's hand and ordered a Jack Daniels.

"No Jack Daniels." Arabela popped her gum loudly.

Then he'd take beer.

"What kind?"

"Lone Star."

"No Lone Star."

"Then make it Bud."

"No Bud."

"Well, what have you got?"

"Coors and Carta Blanca. We're out of Carta Blanca."

136

"Okay, make it Coors."

Narcissa ordered a margarita.

Arabela pulled a Coors from the cooler for JD and began to concoct the lady's drink. She slid both in their direction and placed her hands on her hips.

JD took a deep swallow.

Arabela chewed her cud. Tecolote began to strum softly. Rico cleared his throat and turned to Narcissa. "Let me find you a table."

She toyed with her margarita, primped at a curl, gazed about the room, and saw Serenity. "There's a lady," she said, and her voice carried in the silent room. "I'll just go sit with her." She was still affecting the exaggerated drawl. "If she doesn't mind."

"Sure, ma'am." Serenity stood. "I can see you're the same kind of lady as me." Wesley, stiff as an English butler, held a chair for Narcissa. Serenity's freckled face flashed a look of amused mischief. "Guess we're two of a kind, all right!" A small laugh from somewhere burst like a match to dry tinder and it caught and raced from grin to grin around the room.

Rico banged the tequila bottle on the bar again. "Okay, okay, let's get serious now."

"Sure." JD was assuring Rico. "We both want the same thing—the best for these good people," and Rico was nodding, assuring JD that no one in his group was trying to block progress, and he certainly hoped JD hadn't taken it that way. "The question is," continued JD, "what is the best thing."

"That's what this meeting is for," said Rico. "You explain what you're planning to do, maybe get a few ideas from the people."

"People don't always know what's best for 'em." JD swallowed the last of his Coors and motioned for another. "Like gettin' a kid to take his medicine."

Arabela plunked his beer on the counter and returned to Joe and Tecolote at the far end of the bar. "Them outsiders know so much. Like that health inspector—remember? Came here nosing around for dirt and bugs—then didn't know a cockroach when he seen one!" They laughed remembering and Tecolote plunked a few notes of *Cucaracha*.

JD made his way toward the trio, carefully stepping over the inert Félix. "Well, if it ain't my friend Joe! Maybe you can help me talk some sense into these—" He glanced at Tecolote. "Beggin' your pardon, mister. I got jobs to offer."

Tecolote's face was expressionless. *"No hablo inglés, señor."*

JD turned back to Joe. "We got to make 'em understand. Like this guy—stuck here bumming drinks."

"No," said Joe, "not stuck and not bumming.. Makes adobes by day—good ones, I'm told."

"Who does he work for?"

"Himself. When he wants to."

"No steady job? Well that's what I have to offer—steady, jack-dandy employment."

"Guess he could have that. If he wanted it." Joe felt irritation rising like summer mercury.

"That's what we got to teach 'em—to want it."

"Count me out." Joe scratched his head and affected a silly smile. "Tecolote's kind of like me, I reckon. Rather work for ourselves. I dig my own post-holes and string my own fence and stay inside it. All I ask is a good well and some rain in July. Tecolote—he just asks to make a little music for his friends in this cantina."

"And that trouble-making Duran?"

"Oh, Toro gets a hair up his ass sometimes," Joe drawled. "That's just his way."

Rico jumped onto a chair in front of the bar. "Okay, let's get this meeting started. I will first let Mr. JD Emmenthaler tell us how he plans to help us."

"Believe me, I will make your lives better. That's why we're here, in Christian brotherhood."

Sure, thought Joe. Kick ass one day, kiss it the next. He stopped listening and watched the reactions. Most looked bored or skeptical, but sat with the courtesy of their heritage.

". . . I will give you good jobs—some of you have already signed on . . ."

Toro shifted restlessly. "Dumb bastards."

". . . modern apartments . . ."

Joe gave Toro a warning glare, swept his gaze over the room as a new arrival slipped quietly in the door, and recognized the strange Indian from the pueblo. The man sat beside Chico, who pushed at him the full can of fast-warming beer Rico had left. The Indian nodded his thanks and, catching Joe's eye, flashed the old wartime V-for-Victory sign. For one crazy moment Joe thought it was Chief, automatically returned the sign, and turned to see Toro returning it too. "Who is he?" he whispered.

Toro shrugged. "He comes sometimes. Never stays long. Drinks one beer and go back to the pueblo I guess."

"Did he know about the meeting?"

Toro shrugged again. "¿Quién sabe?"

"I guess we got to admit," Rico was saying, "you got some fine plans to help Tuceros. When you thinking to start this fine project?" The question slid in casually.

Joe felt Toro tense, heard him breathe heavily, jabbed an elbow into his ribs before he could speak.

"Right away on the nursing home. And the apartments—just waitin' on some materials—and this property. Got my gov'ment go-ahead weeks ago."

Joe and Rico shot quick looks at each other.

"Just one question, Mr. Emmenthaler." It was Serenity. Wesley on one side and Narcissa on the other turned to her startled. Her face was pure innocence. "What about the cantina?"

"I have offered a fine price for it, ma'am. More'n it's worth by one helluva lot."

"JD!" It was Narcissa.

"Sorry, pet. A sight more'n it's worth."

"But what about it?"

"You need to ask Ysidro that, and his missus."

"She don't need to." Ysidro threw his toothpick on the floor and crossed to stand by Arabela behind the bar. "We done said no."

JD sighed, gestured widely, and shook his head. "I would hate to see it condemned."

"Can't nobody condemn a building just because you want it." Ysidro was stony faced.

"Oh but they can. It's what's called a 'mandatory acquisition area' if they consider it a 'threat to a program for the public good.'" Of course," he added generously, "you can appeal—nothin' to stop you."

"Nothing," muttered Joe, "but lawyer's fees and court costs and money under the table to try and top yours."

"I'm tryin' to save it from that."

"¡Piojo!" Toro jumped up before Joe could stop him. "You want to save our cantina, you can by-god butt your puff-toad ass back to Big D!"

JD turned his eyes sorrowfully toward heaven. Rico closed his. The Indian in the corner fixed his on the table before him, but a quiver like an amused ghost floated around his mouth. Tecolote strummed a few soft, conciliatory chords.

JD recovered quickly. "Let's act reasonable. This shack's fallin' down." He smiled sadly. "But I'm a Christian man, and I'll shore it up for you if it's so important." He turned to Ysidro. "I'll give you a fair price, gussy it up—been plannin' to do that anyways—let you run it."

Arabela and Ysidro stared back hard-faced.

Wesley jumped up. "What about my art gallery?" His voice was hoarse.

"Art gallery?"

"Yeah. Outhouse to you."

"Why, I wouldn't dream of destroying that building, with all that fine painting. Wouldn't consider it!"

The look of sudden hope on Wesley's face hit Joe like a slug in his gut. So did most of the faces around him, like they'd just heard the all-clear after the air raid. Joe looked at Ysidro and Arabela, staring at each other like two cubs in a steel trap. He looked at Tecolote's dark inturned face, then at Toro's silent fury, a volcano about to blow.

He felt a river rise within him, slowly at first and then it rose to his chest and flooded his throat, and the words began to spill. "Mr. Emmenthaler."

"Hey, friend, call me JD."

"I'll call you what I damn please, and the first thing I'll call you is liar."

The room hushed.

JD stiffened and brushed his lapels. "What on earth might you be insinuatin', friend Joe?" There was a hard edge beneath his joviality.

"Yesterday—only yesterday—you told me you were going to level the outhouse and the cantina."

JD laughed. "You must've misunderstood."

"I misunderstood nothing. Now you're singing another song."

"Looka here, Joe, I don't have to explain myself to nobody 'cause ain't nobody can stop me doin' what I aim to do on my own property."

"This ain't your property." Ysidro pointed a stocky finger at the Texan.

JD ran his fingers through his hair. He smiled and shrugged. "It will be. Talk sense, man. You'll take my money before you let it be condemned." He turned to Rico. "I didn't have to come here tonight. I ain't accountable to anyone here. And I am going to build this development, whatever. Me and my little wife came here tonight in friendship, to make you see this is all for you. This face-liftin' will attract more people, and industry, and that means more jobs—economic growth. There's river water here, and land—wide open, room to grow, down to the river, and across it—and that mesa out there, just beggin' to be developed!"

"Bull-shit!" Joe shouted.

JD looked startled. "I beg your pardon!"

"All you damned developers cry the same blathering idiocy—more jobs, better economy, industry, more goods and higher prices. For who?

"For you, Mr. J.D. Emmenthaler. Not for these people. Because as you come in with your rising prices, their buying power goes down. With your development come higher taxes they can't pay, which means they're either forced onto the welfare rolls and made more dependent—on the government, on your low-cost housing, meaning they have to dance to your bureaucratic tune, or they—the ones who won't bow under—are pushed into more poverty. Either way they're forced from the homes they and their forefathers have lived on for generations.

"You call yourself a civilized man. I call you a barbarian—a barbarian who destroys anything you can't understand—a building or a way of life. And in its place you give them nothing. What you're bringing these people, Emmenthaler, isn't economic development. It's economic cancer that grows cell by cell until it destroys the organism."

JD had stood stunned and his face had taken on a deep hot shade of pink. "I see no connection—"

"No," said Joe. "I'm sure you don't." He turned back to the bar, ordered three more beers, and carried them to Chico's table. But the Indian had left. Joe sat down. "Party's getting wild."

"Like Arabela said—full moon."

"Toro's done it again. In the army he was always starting fights, pulling me in."

Toro was yelling now. "My frien' Choe is right!"

"Your friend is dead wrong!" JD was yelling too now, and his thick hair was bristled up like tumbleweed. He spread his arms. "It's up to you! You can accept my generosity or you can be on the losing end. Because either way, I am going to build my project. And Uncle Sam is right behind me."

Still at the bar, Rico stood contemplating his beer, but looked up as someone yelled, "I say we give this man a chance. He just trying help us."

"*¡Chale!* You bray like a burro," Toro yelled. "And this man going treat you like one—like he treating them burros he got penned up in barbwire."

Voices began to rise.

"Toro's right!"

"Toro's plumb loco!"

The fight was on. A beer can sailed through the air. Another arced back. The yelling rose as others joined. Leaping onto his chair again, Rico roared for order.

Tecolote watched quietly.

Félix stirred, looked around blearily, and raised his empty shot glass high. "*¡Olé!*"

The din also aroused the puppies from the torpor of their spiked milk. Yipping shrilly, they began to erupt from their box and stagger drunkenly through the crowd.

Rico kept calling for order and gradually the shouts subsided.

"Mr. Chairman. Rico."

Rico pointed to Serenity. "The lady wants to speak."

"I want to talk about art." The room hushed as Serenity pointed at JD. "You say you will fix up the cantina. What about our walls?"

JD smile benignly. "Some shoring up, some plastering and painting should do it."

"To cover our pictures?"

"You'll like what we do better."

"These are originals. They can't be replaced."

Narcissa laughed. "Honey, they may be original, but you obviously don't know what good art is."

"Well, I know a few things about men!" Her freckled cheeks flushed and her voice rose. "In my profession I knew a lot of men. I could always spot a phoney. And your husband—" She pointed at JD. "Your husband is a phoney!"

Joe began to chuckle softly. "Lay on MacDuff."

Narcissa jumped from her chair. "I thought you were a lady!"

"Same kind you are, sister. Which house did you work in before you snared your rich gigolo?"

Narcissa prepared to spring, and the tassels on her pink vest swung with her furious breathing. Wesley leaped between them, pushed Narcissa back into her chair. Serenity kept her dignity and sat, composed, to laughter and applause.

JD stood twisting his ring.

Toro was striding up and down. "You ain't nothing but a by-god tumbleweed blowing in here on your hot Texas wind. You know what we do to tumbleweeds? We catch 'em on our own barb-wire fences and we burn 'em out!"

"Please, Mr. Duran, can't we act civilized?"

"You don't know a civilized man from a pile of shit. Like Choe done told you. No people ever got theirselves civilized without they endured first."

Rico nudged Joe. "Get him out of here."

Joe elbowed his way toward the bar and grabbed Toro's elbow. "Great exit line, buddy. Let's head out."

Before Toro could protest, one very drunk puppy became a very sick puppy, all over JD's shiny black boots. Toro began to laugh.

Arabela started wiping the counter, Ysidro fished another toothpick from his pocket, and Tecolote started a song.

JD gestured to Narcissa, and started for the door. "Your meetin'," he said drily, "was about what I figured it would be."

Tecolote's song followed them out the blue door.

> "You may forget the singer,
> But don't forget the song."

"Full moon rising," said Arabela.

18

EVERY TIME JOE FLOATED TOWARD sleep a replay from the evening jerked him awake.

They hadn't said much driving home. Toro had left the cantina grinning at his own performance or Joe's unexpected tirade or both, and probably kept grinning in the dark of the cab. Disgusted with his flood of words, Joe kept his eyes on the moon-whitened gravel ahead.

"Know something, Choe?" At his lane he shifted and turned in. "That JD, he don't even lie good. You got to be a by-god artist to tell a good lie."

"Guess you've had some practice."

"You know it, man." In front of his house Toro cut the engine, leaned back, and laced his hands behind his head. The smell of manure and ripening apples floated through the cab window. The dogs came bounding from behind the house. "I'm a honest man, Choe." He scratched his head. "Most of the time. Unless some sonofabitch come around poking into my business. Then I cook me up a good one."

"Going to sit here all night?"

But Toro was bent on philosophy. "A good lie gots to be original— interesting—and every little piece gots to fit together else it ain't worth the trouble. And if you get pushed in a corner and got to throw some truth in, you laugh a lot and sidle your eyes round and they think it's a lie! Yeah. I lie artistic as any."

"Yeah, you do." Joe opened his door, petted the dogs, and yawned. "I'm for bed." But once inside he paused. "Okay, Toro. You pulled me into your fight."

"Amigo!" Toro pounded Joe's shoulder. "Like always you there when I need you."

"Now it's my turn." Joe planted himself on the couch.

"I get us a beer. *Dos mas cervezas*—"

"No. All I want is, what happened on that raid?"

Toro, standing in the middle of the living room, shrugged. "I done told you."

"Not what I want to know."

"Tomorrow, Choe."

"Tomorrow I head out."

Toro sighed, dropped into a chair, fumbled for a cigarette. "Okay, Choe. What it is bugging you?"

"The blank spots. I'm okay up to the barrio. We found the stone out on the far edge, cut it loose." He pulled a handkerchief from his hip pocket. "Easy as robbing a hen's nest, right from under their damn noses!" Toro lit his cigarette and inhaled deeply.

"So we got the stone, were fairly away, dragging it, beyond the clearing, into the jungle, when—"

"They open fire and all hell breaks loose. We dive for cover, push the stone under some tangle-vines. You remember that?"

Joe rose, moved to the window, turned. "I—think so. Vaguely. And then?"

"Then we spread out, you and me and Cholly, hunkered low and—"

"Crawled. I remember the shooting, and Cholly calling out, and then more shots."

"And we was crawling for him. Japs heard him too, started closing in— not too many, though."

"You were crawling toward him. But—" Joe was sweating. "What I've got to know—I've buried it all these years—Toro, which way was I crawling?" Joe wiped his forehead and stood knotting his handkerchief.

"Which way?" Toro inhaled, leaned back, and took a long look at his friend. Smoke streamed through his nostrils. "We was spread out, remember? Cholly was farthest to our right. I was between you and—"

"Yes. But was I crawling toward Cholly? Or away?"

Toro looked at Joe straight and hard and said nothing.

Joe sat on the sofa, on the edge, arms on knees, looking at the floor. He felt tears start down his cheek, or maybe it was sweat, and he dabbed at it. It was the old question again, the old plaguing doubts still nagging on the undersides of his mind and he was asking, silently, though his lips were moving.

"You talk to yourself often?"

Joe snapped back to himself. "I like to get a second opinion."

Toro stubbed out his cigarette. "Choe, you are one hardheaded sonofabitch. But you never run from a fight yet."

"That doesn't answer my question."

"Like you jump in tonight—tore into that lying rat!" Toro jumped up flinging his arms wide. "And that fight ain't over yet."

"It is for me."

"That fight is just beginning!" Toro's eyes burned bright fire and he looked like a hungry man with a big T-bone. Planning something, Joe thought, and it was not a soothing thought.

But Joe's mind was on its own track. "Which way was I crawling, Toro?"

"Hell, man, I was doing my own crawling, couldn't be wet-nursing you. Can't you remember?"

"I remember—I have this image—I told you I can't remember except in flashes. You got to Cholly."

"Yeah." Toro was cruising the room, straightening a picture, adjusting the TV antenna.

"Grabbed him. Picked him up. And there was more firing."

"They was moving in—heard Cholly same as we did."

"And you. I saw you. You dropped him. And you ran."

For a long time neither spoke. Toro's eyes widened. "That what you lit into me for? After the war, waiting for a boat back home, called me ever' name but nice—and never did say why!"

"You didn't know why?"

"How could I? You was yelling like you done bust a gut. I thought you gone loco. Lots had."

"You dropped Cholly."

Toro picked up an ashtray, set it down again. "*Sí,*" he said, "I did."

"And ran."

"Dived for the brush. Damn right I did!"

"You left Cholly."

"Choe." Toro opened his mouth and closed it and started for the hall. He turned at the door. "You got to do your own remembering, Choe." His voice was soft. "I'm going to bed. You better start thinking. Hard. Remembering. The whole picture, Choe. All of it."

Joe lay awake still and Toro's words played through his mind. He tried to remember what had triggered the attack after they'd cleared the barrio, were well away, or thought they were. He remembered that much. Then something ignited the wild firing. What?

He tried to remember crawling back for the stone after the Japs gave up the hunt—shaking with fever Toro said—but nothing came, except toward the last, pulling the load, and Chief appearing suddenly to help. No matter how he probed, his memory slid around it, slippery, like a snake in a rock pile, and vanished.

The moonlight streamed across his bed, and he thought how he and Beth sometimes lay in such a moon puddle, talking quietly, staving off sleep to watch the pool of silver glide over the bed. Like a magic spell, Beth said, and he felt suddenly lonely. But he'd be home tomorrow.

Sleep began to wash through him and slowly he let his mind drain empty. The cloud-dappled moonlight flowed over the bed.

It was only a small sound, but it awakened him instantly. A footfall. Toro going to the bathroom probably, but why would he put his boots on for that? Joe lay listening for the flush, but he heard only rustles, too quiet to be normal, sounds that related to something or nothing. Why was Toro moving so furtively?

Joe lay still. Soft steps toward the kitchen, the squeak of the floor. A drawer opening. Toro rummaging softly. Then no sound at all, and it seemed a wrongness, and then the kitchen door scraped. From the orchard the burro brayed. Something clicked and the door closed, too softly for Toro, unless he was trying not to be heard.

Joe pulled up quietly, sat on the edge of the bed listening. What was Toro up to in the middle of the night? Damn him. Because Joe knew he was racing down another of his one-way trails to outrage.

He dressed quickly. Pulling on his boots he saw Toro in the moonlit yard. He was buckling a tool belt around his waist, and on it hung an extra something

Joe took to be his little pouch of birdseed. The glow of Toro's Zippo lit his face briefly as he touched it to his cigarette. Then he walked on.

Joe ducked quietly out the kitchen door, following at a distance. If Beth could see him now she'd ask if he'd lost his mind.

Avoiding the road, Toro cut straight through clumps of sagebrush and chamisa that swayed eerily in the small breeze like a chorus of ghosts. The sharp sweet smell of the sage rose as Joe's jeans brushed through it. Sporadic clouds fluttered like lace curtains across the moon. The rustling of small night creatures and the cry of a coyote cut through the pale silence.

They had gone perhaps a quarter of a mile when Toro reached the barbed wire bounding JD's property. He walked another fifty yards or so to a break in the fencing—an opening Joe thought he seemed mighty familiar with.

Toro ducked around an outlying shed, sticking close to the wall. He glanced quickly around. The big house was dark, the compound silent except for the brays of unhappy burros.

Joe closed the distance, watched from behind the shed Toro had skirted, and prepared to rush for a tackle.

Keeping largely in shadows, Toro advanced with bull-headed purpose past the little house where he had once lived with his *abuela*. On the far side of the corral he stopped and looked toward the big house. Except for the patchy cloud shadows nothing moved.

He sprinted for the burro pen, stopped suddenly and stared. So did Joe. Burros were crammed mercilessly behind barbed wire as binding as sin, without space to move. If food or water had been placed in the pen, few in the surging mass could reach it.

"Filthy sonofabitch." Toro pulled something from his tool belt. Joe didn't need to see to know what it was or what Toro was up to.

Before he could close in to stop him, Toro cut the top strand, and with the quick movement came the glint of his watch in the moonlight and the sharp ping of the taut wire springing loose.

Joe froze as the second wire snapped, and the third, and he was back on Bataan, and memory burst through bright as moonlight through parting clouds.

They were dragging the millstone—god it was heavy—were almost across the clearing. There was a pen, a wire pen, and there were horses in it, gaunt starving horses, some bleeding from abuse. He saw Toro's face drawn with shock and hatred, and Toro was striding toward the pen, and Joe and Cholly were pulling him back, and him jerking away, muttering about the cruelty, and he had the cutters he'd used to free the stone. A flash of his watch in the Philippine moonlight, the ping of the wire, the frantic neighing, the pounding of hooves, and then the lights flashing on and the explosions of rifles.

But it was burros braying now, and Toro inside the pen herding them out toward the cut in the property-line fence, and the sagebrush and chamisa and the rolling grassland toward the river, toward freedom.

"Ride, Vaquero!" The shout split the night and Toro laughed the wild laugh from deep inside him. Joe had heard that laugh before.

Windows in the big house flared with light. Floodlights burst on in the compound. Shouts erupted. Toro sped with the burros toward his own land.

Behind him trailed Joe, outraged. Damned grand-standing little bull. What good did he think this stupid stunt would do? What good did cutting the fence in the war do, except to snafu the raid and get Cholly killed? But then Toro glanced back toward the compound and Joe saw his face in the moonlight and it glinted with tears.

"Ride, Vaquero!"

Joe waited for shots, but none came, and he was running not crawling and no jungle pressed in, only sagebrush and chamisa, and with it came the sane and sardonic reflection that he'd come to prevent a crime and ended as an accomplice.

Toro had done it again.

Reaching his own turf, Toro jumped into his pickup, revved the engine, U-turned, and roared gravel-scattering down the lane.

Joe sprinted toward the dusty blue Olds. Keep your distance, he told himself. No headlights. The chase must continue to whatever field of battle Toro might be charging. Where next?

19

A DRIVE ALONE THROUGH THE
night invites the flow of thought. Like a journey from a half-dimmed past to a
shrouded end come subtle images—a shadow of what has been or may be,
intangible, undefinable. In the attic of your mind you come on bits and pieces
of your youth, seldom visited but always there, heaped in the debris of forever.
For the past is not biodegradable.

There were the summers at Chapman's ranch (that later became your
ranch) learning to herd, mending fence, swimming in the stock tank. And the
time you and Ben set the hay barn on fire—an accident, but you knew better
than to be making Indian smoke signals on a windy day.

There were the long boyhood hours you spent reading—in the apple tree,
in bed under the cover with a flashlight, in arithmetic class, on horseback. And
you read everything—your mother's magazines (how sophisticated they made
you feel) and your dad's medical journals (how scholarly). You read
Shakespeare, and Tennyson's *Idylls* and Keats and Burns and Robert W.
Service. And you read Homer and fought round the walls of Troy (how you
ached over Hector's death), and you read Thurber and Fitzgerald and
Hemingway, and you panted through Faulkner's unpruned sentences eager to
get on with the story which you didn't always understand. And from them all
you acquired some sort of eclectic taste, some sort of unsorted wisdom, and a
stirring, however muddy, of your mind.

There was your freshman year in high school when you and Ben and the
Reedy boys pooled your resources and your courage to visit the pink whore
house with the big black bull painted on the sign in front and the three of you
sat popeyed in the front room while Jimboy Reedy who was oldest and bragged
the most disappeared with one of the ladies, and you heard the creaking of
springs through the wall until Jimboy came out red-faced and cocky and all of
you held your breath scared spitless that your pooled money wouldn't be
enough and then what would you do. And when the lady sent you away without

any charge you were first off relieved and then suspicious until Jimboy finally admitted he hadn't done anything—she'd only sat on the bed and jiggled it to save his macho image—and the ragging you gave him after.

These and smaller moments return, the building blocks of mortality, the cells of your life, held together by memory, every minutest detail—a bird wheeling against a white cloud, the sound of falling water, the taste of apple butter on brown toast, the smell of saddlesoap on leather—even these are with you forever, recalled by a scent, a sound, a sadness.

There was school in the East, and Beth, a little kooky from too much college, but willing to risk the West and happily ever after with you—still willing even after the war had split your life in two. Beth, still a little kooky, but she glued you together.

Because after the war things weren't the same again. The world was different, not as nice, or maybe it was you who were different and not as nice. The simple things you'd thought about in prison camp and hoped to have again one day weren't so simple any more. There were more rules and less decency, and the ice cream melted faster. You had more money and more junk to spend it on. You partied more and enjoyed it less, and women had liberated themselves from grace and innocence and few bothered any more to be charming. Except for Beth. A handshake wasn't enough any more to close a deal, a man's word was no longer sacred, and the sense of wonder was gone from the faces of children.

You found America progressing itself to destruction, into a state of limitless rinky-dinkery, overpriced but what the hell, put it on my Visa, they got more money than I do. An America focused on trivia, a mad pursuit of fun instead of happiness, of the cute instead of the beautiful, where men relied on their shrink instead of themselves, and middle-aged women spent their meaningless lives playing bridge.

But life was good on the ranch with Beth. Until you saw your dry land sucked drier by the post-war plague of new population there wasn't enough water for, and you watched appalled while the Emmenthalers of the brave new world lit like hordes of locusts, and the water dropped and your well with it, but what the hell, shrugged the brain-dead bastards, let them drink Coke.

So you turned to repolishing your tarnished world. You got elected to the state legislature, and you found it an eddy of hot air and false promises and mush-brained debates and you refused to run again.

Beth agreed with your despair but she wouldn't let you retreat. She picked you up and turned you back toward life and you began again to listen to the windmill's creak, and you set about being the best sonofabitch in the business.

You prayed for rain in July and you read your books, and you held Beth's hand while together you watched your son grow to his own manhood.

You pushed the war behind you, except for a small box still undelivered, an image you couldn't get past, and a gap you couldn't fill in. But you tried, because you knew man is nothing more than the sum of his memories, though still it wouldn't come. But you rode your fences and kept the world at bay and found your freedom there.

Until Tomcat Little jumped the fence and broke the peace and pulled you down this road with all its mass of memories, and with every breath you take you're grinding out more to remember. You see the glint of Toro's watch and hear the ping of the snapping wire and the rush of pounding hooves, and one more forgotten memory flashes, one more picture in the sequence. You hope the rest will come, and meanwhile you'll go on arguing with Beth about the little things and loving her in your barbed-wire way. You tried to close the gap. You faced the fear that's haunted you, and facing it, you can go home again.

As soon as you complete this one last mission. For your old buddy. For Toro. For Cholly. For Tomcat and Chief. For the Fearsome Foursome. And for Tuceros and La Mancha and High Lonesome.

For Beth.

So you speed toward a mesa, somewhere west of dawn and east of sunset, which is the span of all our lives. Our day in the trail to eternity. Where some build fences and others cut them.

And in these thoughts that whirl in the dark like blowing sand it comes to you that though you and Toro ride on opposite sides, maybe it's the same fence you're riding after all. Toro's an outlaw, always has been. He is also, you have to add, the most civilized man you know, a man of original thought and courage to act, which is to say the talent to survive. For civilization is built on survival.

But still you wonder who Toro is, saint or devil, charlatan or avenger, wise man or fool? But more immediately, what in hell is he up to now?

20

AHEAD LOOMED THE MESA, DARK in the silvered air. Joe wondered what the hell he was doing bumping along without lights behind Toro Duran because of a friendship eroded by forty years and as weed-choked as the ruts beneath his wheels.

Just east of the bridge he'd pulled off the road—didn't want to follow too closely. He knew where Toro was headed. Why was another matter. He didn't know why he was trailing him so surreptitiously, either. There wasn't much trouble the guy could stir up out on the mesa.

Past the river the pickup turned south. Joe drove a mile or so past the turnoff before he U-turned, retraced the distance, cut his lights, and turned onto the dirt road. Stiff weeds scraped the underside of the Olds and moon-bleached chamisa scratched against the side. Jackrabbits bounded before him. The dust from Toro's pickup hung unmoving in the air.

In the eastern distance shone points of light that were Taos, and farther down a few dots gleamed that could be La Mancha and Tuceros. The stars above, going about their cosmic business, seemed as close.

Bypassing the turn he'd taken earlier toward the hills, Toro kept straight toward the mesa. Nearing its base, Joe stopped behind a rocky outcrop large enough to hide his car. Ahead, the pickup bounced another few hundred yards before it stopped.

Toro stepped out and a battered canteen hanging from his shoulder caught glints of moonlight. He swept his gaze toward the river and across to the lights in the valley, and beyond that to the Sangre de Cristos, misty in the silver light, and in the other direction to the austere range of the Jemez.

The world about lay empty, silent, motionless. From the high desert the mesa reared like a whale from the sea, dark and massive and strange. Then, wrapping his dream about him, Toro disappeared into the cleft that marked the beginning of his climb to meet the sky.

I will lift up mine eyes to the mesa, whence goeth mine old comrade, Joe thought, and I'll lift up mine feet to follow the old coot.

Keeping boulders and rocky outthrusts between himself and Toro, Joe followed by sound—a dislodged rock, the scrape of a boot, an occasional muttering. As the ascent grew steep Joe stopped to catch his breath—not as young as he once was—and circling his gaze like a low-wheeling eagle, he skimmed the world below.

But like the eagle, Joe knew the seeming void was a plenum teeming with field mice and kangaroo rats, horned toad and lizards and hollow-fanged desert rattlers, plump quail and cheeky prairie dogs, jackrabbits and coyotes and a thousand other breathing things.

Joe knew too that Toro's trek was none of his business, that however hard Toro had maneuvered to pull him into the Emmenthaler fracas, he hadn't invited him on this night's adventure. Whatever Toro was about, he was about it alone.

The call of a coyote rose in the west, and from another direction came an answering call, and then another, until a paean swelled to the moon. Beyond rose the mountains dark and strong, featureless in the night, concealing dark secret chasms and the night-prowling mountain lion. An occasional flash of lightning deepened their mystery.

"*¡Hola, Señor!*" Joe froze as Toro's shaggy voice continued. "I don' mean to disturb you in your own home."

Joe edged warily up, crouched behind a boulder, and peered around. Toro was standing on a narrow ledge beside a small piñon growing from the mesa wall.

"You got a fine big nest here, *Señor* Rat!" Had Toro lost his frigging mind? What was he talking to? "You not need to worry, *señor*. I not like a lot of people what would steal what you worked so hard to store. I ain't going take your good nuts. I ain't got no *masa*, but I give you a little grain. I bring it for the birds, you know, but you are my friend too." He reached into the pouch hanging from his belt. "*Señor*, I understand. There is a sonofabitch wants to rob my nest too—my land and my house, and our cantina. But we going stay, you and me, ain't we? Your people and my people, *Señor* Rat, we will survive. On account of, we belong."

154

Joe smiled in the dark.

A shower of dislodged pebbles marked Toro's resumed ascent, and the moon lit his wiry body as he pulled himself over the lip, and gained the mesa. Joe spit on his hands, wiped them on his jeans and started up behind him.

Gaining the top, he kept low, slipping quietly from clump to clump of mesquite. A few piñon trees squatted in the flat expanse. They too were survivors, slow growing and patient. Ahead, Toro seemed to be floating, detached, aware only of his own misty night.

The moon passed its zenith. It would be setting before long, and descending the scarp would be a lot harder in the dark than climbing it had been. If he had one good hunk of horse sense Joe knew he'd give up this insanity and get back to his car.

But something held him. Some half-assed notion of sticking with his old amigo? Or was it the fear that once in a forty-year past he'd turned his back on another buddy?

Toro stopped again. He gestured widely to infinity, and Joe grinned at the theatrics. Then Toro began to speak.

"I see you, *Señor* Snake. I see the moon on your shiny skin. Like a long thin river I see you move from under that rock." Joe knew these words were not for him to hear. But hear he would, for this was a Toro he didn't know, a bolted door whose key might unlock his own.

"You ask me what Victorio Duran is doing here this night? *Bueno*, you have that right. I am looking for someone."

Joe heard the buzz of a rattler, or thought he did, that soft unmistakable sound like no other, and the hairs on his arms prickled. He trained his ears toward the spot, but hearing nothing decided it was his imagination.

"Did you see a small burro pass by? A little shaggy one he is. He may be waiting for me."

Joe stood, hitched impatiently at his jeans, wanting to jerk Toro back to his senses.

"You may be right, *Señor* Snake. It is maybe I try to find the little boy I used to be. To find him with Panchito. I love *mi abuela* then. She was good. But she let the lion man have Panchito. She did what she had to do. But never could I make the little knot of hate go away.

"Why do I tell you this, *Señor*? Is it because you shed your skin, like I want to shed my hard little knot? They say you never die.

"Well, snake, I don't think I believe that! I seen plenty of your brothers die. And I guess you can't get into heaven to live, 'cause the Lord done fenced you out. Still, you gave us that apple, and the smarts to go with it. And I am sure in favor of good sense, even if it did get us kicked out of that garden. Eden wasn't nothing but a welfare state anyways, and them people that stay on welfare all their life never amount to nothing. Anyhow, all you did was offer. You didn't make them take that apple. They done it theirselves.

"So maybe you ain't all evil, *señor*. Chief used to say you bring life, show us where water is, bring the rain. Maybe you don't never die after all, old snake. I don't think I like you too much, but I respect you.

"I got to go now." Toro laughed. "Maybe I find my burro now, and he carry me to heaven." He laughed again. "Oh yes, *Señor* Rattler, you could send me there quicker. Maybe I come to you for that, but not yet. I got something first I got to do."

Toro walked on. Joe stretched his back to get the kinks out and started after him. How long they walked Joe didn't know, for time had drained away. Somewhere they began descending a gradual slope, marked with boulders and wind-contorted junipers. The slope was cut through with arroyos, and the night seemed to drain into their black hollows.

Toro twisted through the rocks and sometimes Joe lost him and followed by sound until he caught his silhouette moving ahead.

The sudden sound of loud neighing close ahead jerked Joe to attention. Here stood a horse, his nostrils flared, his eyes fixed on Toro who stood motionless, hand out. The stallion stood ready to bolt, ears forward, muscles tensed.

Joe inhaled deeply, taken by the power and beauty of the untamed steed.

Toro's hoarse voice came low and gentle and rhythmic. "Stay, horse, I ain't going to put you inside no fence. I saw horses in the war, your brothers, *caballos padres*, sick and hurt, and them Japs working them till they drop dead. One night we freed some. Cut the wire."

Again the raid rushed through Joe's head. Again he heard the twang of the cut wire, saw its glint in the moonlight, heard the sharp crack of erupting gunfire. Again he remembered the crawling, the sweet smell of the jungle. But it gave way to the clean sharp resinous smell of the wind on the mesa, and Toro's shaggy voice resumed its hypnotic rhythm.

"Just tonight, *Señor Caballo*, I cut another fence."

Joe inched in closer. He watched the stallion, motionless, only its mane moving in the breeze, and he marveled at the wild beauty of this creature that accepted the land and adapted.

"You ain't seen a little burro? I thought he might be here." Toro laughed softly. "You wonder why I should want a burro when you are here. I tell you why, *señor*. It is true how you are fast and strong and beautiful, and whoever can ride you can run the world. And I am one could ride you.

"But I wouldn't take away your free life, horse. When I ride the burro, he don't lose no freedom. He carry me because he want to.

"Oh *sí*, he pretty slow. But sure-foot. You are fast, you can gallop far— around the whole world maybe. But beautiful horse—and I ain't bad-mouthing you none, 'cause I respect you, and I love you—it was the little burro that carried the mother of Jesus to where He could be born."

Man and stallion stared at each other some moments. Finally their gaze broke.

"*Mira!*" Toro said softly, pointing.

A dot of white light streaked through the black, a meteor hinting at some distant disorder in the cosmos, and then another, and as they watched more appeared. Joe stood fascinated by the celestial show, and he wondered as always at the sudden glimpse into infinity.

Toro was laughing.

"Look at that one go! Ain't nobody tell him what to do."

Another smear of light flared and was gone.

"Now there's something to ride on, horse!" Toro laughed. "Know what, horse? I'd give my best red boots to go riding on some shooting star."

The stallion snorted, shook his mane, and galloped into the night. Toro watched him go and laughed again.

"Ride, Vaquero!"

Somewhere along the trail the Indian appeared. How long he'd been climbing behind him Joe didn't know. He smiled, remembering how Chief had always appeared the same way, a sudden strength in fray or frolic, with a quick grin and a ready shoulder.

Why this strange dark man should appear this night on this mesa Joe didn't know—didn't question even—but he nodded and paused as he drew abreast, and they climbed together. A ragged path, perhaps the eroded remnant of some ancient trail, made a few turns on itself and then gave up. The air seemed to lighten as they gained an extensive ledge.

They saw Toro angling to the right, skirting the low eroded walls of what seemed to be an ancient pueblo silhouetted against the west-arcing moon. Beckoning Joe to follow, the Indian started toward them. Joe watched Toro disappear behind an outcropping some distance north of the walls, then followed the Indian to the periphery of a small ruins.

"The Old Ones lived here." Chief kept his voice low.

"And left. Enemies? Disease? Drought?"

The Indian grinned. "Maybe all. Or too many people crowding their streets. They got no orange barrels, you know!" It was the same sort of humor Chief had often used to puncture a serious conversation.

"I called you Chief at the pueblo."

"Outsiders call all us Indians Chief. Like they call you Tex."

"You didn't tell me your name."

"Chief is okay." He grinned again. "Puffs me up. My people don't promote me so high!"

"You come here often? Touch base with your ancestors?"

Chief shrugged. "They lived pretty simple. Farmed down below, carried up their beans and squash and corn. And water—used to be a stream down there. Dried up now. Good defenses up here. When they saw enemies, they went below and drew a line with cornmeal—sacred you know. That meant keep out. If the enemy crossed that line, then the Old Ones fought."

"Maybe we're both looking for our pasts—for the men we used to be." Joe stood a moment in the deep quiet, contemplated the pools of moonlight cupped inside the low-worn walls.

"The man I used to be?" Chief's gaze swept the ruins and his lips twitched on the brink of a laugh. "You must think I'm awful old!"

"We better hit the trail. Before we lose Toro."

"We won't. I know where he's going."

"What are you after him for?"

" Keep him out of trouble. Like your old friend used to do. Chief."

"Is Toro in trouble?"

"Could be."

"Meaning?"

"Emmenthaler plenty mad. From the meeting. Then when Toro cut his fence—"

"You know about that?"

"All Tuceros knows. Emmenthaler came roaring to the station—made the deputy roust out Rico. And Rico, he knows where to find Toro. So do I."

"Where did you hear this?"

"Scouting around."

"So they're on their way to arrest Toro?" Joe hitched his jeans irritably. "Well, he asked for it."

Chief nodded. "I won't stop them."

"So why are you here?"

"Make sure they get him. Before he does something worse."

"He can't do much up here."

"He can get away. Slip back to Emmenthaler's while they're up here looking."

"I get you." Joe began to laugh, visualizing the absurd procession up the mesa. Toro talking into the air, Joe stalking behind, Chief shadowing both, and a sheriff's posse trailing them all. "What's Toro's game?"

"Game?"

"He's not just running. What's he after?"

"Maybe—like you said—the man he used to be."

Winding through a stretch of gnarled cedars, they followed closely to the next boulder-strewn rise. Coming on a group of free-standing palisades, Chief pulled a handful of matches from his pocket, lit a piece of cedar bark lying close by, and held it near the stone to show a population of small figures etched pale on the surface—masked human figures, stylized animals. Messages from Chief's ancestors, if one could read them.

They heard Toro muttering ahead, and then the crunch of his boots, and they moved on behind him. The long night wasn't over yet.

Again he stopped, and silhouetted against the low moon, his figure rose black and solid. A growl of thunder rolled from the north and Toro looked toward the peaks off which the lightening danced its dance, a little closer now. He watched for a time, and then he turned again westward, past the palisades. The moon hovered just above the horizon, already meeting the line of earth, and Toro's shadow was very long.

Sudden gusts began to tumble from the north sporadically, in surges, bringing the sharp resinous scent of the mountain. Joe's scalp prickled and his nostrils flared to catch the sweet scent of distant rain, and the closer smell of rain-stirred dust. The wind carried the chill. The feel of September.

"Thunderbird's flying," said Chief.

Clouds spilled from the mountain and swept onto the mesa, shrouding moon and mountain, and in the rain-scented air there seemed to hover the Holy Ghost. They stood watching the fire, deafened in the barrage of nature's artillery as it crashed closer, and earth and heaven joined on the mesa. Creation and destruction.

"Water and fire," said Chief, and in the nearly constant flash Joe saw he was grinning. "You and Toro."

A bolt struck snakelike through the roiling clouds and the thunder exploded. Without thought Joe dropped to the ground. Something cold seemed to clot inside his brain, like an ice-floe that would choke all thought. He was back in the jungle, enemy fire exploding around him, and then the clot in his mind seemed suddenly to burst free like the *acequia* in spring cleared of its winter debris, still muddy in sudden spate.

But flowing. He saw the horses running free from the cut fence, and something primitive, something sensual, almost sexual rushed through him, something he couldn't understand, something strange and new but very old, and it was the feel of battle. Of survival.

And then he saw Toro running through the bursts of fire and bullets, diving toward Cholly, grabbing him up, then dropping him, falling behind him.

And the mud in Joe's mind began to settle and clear water flowed through his memory and he saw Toro beginning to crawl toward him. Away from Cholly.

They were both crawling. Away.

Time passed, a minute, an hour, Joe didn't know, only that the fever had washed through him and he and Toro were angling back to where they had pushed the millstone into the jungle growth. Then they were tugging, pulling, and god it was heavy.

"You okay?" It was Chief, coming to meet them, to help with the stone, only he was back on the mesa now and the Indian was reaching down to give him a hand. "You okay?"

"Sure." Joe grasped the outstretched hand, pulled himself up. "Dumb trick, hitting the dirt. Thought for a minute—"

"I know."

"Storm's passing over." It was always that way. The smell of rain, but none fell.

Within minutes it had blown through, the lightning receded south, the thunder now only a grumble. The moon too had gone to its grave. The mesa lay silent and black around them, and stars burned above in the black sky.

Walking was more difficult in this darkened world, but Chief knew the terrain. Plodding behind, Joe felt the long night's exhaustion dissolve into a sort of numbness, as if he moved outside his body.

They walked for a distance, not talking, not even thinking. Then dawn hung beneath the eastern rim. Vague shapes so recently part of the night began to solidify, black nodes that in the measured rhythm of quickening day would lighten into brush or piñon or jutting rock. The two men paused and turning could now make out the black silhouette of the Sangre de Cristos against the pearling sky. With the light would come reality—sanity maybe.

And deputies with a warrant.

Chief scanned the terrain. "He can't go much farther."

They plodded on, up a steady incline now, and the amorphous thoughts in Joe's mind began to take shape like the growth in first light. He asked himself again what Toro sought, beyond defeating JD and saving the cantina. What was his wild gibberish?

He was sorry for Toro, searching forever for a small brown burro, seeking a dead past and an unborn future. Taking on the whole world in the person of JD Emmenthaler. Following his own strange vision.

But did it matter how strange or impossible? And Joe knew it didn't. What mattered was that Toro had a vision, dreamed a dream. And it came to Joe that it was JD Emmenthaler he pitied. The man who had no vision, who sought no beyond and regretted no past, but only parroted a fake piety. A man who would rather wreck a privy than gaze on a comet—a privy painted with dreams he couldn't see.

The storm had moved south. Watching the distant flashes Joe thought again of creation and destruction, of the cataclysms that built mountains, and of the winds and waters that wear them down. And he thought that man too is worn down more often by society's erosion than by its violence.

The spent thunder was only a distant growl now. His own footsteps and those of the Indian ahead of him crunched louder in the dry grass, small sounds that only intensified the mesa's vast silence.

Louder too droned the rumble inside his own head.

Crawling away.

But that too dulled as the silence spread over him like a salve.

Slowly a streak of pink threaded through clouds on the far horizon. The men stood still, two lone figures in an opaline world. Instinctively Chief turned toward the rising day, stood for a moment as his people had stood each dawn for centuries to be one with the light, then turned to resume the trek.

Through thinning piñons they passed and emerged onto a flat sandy stretch, bald of growth, its sharp lip dropping sheer into a deep chasm. They had reached the western finality of the mesa. Across the narrow ravine rose a line of cliffs, the face of a giant rise that labored toward the mountain beyond, and as they watched, the first rays of the new day's sun kindled in the tops of the crags.

They saw him then at the mesa's edge, arms lifted toward the sun-touched rocks.

"Like that cornmeal line." Chief's voice was low. "We don't cross."

They edged back into the line of piñons and as they watched Chief pointed. Something—bird or spirit?—shot gun-gilt from the opposite cliffs, dived into the mists that rose shimmering from the crevasse, soared again above the mesa's lip, and his great wings caught the sun and spread strong with morning's yellow life. Reveling in his power the eagle soared and dipped and soared again and they marveled at his flight.

The great bird began to circle, high at first, slowly descending in narrow spirals, his wings spread as wide as a tall man's height. Toro stood watching. Two strong lives seemed drawn together as in a magnetic field.

The early sunlight flooded the cliffside now, hot, seminal, pure spirit, the eagle its embodiment. "He takes prayers to the sun," Chief said. "And souls." He grinned. "Nothing else has the guts to go that close!"

"Or wings like that to get there."

Toro was calling to the circling bird. "Ain't nobody ever going fence you in," he shouted. "You fly clean and free. Someday I will too."

The eagle circled lower and his fierce eyes reflected the yellow morning.

Then, his great wings flapping, the bird began to rise, and Toro's cry followed. "I can ride you, *águila*, high as I can go! You think I can't? Try me, eagle! Try me!"

The bird swept high and higher, sun-fired in the turquoise sky, and then he seemed to pause, to survey the mesa, sun-drenched now in the quickening morning, and then to focus on the man standing below.

"Test me, *águila*! I am man enough. Test me!"

Now the bird dropped into his dive. Straight he plunged, arrogant in his power, angry, driven to charge the man who dared him. Fast he plummeted, taloned claws flaring.

For god's sake, Joe pled silently, dash for the piñons, fast.

Toro stood like granite.

The piñons, you damn fool!

The eagle angled for the attack, giant wings slashing the air, talons spread.

Joe bunched his muscles to run, to yank Toro from the great bird's path. He felt his own arm gripped.

"No," whispered the Indian. "It's his fight."

Joe jerked away, but he'd lost his few seconds' chance. The eagle closed in, every sinew coordinated.

Still Toro stood.

Then, unbelievably, the bird pulled out of his dive, and the wind in his wake roiled the hair on Toro's head like white seafroth. And as the eagle in his steep climb rushed over his own head, Joe heard the whining noise of sliced air.

The sweat ran down his sides and his shirt stuck to his wet skin.

The eagle circled wider.

"The spirits of dead warriors. My people say they fly as eagles."

"Maybe your people are right. They know a lot of things. What are you, old eagle? Live bird of dead warrior?"

The creature made one last circle, and his strong beak shone in the fierce light of the full-risen sun. Then, with a rush of wind and power the mystic bird rose, leveled, and shot straight for the eastern light.

A single feather floated earthward in his wake, slowly, gently, settling on a piñon branch between the men.

Chief looked at the feather, at Toro still standing on the promontory, and then back at the feather, and Joe saw the lines around his black eyes crinkle a little, but what any of it meant he didn't know.

He was still wondering when he heard the voices and the crunch of footsteps on the dry grass.

21

"I FIGURED YOU'D BE ALONG."
Toro grinned.

There were two deputies and Chico. "You knew damn well we would."
Chico fished in his breast pocket. He flourished a warrant.

Joe looked around for Chief. The Indian had disappeared. He lifted his
hat, ran his fingers through his hair, and wondered where. And why. He
replaced his hat thoughtfully, and walked into sight. No one seemed surprised.

"Okay, let's go." Chico assumed a hard-boiled pose. "And don't try
giving us the slip."

"I done had my fun, amigo."

"You can't win this game. You know it."

"I know." Toro began to chew on a piñon twig. "Like I knew in the war.
I knew we'd lost the battle. But we also knew we'd win the war. Right, Choe?"
He turned toward his old buddy.

"Yeah, well that was a war for chrissake."

"You think this ain't?" Toro threw his twig to the ground and spat after
it. "You think that Emmenthaler outfit ain't out to take over Tuceros same as
them Japs? Only difference is they let us fight back in the war—didn't have no
piddle-assed sheriffs getting in the way."

One of the deputies grinned. The other was picking his teeth.

"Okay general." Chico yawned. "Meanwhile you can consider you lost
this battle. And I lost a good night's sleep, and we are taking you in."

" I hope you got better by-god coffee than last time."

Thumbs hooked in his belt loop, Joe looked at Toro. "You don't act
much surprised to see me."

"I ain't. Only one missing is Chief."

Joe looked at him sharply, and then they were starting back across the
mesa. Chico tramped doggedly in the lead. Behind him Toro pranced like a
morning-fresh goat. Stiff and tired, and squinting in the glare, Joe fell in beside

him. The deputies made small talk in the rear.

Ahead Joe saw the tips of the tall rock palisades rising from the level below where the ancients had carved their legacy in stone for whoever in ages to come could read it. Then they were descending through the narrow cleft, twisting through the boulders single file, and Joe glanced quickly off the path, half expecting Chief might be standing silently near but knowing he wouldn't be.

Reaching some cedars, Chico stopped for a breather.

"Played out already?" Toro pulled a couple of Marlboros from his breast pocket, passed one to Chico, and patted his empty jeans pockets for his Zippo.

Chico lit their smokes grumbling. "Can't get a night's sleep anymore."

"You getting old." Toro smoked a few moments. "I wasn't half that old when I was your age." He turned to Joe. "Chico'n me used to have some gut-busters. Till he decided to get old." He kicked at a dirt clod. "Took the fun out. Hell, this wasn't no chase at all."

Chico started walking again and Toro fell in beside him. "You didn't have to come after me."

Chico yawned.

"You knew I'd be back—got my dogs to feed. Blowed this whole thing up, amigo. Could of got your by-god beauty sleep."

"¡Chale! With Emmenthaler raising hell at midnight, demanding I bring you in pronto, before you tear up his whole damn compound?"

Toro threw his stub on the ground and worked it into the sand with his boot heel. "His whole compound! Now that's a idea to think on!"

"Well, you just think away. But I ain't going to spring you till Rico fences Emmenthaler in. Legal."

"Hell, that's permanent residence you're offering me." Toro directed a stream of spit at a chamisa bush. "Ain't any sidewinding Texas sonofabitch ever yet been fenced in with legal papers."

"That's Rico's problem. Mine is you."

"Oh hell. You like to play cops and robbers."

Chico grunted.

"Bust my gut trying to help."

"Sure. Like when that Utah killer was loose."

"Now that was one good chase!" Toro chuckled. "You ever hear that story, Choe?" He motioned Joe to come abreast. "Guy been shooting up the

166

countryside. Gave the Utah cops the slip, cut a corner through Colorado, and headed this way. Killed nine people."

"Two," said Chico. "And one was only his mother-in-law. Self defense."

"Yeah? What about old man Lucero? Up at Chama?"

"He died of a heart attack."

"That was the cover story. You hear about that killer, Choe?"

"Can't recall it."

"'Bout ten years ago. Seven-Finger Silva, they called him."

"You called him," said Chico.

"Seven fingers on his right hand."

"Rumor."

"Born with eight but one got chewed off by a mountain lion before he could choke that critter to death."

"Bullshit," said Chico. "Give me a smoke."

Toro pulled two more cigarettes from his pocket. "Saved the finger, though. Wrestled it right outa that lion's mouth. Carried it around to stir his coffee with." He passed a cigarette to Chico. "So next thing we know, he's seen around La Mancha."

Chico halted the procession, lit both cigarettes, exhaled a long plume of smoke, and resumed the march. "Nobody proved that."

"Hell, how many people plunk theirselves down in Manny's coffeeshop and pull a loose finger outa their pocket? How many people got seven fingers and only wear one glove 'cause they can't buy any they can get their other hand in?"

They were now skirting the ancient pueblo and Joe's mind wandered from Seven Fingers to Chief—to both Chiefs—the one he had soldiered with, and this new one, whoever he might be, and to their Anasazi ancestors. The ruins were less ghostly by morning light.

"So when I went out scouting and found the ashes from a still-warm fire, I high-tailed back to report it. Chico and me and a posse saddled up and started out."

"On a four-day hunt. December and colder'n a witch's tit." Chico sighed. "Crisscrossed the whole damn country." He glared at Toro. "Come to find out he'd been caught already. In Colorado. Never been close to Tuceros."

"Then who the hell was it I seen?"

"Said you seen."

"Well, I done tried to help you." Toro assumed his crucified Christ expression. "And just think, if you'd caught him, *cuate.*" He grinned his long white grin. "You'd of been famous!"

It seemed to be an old and often-repeated argument. Joe thought too that the story had some familiar details. Hadn't there been something about a seven-fingered Jap sniper they'd taken after?

Reaching the vehicles, they drove in tandem back to La Mancha, Chico leading in the patrol car, Joe following in the Olds with Toro beside him, the deputies clanking behind in Toro's pickup. They parked in the same order behind the sheriff's office.

"You ain't said two words," said Toro.

"Haven't had a chance." Toro had gabbled gaily all the way, his monologue a blend of gossip-column commentary on life and law in Tuceros, laced with philosophic asides on fences and freedom.

He was still on the latter subject when they entered the sheriff's office. Chico sank into the leather chair behind his desk. He straightened his carved name plate, folded his hands under his chin, and eyeballed Toro.

"What authority you got to come chasing me?" Toro asked.

"This warrant, that's what. Issued on the sworn word of Mr. JD Emmenthaler, who routed me and the DA and Rico out of bed for, whose property you trespassed on, whose fence you cut, and whose stock you rustled."

"Hell, I just turned a few little burros loose."

Chico snorted and headed for the coffee pot.

Toro spread his hands wide. "Okay, then, I swear that JD Emmenthaler is a certified Texas bastard that is out after all our by-god asses, which is all you need for another warrant to go get him."

"You catch him in any illegal act? See him committing it?"

"You see me cutting the goddam fence?"

"Didn't you?"

"Hell yes, I did. Which has nothing to do with the by-god subject."

Chico filled two styrofoam cups, slopped coffee onto the cart, mopped it up with a greasy bandanna, and handed the least-stained cup to Joe. Back at his desk he assumed an official expression and tilted the chair back. "Now," he said looking hard at Toro. "Time to tend to business. Which is you."

Later Joe wondered why he did what he did. He'd botched his job of keeping Toro under wraps, but they had him now, if they still thought it necessary. He'd had his fun and proved his point. They'd placated JD. And Joe had the feeling the whole thing was a game between them. At any rate, the usually deliberative Joe Steele yielded to impulse.

Chico and Toro had progressed into a long-winded argument about where Toro was to spend the weekend until court Monday. Toro opted for home. Chico preferred the calaboose, but seemed to be wavering. Emmenthaler had insisted they lock him up. On the other hand, he, Chico, had done his duty bringing him in. He could grant bail—a duty he often preempted—saved Rico the trouble, and nobody in Tuceros wasted time arguing over legal fine points.

A horsefly that had been buzzing around Chico's head lit on his left arm. A fast swipe with his open right hand made contact. "Got 'im!" He brushed the fat green corpse onto the floor, came to a decision, and looked hard at Toro. "Okay. Go home." His eyes were crafty. "If you can make bail. Five hundred dollars."

Toro bristled. "Five? That's more'n that shitass paid for all them burros and his goddamned fence."

"Take it or leave it. Five hundred or the hoosegow." Chico glanced sideways at Joe.

"Let's play for it. One hand of stud. Deuces wild. Five hundred or home free."

"Nope. You ain't got five hundred."

Two pairs of speculative eyes lit on Joe. But Joe was a poker player too. "No way."

Joe sat unmoving. It was Chico's turn. "Okay. Two-fifty. On account of the drought."

Joe knew he was being had. But this could go on all day. He was dog-tired, wanted only a shower and a nap. And there was that one other matter he had to clear before he took off for High Lonesome. At any rate he sighed heavily and gave in.

"Take my check?"

22

"DID ANYONE EVER TELL YOU," drawled Joe, "that only a genuine asshole would cut a man's fence, then yell bloody murder blaring to the whole frigging world that he did it, and lead half the county on an all-night chase to nowhere?" They were cutting across Toro's yard.

"Guess not," said Toro cheerfully. He was ruffling the ears of the dogs jumping to greet him. "When I itch I scratch."

Joe gave up. At the moment he only wanted a shower. Ten minutes later he was reflecting there was nothing like soap and hot water to restore a man. A few minutes after that at Toro's kitchen table he concluded that nothing comforted a man's belly like hot coffee, fried eggs, and chorizo. A short nap and he'd be fit to hit the road. He'd already called Beth to expect him, and she'd promised him apple pie for dessert.

"We need to talk." Joe looked hard at Toro and fingered a small leather case in his breast pocket.

"For sure, Choe. But you ain't leaving today."

"Got to."

"We got a party tonight, man!"

"You have."

"Us, Choe. Big night—got to celebrate."

"Celebrate what?"

"We freed them burros, didn't we?"

"He'll just get more."

"And there'll be more battles."

"Which you'll lose. Hell, man, you'll lose this one in court Monday."

Toro swallowed a mouthful of coffee and smiled gently. Amused.

The warning bell shrilled in Joe's brain. He'd seen that look before. "I should never have bailed you out." He always had, though. Once, just before they'd shipped overseas, Joe remembered, Toro had bought a bunch of cheap

170

tee shirts to sell off base. "Remember the Alamo," they had read. "Next Time Build a Back Door." The citizens of El Paso didn't buy, the city closed him down, and Toro crossed the border with them. They still didn't sell and Toro, stuck with five hundred shirts and in the spirit of good will across the border, gave them away.

"How was your sale?" Joe asked later.

"Not a shirt left!" crowed Toro.

"Good," said Joe, "because the city of El Paso is about to fine you for selling without a license. It'll cut into your profit. And the sergeant's after your ass."

"I got no profit." Toro was indignant. "And I spent all my army pay on them shirts."

Joe had smoothed it with the sergeant. And paid his buddy's fine. There had been other times too.

They carried their dishes to the sink. "Let 'em soak." Toro refilled their cups and Joe followed him into the red-curtained living room peopled with Toro's eclectic art.

Toro sat in his worn chair. "So where were we?"

"At a crossroads. Between common sense and insanity."

"Ain't no crossroads in a war, amigo. There is only charge and keep firing."

"This isn't a war." But Joe knew better. For Toro there would always be a war. He knew it as he said it.

"There is a war, Choe." Toro learned forward intensely. "Always has been, since our great grampa got busted out of Eden. War between the men that makes the adobes and builds the walls and grows the beans and paints the pictures and sings the songs—between them and the men that comes to steal and ruin what the good men built. Or buy us out and bulldoze us under."

"Dammit, Duran, there are laws! And they're on our side—if we stay inside them."

"You always do that?"

"I keep my nose clean."

Toro smiled. "Well, it's your nose, amigo." He watched a spider in a high corner. "You got your nose, I got mine."

Suddenly Toro jumped up. "Choe—them mungo beans with Saint Christopher, that protects travelers." He was pacing up and down, energized. "I give him to Tomcat when he was going through the jungle, straight into the jaws of them Japs. He brought Tomcat through safe. And now. It's a omen, Choe. You bring him here to me, just when I need him!"

But Joe's mind was elsewhere. He leaned forward, elbows on knees, looked at the floor, then stood, and walked to the window. "Last night on the mesa I learned something." He turned toward his old comrade. "Lots of things a desert can show a man. Toro, when Cholly got hit." His eyes locked with Toro's. "I was crawling. Away."

"Yeah. I know it."

"Away from Cholly." Joe pulled the little case from his pocket, snapped it open, lifted out the medal. "For bravery in action. Here, take it. You're the one who earned it." He tossed it to Toro.

Toro caught it and cocked an eyebrow. "What in hell for?"

"I was crawling away."

"Sure. I was right behind you."

"You're lying. You went to help him."

"Choe, listen to me." Toro dropped the medal next to the box of pictures that still lay where they'd left them. "You seen me pick him up."

"Yes. And drop him, and I haven't forgotten that either. But you—at least you went to him. I didn't even do that." Joe turned back to the window.

"We was spread out. Remember? I was closest to Cholly. And got there first.

"While I—"

"You seen me pick him up, right? And drop him. *Bueno*. Well, you dumb-ass, if you hadn't of been heading in the same by-god direction, right behind me—toward Cholly—how in hell could you of seen that?"

Joe turned and looked at Toro.

"Keep your fucking medal." Toro picked it up, looked at it a moment, and tossed it back. It hit the floor. "It ain't worth a good case of beer. I got enough on my mind trying to keep my own act going. I ain't going carry your problems too. Or your medal."

"That damned medal's bugged me for years," Joe said slowly. "You've had

172

your own hell too I guess. You did drop Cholly. And run."

"We was both trying to get to him. I got there first. And when I picked him up—Choe—Cholly was already dead!"

Joe stared at Toro through the smoke in his brain. "Dead?"

"Machine-gunned. Right across his chest. Riddled, Choe. You saw that. There wasn't nothing to do for him. And we had that stone to drag back."

Joe walked to the couch, sat like a robot, trying to remember. He stared at the floor and he was asking silently if he could believe this after all the doubts nagging for so long. Or was this one of Toro's artistic lies?

"Did I know Cholly was dead?" He looked at Toro and his voice was hoarse. "Was I close enough to see it? Before I started away?"

Toro looked square at him. "Choe. Only one person can answer that. And that's you. Maybe it'll come to you."

It was all the answer Joe was likely to get. "But why," he asked slowly, "didn't you tell me all this in the beginning? When I lit into you—right after the war?"

Toro shrugged. "Well, Choe—I guess because I am just one dumb Mexican!" He yawned. "Let's get a little siesta. Before the party."

Suddenly the weight of old comradeship settled around Joe like a blanket in the night. He guessed Beth's apple pie would keep one more day.

"You win," he said. "What time's that shindig?"

23

"RIDE VAQUERO! THE STETSON arced into the room and the cheers rose. Toro stood framed in the blue doorway and the red glow of the Coors sign lit him like an imp from hell. He stomped his red boots. "We done it, amigos! We cut his fence and stampeded his by-god herd! Me and Choe!"

Joe took a deep breath and followed Toro to the bar through a barrage of shouts. Notes exploded from Tecolote's guitar.

"¡Cerveza! For ever'body!" Toro shouted. "On me!"

"Not on credit!" Arabela cocked an eyebrow at him and continued mopping the bar.

"I figure," said Toro stroking his upper lip, "that I have bought seven million and forty-four cans of Coors in this cantina."

"Cash only." Arabela pushed back a stray lock.

She had dressed elaborately for the party. A silk rose perched over her left ear and the matching fuschia blouse dipped low beneath her generous cleavage. Joe wondered how everyone seemed to know there'd be a party. Many had brought their wives.

Joe ordered beers for himself and Toro, who had skittered to the end of the bar to guffaw with Patricio. "And a copita for the guitarristo."

Tecolote nodded his thanks and geared down to a softer melody. Too soft for the keyed-up Toro who, clapping Patricio on the shoulder, called for a livelier tune as Wesley and Serenity stepped through the doorway. They too were dressed for a baile, she in white ruffles and high heels, he in his pointy-crowned black hat with the trailing pheasant feather.

"La Bamba!" called Toro scooping Serenity onto the floor.

Tecolote responded. "Para bailar La Bamba," he sang thumping the guitar loudly between beats and everyone backed into a circle clapping as Toro and Serenity swept into the rhythm.

Ysidro stepped from behind the curtain, grinned, and leaned against the

174

ice tub. Patricio, still laughing, ducked through the door to the outhouse.

Guitar and dance grew wilder.

Until Patricio raced in, dark-faced and roaring. "He's attacked the outhouse! The pictures! He's smashed in the end of our privy!"

The music stopped in mid-beat bang. Everyone froze. "I been waiting," said Arabela in her rich amber voice, "for somebody to discover what he done."

"You seen it?"

"We seen it." Ysidro threw down his toothpick. "He been saying we're on his property."

A stampede to see the damage jammed the door. Wesley turned to Patricio. "My portrait of Serenity?"

Patricio nodded.

"He been threatening," said Ysidro.

"That's why I put the sign on it," said Wesley. "No trespassing it said."

The room had nearly emptied. Arabela, Félix, and Tecolote remained at the bar. Joe, seeing Rico gesture to him, carried fresh cans of beer to the table.

"Got something to tell you." Rico's voice was dark brown.

"I'm listening." Joe pushed a can toward him, sat, and popped his own.

"I been in Santa Fé." Rico took a long swig. "This Tuceros project is not Emmenthaler's first development."

Joe pulled his pipe from his pocket.

"And this charity crap is only part of something lots bigger. A front maybe. Or a play-pretty for that baby-doll wife." He leaned forward and his words began to slap on the table like cards in a game for high stakes.

"That sonofabitch—using his company's name—has bought up a spread probably bigger'n your ranch. Worthless land—no water rights. Got it cheap, had it appraised about three times what it's worth."

"Who appraised it?" Joe knocked his pipe against the ashtray.

"Guy over in Santa Fé. An import. From Dallas." Rico took another swig and flashed a conspiratorial smile at Joe.

"Ah." Joe started tamping tobacco into his pipe.

"So JD goes back to his bank in Dallas, gets an eighty-percent loan on it—"

"At the falsely appraised value?"

"Sure. Subdivides it, bulldozes a few roads, gets it reevaluated, draws up some classy house plans, sells some lots—"

"Where is all this?"

"Upriver. Only none of those houses will ever get built. Leastways the ones in Texas didn't. The sales were all phony. But he gets another appraisal, still higher."

"And another loan. I get the picture."

Rico nodded. "Shifts these funds through a couple of dummy companies. This is his Texas pattern, but I'd bet my last shirt and britches he's doing the same thing here—and funnels it back to his pals that bought the lots."

The congregation was drifting back into the cantina now, sad, angry, muttering. Serenity with flowing eyes was lamenting the destruction of Wesley's art, and her memories of the path alongside where he asked her to marry him.

Rico took no notice. "Gets another appraisal, sells it to another company, then another. They're all in the scheme. And buys it back for a larger sum."

"On a larger loan."

"Hasn't done that here yet—ain't sold it—this is just his Texas pattern."

"And got by with it?"

Rico shrugged. "He got friends."

The cantina grew noisier. Everyone was talking and no one was listening but it didn't matter because they were all singing variations on the same song anyhow. Arabela was sliding dripping cans down the bar like a production line, pocketing cash, making change, swiping at the bar, popping her spearmint. Tecolote strummed deep vibrating chords, sipped his wine, and watched.

Rico lowered his voice. "So he buys it back. The Texas land I mean, on that last loan, and then the bastard declares bankruptcy."

Joe whistled. "You got proof enough to corral him?"

"Not yet. Hell, they're still investigating in Texas. Books all screwed up. Anyhow, this Tuceros thing's a separate matter from the upriver land-grabbing. Government loan to benefit us poor *chicanos*, all that shit."

"But if you can expose the pattern—or even threaten to—scare him with a bluff—"

Rico's face lifted into an angelic smile. "My friend, you are beginning to think like us *mexicanos!*"

176

Toro suddenly burst into the room, banged on the bar with an empty can, and jumped onto a chair.

"Amigos!" His red words rolled through the cantina. "The war in on! Mr. JD Emmenthaler done fired the first by-god shot! Now it's our turn!"

Tecolote, idling his strings in a soft tuneless rhythm like rain on a tin roof, smiled a little and his lips began to move in silent composition.

"—win or lose!" Toro's voice was rising like an oilfield gusher, hot and triumphant. "Are you with me, amigos?"

"*¡Sí, sí!*" "*¡'sta Torito!*"

Félix raised his beer toward heaven, gave a last ragged "*¡Olé!*" and lay his head gently on the bar.

Toro held something up. "See this?" It was Joe's medal. "For bravery in action. Choe and me. It was like this."

Tecolote stopped singing to listen as Toro told his tale, and he watched Toro closely, perhaps even then thinking here it was, he had at last found his great *corrido*.

Rico took a deep swig. "We need time—a little time to get some proof. If—" Jerking his thumb at Toro he looked a question at Joe.

Joe didn't answer.

"Tonight we have the *baile*," Toro yelled. "We dance! *La Bamba*! *Eeeeeeeh-hah*!"

Toro was really keyed up, Joe thought. Too much. He'd seen him this way before, at the start of a raid.

But this wasn't Joe's fight.

He looked around. At Patricio dancing with his wife, or maybe someone else's. At Chico, and Rico who bent the law to whatever shape best fit the needs of Tuceros. At Arabela who always had green chile stew for the tired or lonely, at Ysidro, host and padre for all his flock, and at Félix who slept without care in his cantina knowing his friends were real friends who would see him harm-free home. At Wesley and Serenity and at Tecolote, a wandering minstrel from the tortured soul of Mexico with a spirit as ancient, a medieval man, a man of earth who made mud walls by day and song by night like life-giving water in the desert.

And it came to Joe that this was his fight, it was the fight of all men who had ever fought for a heritage worth preserving, that the fight for Tuceros was the fight for every little village in America and the fight for the cantina was for every home and church and corner grocery, for every sand-lot ball field and county courthouse and backyard tomato patch that someone loved because it was his, it was his childhood and his present and it was, as Toro would have said, his by-god future.

A future endangered, and it wasn't the bombs and tanks and artillery of war that threatened the wondrously varied ways of life that are America. It was the far more destructive forces from within, the tyranny of the nonthinking majority who would dictate a sterile sameness to every village in America, and the JDs of progress, armed with their bulldozers and government subsidies, and all the robot people who follow the slick prosperity and suck the land dry of its precious water and drive out the people who've tended the land and loved it and protected it.

And it was a war, and harder to fight than any had ever been in America before, because so few recognized the enemy.

Tuceros was only one foxhole in the fight, but Joe knew about foxholes, how each small dug-out hole was for the moment each soldier's whole damned war. But the fight for the wider world was always with you, because that was the reason for your foxhole. And, he acknowledged wryly, it was the reason he rode fences. And Toro cut them.

So here he was, stuck with his old amigo so long as Toro needed him.

"Okay." Joe knocked his pipe against the glass ashtray and pocketed it. "I'll try to keep him under wraps till Monday."

Rico raised his can and smiled.

There was a pause in the music for the dancers to catch their breaths. Some ducked for the back door and the part of the outhouse still standing, Toro among them. Joe sauntered to the bar to talk to Tecolote and keep his eye on the door.

Tecolote was singing softly, composing as he sang, and for Joe he switched to English.

"*Into the enemy's lines he charged,*
He and his buddy alone.

To save their comrades hungry and gaunt,
They crept to capture the stone."

"How do you make up songs that fast?"

Tecolote shrugged. "You know, Toro never told us that story before."

"No, I guess he didn't."

"The bullets flew but they made it through,
Charging across that field,
To save their comrades their only thought,
And courage their only shield.

"That the way it was?"

Joe smiled. "I guess the reality's in the singing. What would Troy be without a Homer? Does the song make the hero or the hero make the song?"

"¿Quién sabe?" Maybe it's like man and woman. Takes both to keep life going."

But where was Toro?

And then a shout rose from outside and grew and swelled and flooded the cantina.

"¡Fuego! At Emmenthaler's! *Fuego!"*

24

THE CANTINA'S CITIZENRY STAM-
peded toward the blue door and funneled through. Rico's face sagged with sad
fatality. Locking his paunchy-eyed gaze with Joe's, he nodded, and they too
rushed with the exodus, just managing to leap into the patrol car as Chico
shifted and swung into the jam of battered pickups racketing toward the
smoke-laden glow that rose from the village center.

The din of racing engines and honking horns battled with the screaming
of La Mancha's two firetrucks. From houses and courtyards the people of
Tuceros erupted, from the McDonald's and the Burger King and the Pizza Hut
in the town proper they streamed food in hand, and from the drugstore and the
Geronimo movie house they poured in the wake of the wailing sirens. It was a
first-rate fire, the biggest event of the summer for all La Mancha.

The JD Emmenthaler Construction and Development Company was
toweringly, roaringly, magnificently ablaze.

"I knew it, I knew he'd do something," Rico kept muttering.

Chico opened up the siren to force a path through the snarl of vehicles
and he was grinning. " Hot damn, what a fire!"

Veering onto the cracked sidewalk, he pulled around the bottleneck,
sluing sideways across the street, and lurched to a stop, blocking the traffic that
had already reached a tangled impasse. Leaving the keys in the ignition, Chico
ran toward the firemen manning the hose. The enormous warehouse was a
roaring flame, already spreading toward the main office and outlying buildings.

Joe and Rico stood by the patrol car watching. Black smoke gushed
skyward, veiling the rising moon. From time to time the sound of splintering
glass punctuated the roar of the fire, and Joe thought of that last violent night on
Bataan. The infantry lines had broken against the massive Japanese advance, and
knowing the end was near, the Americans were torching everything. A hundred
fires lit the night around them. Ammo dumps were exploding. Climbing the hill
to form a last line of defense, Joe's regiment walked as if in sleep.

Except for Toro, whose flame seemed to burn more passionately as he ran from group to group, stimulated by the thrill of the game. And Joe remembered how as dawn was graying the sky the word came down that there wouldn't be a battle after all, because the general was surrendering them, and how instead of relief they'd all felt shocked, unbelieving. But it was Toro who boiled with fury. Toro, who'd rather be destroyed than defeated.

But where in god's outhouse was Toro now?

Little knots of bystanders clustered around the periphery.

"Wonder what started it?"

"Or who?"

"¿Quién sabe?"

A few sly grins passed around, a few knowing winks, some covert giggles that grew to guffaws, nourished by flames and noise and a growing holiday mood. All knew, but none spoke his name. From somewhere came a tune from a lively guitar, but it wasn't Tecolote's.

Rico was furious. "Just when I nearly had Emmenthaler," he grated. "When all I need is a little more time."

Joe leaned against the patrol car. "We don't know Toro set this."

"Maybe you don't know," growled Rico.

"Could've been JD himself. For the insurance."

"Could of been. Wasn't."

At this point a raucous laugh sliced the air, a chorus of high-voiced shouts, and the crowd parted as the girls from the whorehouse, with Lily at their head, pranced down the street to join the fun. A cheer erupted.

"Well," Joe continued, "throw the book at him."

"I could sure charge him with this." Rico ran his hand through his hair.

Lily bore down on them like a full-rigged galleon. "Charge who, Rico?"

He looked up. "Anyone the evidence may point to, ma'am."

"Like—Toro Duran?"

"Now, Lily, don't start naming names."

She grinned. "Well, I'll testify he couldn't of done this—because he was with me all evening!" A chorus from Lily's girls all agreed that Toro had indeed been with Lily all evening. "Since sundown," added one. A group was gathering around the girls and everyone laughed, even those who'd seen him in the cantina.

"Sure," continued Lily. "He was with me, and I'll swear to it in your court." She winked. "And you won't say nothing, honey." He wouldn't, either, for reasons both of them knew.

A crash upstaged the music and the laughs and the girls as the warehouse roof collapsed. Showers of flame hurtled through the air and a great *oooooooh* swept through the crowd as a nearby building burst into a wild blaze. A corner of the main office building now flared like a torch. The firemen ran to play the hose on the new flame.

Suddenly a horn blasted a group from their middle-of-the-street stance, the big green Continental charged through, and its furious driver leaped out and sprinted toward the holocaust. Breaking through to the cordoned clearing, he stopped, smitten by the immensity of his burning world. JD Emmenthaler stood on the wet pavement staring, and his face looked as if it hadn't been lived in recently. Airborne debris, black and greasy, fell around him.

Chico left a couple of JD's security guards he'd been questioning and cut across to JD. Whatever he said broke the hypnotic daze. Turning furiously, JD dashed toward the firefighters shooting orders like a machine gun until a spasm of coughing halted the barrage. No one had paid him any attention anyhow.

One of the security guards pounded him on the back until he quit coughing and helped him back to his car. After a brief conversation JD climbed onto the Continental's hood, faced the crowd, and motioned for silence.

"I want you-all to hear this," he yelled, and a few, annoyed or curious, glanced his way. "This fire," he bellowed, "was not an accident!" A few more heads turned his way. "I just been talking to my security guard. And those guards—just as the flames were first licking up—they saw a figure—a man— go skedaddlin' through the buildings!"

"They know who he was?"

"No. But I do!" JD's gaze skimmed his audience but his anger hit a wall of grins.

Like a *politico* down in the polls he shifted tactics from fury to guile. "You're all good people. And I ain't goin' to hold it against you because of one man."

He droned on but Joe wasn't listening, and neither, it seemed, were most of the spectators, whose interest shifted back to the main show. The flames

182

diminished in one spot to leap higher in another.

An explosion shook the air as something in one of the warehouses detonated, and a blast of smaller explosions followed.

Fire was a unifier, Joe thought. Had been since man first discovered it. A center that drew men together into light and warmth, and this one was drawing Tuceros together. But not as JD intended. For those who drew to it now knew whose doing this was, and they seemed to be gathering solidly, admiringly, behind him.

Then a new flurry of movement stirred at the crowd's edge, and the red Corvette screeched to a stop. Narcissa charged, an ash-faced Stevie in her wake. She was screaming even before she reached JD. "Did you get the papers?"

He stared down at her. "Pet—"

"Idiot," she shrieked. Stevie put a hand on her shoulder but she flung it off. "You stupid idiot!"

"Pet. Look at them flames. You expect me to—"

"The office—get in there and get those papers!"

"Narcissa honey. I can't."

"That part hasn't caught yet. Get those files. Now!"

JD looked toward the office building. Speculating. He looked at Narcissa. She stared back, hard, commanding. He looked at Stevie, saw him shake his head helplessly. He looked back to the building. The flames were beginning to spread.

Poor bastard, Joe thought.

JD took a deep breath. Then he leaped from the big car's hood, and charged toward the fire.

Ducking under the yellow tape, he scuffled briefly with a fireman who tried to stop him, tripped the man, sent him sprawling, and plunged ahead. On his feet again, the fireman tore after him.

But JD was already inside.

Smoke gushed through the suddenly opened doorway and pulled by the draft the fire began to spread. Bursting windows sounded like the popcorn machine at the Geronimo.

Narcissa stood like a Prussian sentry, her only movement a tattoo of red nails on the hood of the Continental.

Then an *aaaaahh* announced the exit of the fireman and of JD, with blackened face and clutching something in his arms.

But it wasn't a briefcase of papers. This burden yowled.

So did Narcissa. "A—cat?"

JD stumbled toward her crouching. The animal kept yowling, long, terrified yowls. He held it toward her but she stepped back, arms straight at her sides. Her voice was low and Joe couldn't hear the words, but he could read her stiff stance and sharp expression, etched sharper in the tarnished orange light, and then her voice rose to brass-horn volume.

"We've got to get those papers, you stupid fool. And you come out with a cat!"

"Couldn't just leave him."

Fire gushed from the office as a section of the roof gave.

Narcissa was shrieking. "Now it's too late." Her eyes were wild in the firelight, eyes abandoned by reason.

He looked around, suddenly aware of an avidly listening audience. "Please, Pet."

"I've had it. I'm through with you and this hick town and your whole screwed-up mess. Because I'm not sticking around to pick up Humpty Dumpty." She was poking her fist straight into JD's chest. "You've screwed up everything I've planned, ever since I was dumb enough to marry you, thinking you were so damned successful." The invective rolled on and it billowed through the gleefully listening crowd.

The flames rose into the night.

He was still clutching the wet cat when she reached the Corvette, gunned the engine, and drove away.

By the time Joe started back to the cantina, the fire was settling to a steady burn. A merriment was capering through the crowd, a burst of joy, sparked by the fire. It was Saturday night, it was August, and summer was running out.

And there was the moon. Emerging through the pall of smoke it rode westward, high and full and palest gold.

At the edge of the crowd Tecolote fell into step with Joe. The fire would burn a long time, he observed, and those who had rushed from the cantina would soon be coming back.

Arabela, until now alone in the cantina except for the sleeping Félix, agreed. "Party's where the *cerveza* is, and the *cerveza* is here!"

She slid a Coors to Joe and poured Tokay gurgling red into Tecolote's glass. "Wash out the smoke," she said and waved Joe's money aside.

Joe took a long cold swallow and looked around. "Where's Toro?"

Tecolote was looking at the ceiling. His lips were moving, his nearly closed eyes were pulled up in smiles, and he was communing with his own inner world. And Joe thought, it's men like Tecolote who suckle civilization, who snatch from time a moment and encase it forever in a poem, a picture, a song. And these small bubbles of essence may in the balance of infinity weigh more than the mountain's mass.

The hero must forge the deed. But in the end, the hero is what the singer makes him.

"What do you make of Toro?" Joe asked. "Is he hero? Or hellion?"

The question pierced Tecolote's reverie. "Ahhhh." He tilted back his head and looked from under heavy lids. "Maybe-so they are the same. Toro— he is looking for something."

"The search for the Grail?" Joe sat turning his beer can, his eyes focused on something distant, and then he laughed. "But with Toro you've always got to ask, is he seeking the Grail or making off with it?"

Tecolote sipped his wine and when he spoke his voice was low. "Tell me about your war."

"We fought it, and when it was over we came home. Some of us."

Tecolote perched on his stool and began to strike soft chords. "What was it like to come home?"

"There were some ghosts to lay. Some nightmares. Mostly we wanted to forget. It was over. Time to quit fighting. Oh, we griped some about where our country was going. But not many of us really kept on fighting. Toro did. He was fighting an enemy most of us couldn't see. Toro cut the fences."

Arabela leaned against the ice chest, cocked a black eyebrow at Joe, and folded her big arms over her breasts. Both men looked at her and then Tecolote's gaze slid on past to the curtained door.

There stood Toro. Cocky as ever. He stomped a red-booted foot. "Amigos!"

"Where in hell have you been?"

"Back there." Toro jerked his thumb toward Arabela's kitchen.

"For the last four hours?"

"Eating green chile stew."

"Arson make you hungry?"

"Arson? Choe—what are you meaning?"

"You know damn well what I mean."

"You ever eat Arabela's green chile stew?" Toro pranced laughing to the ice chest and reached for a beer. "You see that sonofabitch squirm?" He popped open a Coor's. "Embarrassing to see a man whine like that." Toro leaned against the chest and took a deep swig. "Catering to that female." He chuckled. "She got hair like scrambled eggs. Scramble-egg brains too. You know, Choe, I almost feel sorry for that weasly sidewinder. He ain't got nothing left now but money. Lost his woman. Got no pride. No friends. No cantina. Yeah—almost I feel sorry for him."

"¡Adió!" Arabela popped him with a loud snap of her bar rag. "It's you we better start feeling sorry for. You have got yourself ass-deep in *caca* now."

"Lay off, mama! I nearly burn my butt off saving this cantina."

"Or dooming it." Joe's voice was dry. He reached for his pipe. "Do you really think you can run Emmenthaler out this way?"

. "Choe!" Toro began to laugh again. "You think that I—?"

"Can it, Duran. Everybody in Tuceros knows who set that fire."

Toro contemplated the painted wall, studied each figure, and finally rested his gaze on the slithering serpent. "Maybe we ain't neither one of us going win." He laughed again. "But he's by-god got the message!"

"Did it ever occur to you that you could be wrong? That you've got a hair-trigger brain?" Joe was glaring.

The blue door opened and Ysidro walked in. "Hope we got plenty *cerveza*. People coming back and they are plenty thirsty." He grinned at Tecolote. "They all set for one gut-busting *baile*!" He turned to Toro. "Except for Rico. That hombre is pure pissed. And Chico, he ain't mad, but he is plenty fired up for a good chase."

Toro darted for the back door. "Yeah. Well you tell Chico and Rico I am occupied. In the latrine."

The sounds of high-pitched voices began to roll toward them, and of converging pickups. Still Toro stood at the exit. He looked at his friends. At Tecolote sitting quietly watching, listening. At Arabela and Ysidro grinning like conspirators. At Joe. "Amigo."

Joe stepped toward him and their gazes locked, and when he spoke his voice was husky.

"Amigo."

Something lit in Toro's eyes, some fire of remembrance, and they both thought of Cholly, and they were both guilty, Joe knew. And he knew too that each of them carried the load of each other's guilt and the burden of each other's heroism, and they were the same, and he said it again.

"Amigo."

Toro started through the door, then turned. He held a small something which he touched to his heart and then to his head, and then he tossed it.

Joe caught it in mid-air. That damned medal! He held the case a moment and then he returned the salute, slowly, heart to head, and pocketed the little package, and with that gesture the old brotherhood was sealed.

Toro stood for a moment in the open door, and he looked toward the mesa, to somewhere beyond the fences and the fenced, where the eagle sought the sunrise and the coyote mourned the night. Then, raising his right hand with elegant insouciance, he made man's oldest obscene gesture, and he laughed aloud. The full-bodied moon hung just above the mesa, and against it Toro's silhouette rose black and solid.

And then he was gone. In that moment Joe knew he would not see Toro again. The little fire-snorting bull who challenged the world with a pair of wirecutters and a pouch of seed for the birds. Quixote on a burro named Panchito. The best buddy Joe ever had.

His impulse was to run after him. Instead he stood looking through the open door. Toro had drawn his cornmeal line. Joe could not cross it. "Ride, Old Vaquero," he whispered.

Then only the setting moon was left, half gone already, that and the mesa and the vast darkness beyond, and somewhere in that darkness streaked a man and a meteor. But without the darkness their light would have no meaning.

The crowd rushed in, in noisy groups.

"*Bamba!*" cried someone. Tecolote struck a loud chord, and the *baile* began. Wesley danced stomping with a gleeful Serenity; some danced with their wives, and others swung onto the floor with Lily's girls who romped in for some of the fun before they went back to work. Some danced without partners.

Bamba, bamba . . . Eeeeeeh-hah!

Their cantina was saved, and their outhouse with the painted walls. JD was defeated, and Rico confirmed it after he arrived. He carried two *cervezas* to the table under the neon Coors sign where Chico waited. They'd done their job. Case closed.

Bamba, bamba . . . Eeeeeeh-hah! Toro had saved the cantina!

The song ended and the dancers gasped for breath, and in the pause they began to talk of a shooting star someone had seen, or thought he'd seen, and they thought of Toro and drank to him. And after many *cervezas* they said it was a sign, a message from Toro, or even (after a few more *cervezas*) that it was Toro himself. They would come to believe it in time, and Joe could see a song rising in Tecolote even now, see the lips moving, the images forming behind the hooded eyes. Someone shouted "Ride Vaquero," but it wasn't Toro, it was just an echo, or a tribute, and the celebration became a grander wake than even Toro would have dreamed.

The Indian was sitting alone in a back corner. Joe carried two beers to the table and sat across from him. The Indian grinned with that strange private amusement he'd shown before, and Joe asked, "Who are you?"

"Who do you think I am?"

"If I knew, would I be asking?"

"Call me whatever you want." The Indian popped open his can. He touched it to his breast and to his forehead as Chief had always done, and the secret amused look crinkled his black eyes.

Talk was bubbling all around them. Those who had not seen the meteor now thought they had, and Joe thought Toro himself was like a meteor, a dynamic part of his little universe that was the cantina, but a foreign body shooting through.

Tecolote struck a rich deep chord and his voice rose, soft, commanding.

> "*Hermanos* they were and as brothers they fought,
> Heroes they were and still are.
> *Mi corrido* I sing *de dos hombres valientes*,
> And of one who now rides on a star."

Yes, thought Joe, it's already taking root. It doesn't matter whether it happened that way, or even if it happened at all, it's how it's remembered that counts. And somehow—the singing makes it true.

Joe smiled.

Then he remembered the medal. He pulled the little case from his pocket. "It's Toro's. Came to me by mistake. But it was Toro who led the raid. Chief ended it though. Dragged that frigging stone the last mile or so into camp. It's his, too. Take it. Put it among whatever else he left behind."

"Chief never put much stock in medals."

"Neither do I. This one's only important because Toro passed it to me. He was telling me—I'd earned it."

Joe raised the lid. He blinked. Then he began to laugh. "That little sonofabitch!"

There, instead of the medal, lay the dried mungo beans, and Joe thought that little string of beans from Toro signified more than the medal ever had. There was a note. *I don't need this ennymore. I gess you do. Take care of my dogs. I got the burro.*

Joe shook his head, saw the Indian watching him with a face as unreadable as the lost language of his ancestors on the mesa. "Just thinking what an ass I am," he said. "Thinking you're Chief for a minute." He laughed. "And the mesa—did that night really happen?"

Chief smiled and reached for a leather bag beside his chair and pulled out the feather the eagle had dropped.

He held it up between them, and slowly he opened his hands and it glided like a prayer until it rested on the table between them.

Joe looked at the feather and he looked at Chief, and each lifted his beer, to his heart and to his head, to the open door and the man who had passed beyond it. To the man with the blue guitar.